SLINGSHOT

Praise for LAMBDA Literary Award Finalist Carsen Taite

"Real Life defense attorney Carsen Taite polishes her fifth work of lesbian fiction, *The Best Defense*, with the realism she daily encounters in the office and in the courts. And that polish is something that makes *The Best Defense* shine as an excellent read."—*Out & About Newspaper*

"Law professor Morgan Bradley and her student Parker Casey are potential love interests, but throw in a high-profile murder trial, and you've got an entertaining book that can be read in one sitting. Taite also practices criminal law, and she weaves her insider knowledge of the criminal justice system into the love story seamlessly and with excellent timing. I find romances lacking when the characters change completely upon falling in love, but this was not the case here. As Morgan and Parker grow closer, their relationship is portrayed faithfully and their personalities do not change dramatically. I look forward to reading more from Taite."—*Curve Magazine*

"Taite is a real-life attorney so the prose jumps off the page with authority and authenticity. [*It Should be a Crime*] is just Taite's second novel, but it's as if she has bookshelves full of bestsellers under her belt. In fact, she manages to make the courtroom more exciting than Judge Judy bursting into flames while delivering a verdict. Like this book, that's something we'd pay to see."—*Gay List Daily*

"Taite, a criminal defense attorney herself, has given her readers a behind the scenes look at what goes on during the days before a trial. Her descriptions of lawyer/client talks, investigations, police procedures, etc. are fascinating. Taite keeps the action moving, her characters clear, and never allows her story to get bogged down in paperwork. *It Should be a Crime* has a fast-moving plot and some extraordinarily hot sex."—*Just About Write*

"Taite's tale of sexual tension is entertaining in itself, but a number of secondary characters...add substantial color to romantic inevitability."—Richard Labonte, *Book Marks*

In *Nothing but the Truth...* "Author Taite is really a Dallas defense attorney herself, and it's obvious her viewpoint adds considerable realism to her story, making it especially riveting as a mystery. ...I give it four stars out of five."—Bob Lind, *Echo Magazine*

Visit us at www.boldstrokesbooks.com

By the Author

truelesbianlove.com

It Should be a Crime

Do Not Disturb

Nothing but the Truth

The Best Defense

Slingshot

SLINGSHOT

by

Carsen Taite

2012

SLINGSHOT

ISBN 10: 1-60282-666-8
ISBN 13: 978-1-60282-666-3

This Trade Paperback Original Is Published By
Bold Strokes Books, Inc.
P.O. Box 249
Valley Falls, NY 12185

First Edition: June 2012

Credits
Editor: Cindy Cresap
Production Design: Susan Ramundo
Cover Design By Sheri (graphicartist2020@hotmail.com)

Acknowledgments

Slingshot represents many firsts for me. First novel written in first person, first mystery, first time tackling a series. Huge thanks to Rad for unwavering support in all my projects. To my editor, Cindy Cresap, thanks for guiding me through this new adventure. A special mention for the other BSB editors who helped me work through specific scenes during our retreat: Shelley Thrasher, Ruth Sternglantz, and Greg Herren. And big hugs to all the other BSB folks that make the publishing process painless—Sheri, Stacia, Sandy, Connie, Lori, just to name a few.

As always I had lots of help during the writing process. Thanks to my beta readers for reading the drafts. Thanks to Mike Bosillo for his insight into the world of the bounty hunter. Lord Herren—you always know just the right time to drop a dead body into a scene. And to my wife, Lainey, your insights were invaluable—I can never thank you enough for your support and commitment to my dreams.

Thanks to all my readers. As I've said before, I save every note, Facebook post, and tweet that you send—they warm my heart and keep me at the keyboard.

Dedication

For Lainey. Always.

CHAPTER ONE

Doritos, two pounds of thick-sliced bacon, baby kosher dills, skim milk, the latest issue of *People* magazine, and three packs of sugar-free gum. And that was just the top layer. Not my first choice of food selections, but once I apprehended Sara Johnson, I was going to be living large on the haul in her grocery cart.

Yes, I could've taken her in before she made it through the checkout line, but part of my finesse, if I have any, is apprehension without a fuss. Besides, some poor store clerk would have spent an hour reshelving Sara's bounty.

I trailed her to her beat-up ride before I made my move.

"Sara Johnson?"

She whirled and planted her small self in my shadow. "Who wants to know?"

I almost laughed at her show of strength. I could swing her over my shoulder with one hand. At least she was smart enough not to reveal too much information to strangers. Too bad she hadn't practiced such discretion in her prior employment. Sara Johnson was charged with felony prostitution, meaning she was a repeat offender who wasn't very good at keeping her profession a secret. She'd missed her last court date and that's where I came in.

I'm a bounty hunter. Some of the suit-wearing types and the state licensing board prefer the term fugitive recovery agent. It is what it is, and since most of what I do involves following lowlifes like Sara Johnson around, lurking in the shadows and waiting for the perfect opportunity to snag 'em and drag 'em to the nearest jail, hunter is a better moniker. But I was smart enough to realize that title was likely to send Sara running out of the parking lot.

I offered a tentative smile and kept my tone easy and even. "My name's Luca Bennett. I'm here to help you with your court appearance. I understand you missed your last one and we need to get that straightened out as soon as possible to keep you out of trouble."

Sara stared me down for a full minute before her wary look softened into relief. "I couldn't find a ride." She pointed at the jalopy next to her grocery cart. "This isn't mine and it barely works most of the time."

I pretended to ignore the inconsistent response, and shook a ring of keys in her direction. "The faster we get this sorted out, the better off you'll be. Come with me now?"

I saw the hesitation in her eyes even as she leaned forward. The struggle played out on her face, and I figured she'd made me. I reached around my waist for the pair of cuffs always attached to my belt, careful not to signal my intent. I needn't have worried; her concerns were focused in a different direction.

"I don't know." She pointed to the cart. "What about my ice cream?"

I'll eat it before it melts. I swear.

A few hours later, once Sara was tucked away for the night in a Dallas County jail cell, I swung by Hardin Jones Bail Bond agency to finish my business. I tapped my foot while Hardin counted out five Benjamins from his gaudy money clip encrusted with diamonds and shaped like the state of Texas. The clip was an anomaly. Everything else about Hardin—ragged western-style shirt, John Deere cap, and well-worn, pointed-toe boots—screamed redneck. Folks on the street would never know him as one of the most successful businessmen in Dallas. Together we were quite a pair, both tall and rugged, with the same square jaw and piercing blue eyes. His hair, like mine, flipped and waved in all the wrong places, and I wondered if he too cut his own dark brown hair to save money. I shared his rough looks, but not his business sense. My worn jeans, plain T-shirt, and scuffed boots accurately signaled my status. Hungry.

"What's the deal, Luca? It's not like you hit the jackpot here."

I held out my hand. "Girl's gotta eat."

"I thought you'd still be riding high after your Diamond heist." His weathered face cracked into a grin.

I shrugged. My favorite bondsman wasn't referring to jewels. Nope, he was talking about the last big jumper I'd brought in. About six months ago. Her name was Diamond Collier, and I was paid handsomely for bringing her in, even though she was actually a federal agent posing as the main squeeze of a Russian mobster and a murderous viper to boot. Long story, the upshot was I didn't get to collect a bounty since she wasn't really a fugitive, but Diamond made sure I got a chunk of the reward money from the Feds. Biggest lesson I learned was ten thousand doesn't go as far as you'd think. New computer, new tires, old debts. Didn't take long before I was back to living by the seat of my pants. The five hundred in Hardin's hand was the key to meeting my personal hierarchy of needs: dinner, beer, and enough of the rent to keep my landlord at bay for a couple of weeks.

In an attempt to appear responsible I asked, "Got any other jobs for me?"

Hardin shook his head. "Mostly crumbs. Most everyone's behaving for once." He studied my face and I put on my best pathetic "feed me" expression. He reached into a drawer and pulled out a card. "Call this guy. Tell him I sent you. He's started writing some bonds, nothing big. He refers the high-dollar stuff to me. Maybe he can toss you some work."

I glanced at the card before shoving it in my pocket. Miguel Moreno, Attorney at Law. "A lawyer?" I picked up most of my work from bondsmen. Lawyers writing bonds wasn't unusual, but I'd always thought it was strange. If I skipped out on my bond, I'd like to think my lawyer would cover for me, not hunt me down.

"Yeah. He's got a huge practice. Mostly small-time misdemeanors, but he's added an associate and they've started taking more felonies lately. They're writing the bonds themselves.

Word is they don't do much in the way of screening their cases—take everything that walks in the door. If they like you, you'll have a steady stream of work."

I shrugged. The Moreno firm's relationship with their clients wasn't my concern. I only needed them to like me. Now that might be a challenge.

❖

An hour later, I slid into a seat at my favorite bar. Within seconds a sharp voice asked, "What'll it be, girl?"

Maggie Flynn rapped a pen on the table as if she actually intended to write down whatever I planned to order from the unwritten menu. Proximity was the reason we knew each other. Maggie owned the only bar within walking distance of my apartment. Today she wore a crazier than usual version of her usual ensemble: spiked red heels, a short black skirt, and a ruffled hot pink blouse with a plunging neckline. I'd long given up trying to figure out how she managed to walk through the bar without slipping on her ass.

"Beer. Blue Moon. T-bone. Rare. Fries." Before she could shake her head, I added, "I've got cash." My tab had reached its limit weeks ago. Maggie would continue to feed me crappy beer and random sandwiches, but I'd need to flash some real money if I wanted to call brands and order steak.

Apparently satisfied I was good for it, Maggie shook her mane of blazing red hair and sauntered off to the kitchen. She could act like she was annoyed with me all night, but I knew better. I'd known Maggie for years and our relationship was deeper than the four or five meals I ate at her bar every week. Twenty years my senior, she kept an eye on me, kept me fed. The only thing she couldn't do was keep me out of trouble. No one could handle that task, not even someone as formidable as Maggie.

The steak was perfect and the beer was so cold ice chunks slid down the sides of the mug, a sure sign I was in Maggie's good graces. Either she trusted I was good for the tab or she wanted something. I should've known trust wasn't the reason for the special treatment.

"What's up, Maggie?"

She slid onto the barstool next to me. I sliced into the steak before she could get started. Maggie's request would come with a story, and it wouldn't be short.

"It's my worthless brother."

I'd heard tales of Maggie's ne'er-do-well brother before. Ten years her junior, Billy spent his life in and out of county jails, living out back time on a number of petty offenses. Maggie griped about her brother's troubles every now and then, but today her usual annoyance was laced with worry. She related the latest installment about his life of crime, ending with, "He's got an outstanding warrant. A felony this time. Aggravated robbery."

I swallowed, ignoring memories of my father's warning about how many times to chew my food. "That's serious." Obvious, but I was just trying to move the story along to the part where Maggie asked me for help since it was clear her tale was heading in that direction.

"I think he's hiding out."

"Probably right about that."

She got up from her seat and walked around the bar. Seconds later, she poured another Blue Moon into an icy, new mug. Maggie never gave out new mugs, especially not to folks like me who ran up tabs they might never be able to pay. I drank down half of the amber freeze while I waited for her to finally get to the point.

"Think you could find him?"

There it was. She acted casual, as if she'd asked me about the weather. I returned the favor by acting casual too while I considered her request. I'd never even met Billy. Finding him would take some doing, and I wasn't sure I was up for a full-scale investigation.

I'm a licensed private investigator, but only because I have to be. Bounty hunters in Texas are required to be licensed P.I.s, but investigating isn't what I do. I do find people, but only people who've already been found once. Once they jump bail, I'm on the job. Bondsmen hire me so they don't have to file a claim with their insurance carrier. My fee's cheaper than a rate increase. On the smaller cases, they usually try to trick the jumper into showing up for court themselves, but occasionally they'll get overloaded and call me in. A recent brush with the law left me persona non grata with many of the local bond agencies. They'd come around, but in the meantime, I had to scrape for work. But no matter how desperate I might be, I wasn't about to veer off my chosen path. Find the jumper, bring him in. My investigation's limited to the where. All the other w's, I leave to real P.I.s or cops.

Maggie's tapping foot signaled she thought I'd had enough good beer to make a decision. She was right, and not for the first time in my life I made a decision prompted by a slight buzz.

"Yeah, I'll find him."

Later, when the endorphins from the steak and the beer haze wore off, I realized I promised to do more than just look.

CHAPTER TWO

I started the next morning at the criminal courthouse. The halls of the Frank Crowley building were teeming with dozens of sloppy souls. Low slung jeans, halter tops, T-shirts covered with profane slogans. Did these people think a court summons was a clever disguise for an invite to the State Fair?

I scanned the halls for signs of attorney Miguel Moreno. His office said he had appearances in several different courts, and lucky for me, they were spread out over four different floors. I'd looked him up online and figured his slick looking self would stick out from the hordes of crime doers lining the halls, but so far no luck.

The courthouse isn't my favorite place. In my short stint as a cop I wasted time kicking around in the halls waiting for a cluster of twelve-year-old prosecutors, fresh out of law school, to decide if they needed me as a witness at trial. Nowadays, I live my life one step away from the folks lining the halls. I keep things in balance by finding crooks on the lam, but I couldn't care less what happens after I turn them in. Well, except for collecting my payment. Speaking of which, I decided to use my finely-honed searching skills to find my new income source.

Moreno was in the last courtroom I checked. So much for my hunting ability. I slid into a seat and watched him argue for a bond reduction for his client. He was as slick as his photo. Despite his polished demeanor and exaggerated arguments, I could tell the judge wasn't buying it. The respectable client with strong ties to the community was back in the pokey because he'd smoked pot while out on bond for a possession case. Brilliant. I was actually surprised that Miguel offered such a strenuous argument to get the bond lowered considering the higher the bond, the higher his fee. Must be tough to work both ends.

When he finally finished, I sprang out of my seat to catch him before he fled the courtroom, no doubt on to the next minor matter.

"Miguel Moreno?"

"I'm in a hurry." He didn't even glance my way.

"Hardin Jones sent me. Name's Luca Bennett. Your office said I'd find you here."

One of the names I spoke carried weight. He stopped in his tracks and gave me a once-over. "You're not what I expected."

"Yeah, well, neither are you. Most of the bondsmen I know wear jeans and boots and hate being in court."

His big laugh surprised me. It was out of character, but made him seem more human. Slightly. Maybe I could work with this guy. "Hardin says you may have some business for me."

He motioned for me to follow him into the hall. "Yeah, I have some work." I waited through his long, hard look at my worn Levi's and heavy black boots. The only concession I'd made to my usual wardrobe for this "interview" was a long-sleeved white shirt with a collar that had seen an iron once upon a time. I wanted the work, but not bad enough to buy a suit to impress this guy.

"I'm not for sale, just my services." I waited until he finally looked into my eyes. "You interested?"

His leer wasn't the kind of interest I needed. I started to walk away. I didn't need this. Seconds later, I encountered another thing I didn't need, his hand on my arm.

"Wait." He noticed my glare and raised both hands in the air in a gesture of surrender. "Look, I do have work, plenty of it. If Hardin sent you, you must be good. If you can hang around a minute, I'll send my associate over to talk to you about a couple of jumpers we need to get a line on soon."

He was slimy, but maybe the associate wasn't. I needed the work. My tab at Maggie's would only go so far. I nodded and he took off like a shot.

Most of the benches in the hall were occupied. I paced to walk off my impatience. Not big on waiting. On my third lap, focused more on the rote activity than the stuff around me, I smacked into a cop. Not just any cop.

"Bennett, what the hell are you doing here?"

I turned to face the tall blonde calling my name. "Nice to see you too, Chance." My tone was sarcastic, but it really was nice to see her. It had been months since Jessica Chance tried to save my ass during a takedown, far exceeding her usual role as my interdepartmental information leaker. And source of occasional late night sexual release. Lately, those occasions had been few and far between. For the first time in our relationship, I wondered if she was seeing someone. What we had was the very definition of casual, which meant neither of us was allowed to care what the other did on her own time. I sidestepped any examination into why I had even traveled this far in my mental journey and kept the conversation light, safe, business.

"I'm looking for work. I do work you know."

"Yeah, sure you do." Chance didn't consider bounty hunting real work. She and I met at the academy. She went on to earn her detective shield. I bailed the first time I ran into a jam. Post-traumatic stress linked us for life.

"You still up for Sunday?" Her gaze morphed into a laser beam as she realized I had no idea what she was asking about. "Softball? League tournament?"

Oh shit. I'd agreed to fill in for an injured player in one of my weaker moments. Team sports weren't my thing, but Chance had prevailed upon the last ounce of mercy in my soul. And she'd promised to buy me dinner. I scrambled for an excuse to bow out, but she was too quick for me.

"I'll pick you up at eight."

"Sure. Bring coffee and not that fru fru shit you drink." I knew she'd show up with a hefty mug of the plain black brew I liked, but I couldn't resist teasing her about her coffeehouse habits. She was a good friend. She was more than a good friend.

I suspect I telegraphed a hint of wistful, because she asked, "You need something else from me?"

Loaded question. I stared everywhere but her face before I answered. "Not right now."

Her hooded eyes met mine with a hint of need, or want. For a second, the teeming craziness of the courthouse hallway slipped away, and I considered finding an empty closet, the stairwell, anyplace where Chance and I could grab a minute of passion. Grab each other.

"Luca Bennett?"

The voice was like a shout into the unspoken conversation I was having with Chance. My first instinct was to ignore it. Slowly, a memory crept its way through me. Miguel. Associate. Work. I turned to face the interrupter. "I'm Bennett."

A tall, leggy brunette stuck her hand my way, completely ignoring the fact that Chance was very much in my personal space. I admired what was either focus or just balls. I shook her hand. "You must be Miguel Moreno's associate."

"Associate?" She raised her eyebrows. "Is that what he said?"

"Yeah, or something like that."

She shrugged. "Okay then. Are you still looking for work?"

I focused on not leering and ignoring Chance's exaggerated grunt. I'm sure she thought "work" was a euphemism for some other form of activity, like the kind we usually shared. I looked her in the eyes to assess her state of mind. All I could detect was a strong admiration for the Latin beauty impatiently waiting on my response.

"I'm available for work if you've got it."

"Great." She reached into her purse and grabbed a card, scribbled a few words on it, and shoved it my way. "Meet me tomorrow at two, and I'll give you the info." And she was gone.

Chance and I both watched her ass the entire length of the hallway. I looked at the card in my hand. *Veronica Moreno, Attorney at Law*. I flipped it over. *Foxy Lady*. A strip club. Interesting. While I wondered why we weren't meeting at her office, Chance offered her own theory. "Looks like she has a special kind of work cut out for you."

"Shut up, Chance."

"Be careful."

Her eyes said she had more to say on the subject. I didn't press. She walked away and I compared her backside to the one that preceded it. Tough choice.

❖

With the rest of the afternoon to kill and no paying gig to fill it, I considered my options. Lunch sounded good, but if I showed up at Maggie's with no report on Billy, heartburn was sure to result. Since I was at the courthouse anyway, I went by the records office and picked up a copy of Billy's Dallas County rap sheet and a printout of his latest mug shot. Luckily, even with county cutbacks, there wasn't any shortage on paper.

Billy hadn't committed any felonies before now. At least none for which he'd been caught. His worst prior was burglary of a motor vehicle—a fancy way of saying he'd busted a window on a car and made off with a stereo. The act was a misdemeanor, but the way judges acted you would think it was a capital offense. Bonds were high and punishments severe, at least compared to other petty crimes. Judges around here had to run for reelection, and doubtless they heard from a lot of constituents about their cars being broken into. I sympathized. My old Bronco may not look like much, but I got really pissed off the two times some punk kid broke in even though they'd left the AM-only radio intact. I wasn't a statistic since I'd never bothered to report the break-in. Too busy being relieved they hadn't taken the time to find the guns I keep hidden under the floorboard.

From the string of property crimes and minor drug possessions, I concluded Billy had a combination drug problem and inability to keep a job problem. He stole things to buy food and stuff to smoke or put up his nose. Up to now, he'd never assaulted anyone, committed any acts of indecency, or used a weapon. He wasn't a complete write-off, but I couldn't figure out why Maggie wanted him found. I tried to remember if she'd ever mentioned any other family. None I could recall. Maybe it was just that simple. Some family is better than none at all. Not sure I bought the sentiment, but I couldn't argue the point since I clutched my own straggling family ties tighter than I cared to admit. I owed Maggie big time. For more than a meal and a beer now and then. Sad to say, she was the most reliable presence in my life. Why she wanted me to find her law-dodging brother didn't matter. I'd find him as a sign of respect.

I scrawled the address listed on his most current charge on the back of a gas receipt and shoved it in my pocket. When I walked out the doors of the courthouse, the hot, dry air hit me with a rush. August was supposed to be the hottest month of summer, but this year June was in the running. Already three weeks with temps topping a hundred degrees and not a drop of rain. I hoped the A/C in the Bronco held out until I got more work.

I drove to East Dallas. Sad to say the address in my pocket wasn't far from where I lived. I don't mind living in a sketchy neighborhood, but I don't generally think about it. Old Man Withers was a pain in the ass, but he kept the place clean and decent. When I rolled up on Billy's last known, the contrast slapped me in the face. This building could barely stand. Pieces of faded siding hung at odd angles, and only two windows appeared to be free of broken panes. If he was here, he wasn't well.

The front door led to a dingy entry complete with an intercom system circa nineteen seventy. I pushed a few buttons even though I knew they wouldn't work. I took the no answers as an invitation to check things out for myself. The stairs were strewn with used syringes, old newspapers, and random articles of clothing. The entire place stank of stale booze and urine. I'm not averse to getting dirty, but this kind of nasty tests even my boundaries. I stepped carefully around the debris and made my way to the apartment listed on the court records.

The open door saved me from breaking in. If there'd ever been anything of value in the place, it was long gone. All that was left was a stained mattress and a few empty bottles of generic booze. I flashed to an image of my dad. Left completely to his own devices, would he wind up like this? I shook away the thought. Didn't want to go there. Didn't want to be here. I spent a few seconds making sure no clues to Billy's whereabouts were lying around and then I left, eager to shed the images of desperation.

CHAPTER THREE

Saturday afternoon, I strolled up to the door of the Foxy Lady. I've seen seedier strip joints. I'd never darkened the doors of this one. I'm not a huge fan of paying money to have women wag their stuff in my face. Besides, most of the clubs around here were owned by Yuri Petrov, and I was persona non grata to him after the last big case I'd worked. This wasn't one of his, so I felt reasonably safe. Still, it was an odd place to meet an attorney.

The place was dimly lit. I supposed the owners were aiming for ambience, but I bet the low lights hid a lot of wrinkles and other imperfections. I was surprised to see almost a dozen patrons, nuzzling their drinks while they imagined other things they could pay to nuzzle. Veronica Moreno was nowhere in sight. I slid into a booth and leaned back to wait.

I didn't have to wait long, but the woman who came calling wasn't here to give me work. She was blond, curvaceous, and barely dressed. I might not spend a lot of time in joints like this, but I knew when I was being groomed to pay big for a lap dance.

"I haven't seen you in here before."

"Maybe that's because I haven't been in here before."

"Damn shame." She straddled my hips and gave a little grind. "Most of the middle of the day clientele are buzzed businessmen trying to work off lunch."

Playing along didn't cost anything so I indulged. "I ate a light lunch and I'm sober as a judge."

She shook her pelvis and lifted it my way. "Thirsty?"

We were halfway into the service I had yet to pay for. I'll admit I was turned on. Who wouldn't be with a half-naked woman rubbing her body all over them? I concentrated on dousing my arousal. I was about to admit I wasn't good for her fee, but a soft voice over my shoulder blew my focus all to hell.

"You look pretty comfortable."

Moreno. Her whisper glided across my neck. I resisted the urge to turn into her voice, sure that her full, lush lips were within striking distance. I licked my lips but didn't indulge. Don't get me wrong, I was interested, but I needed the work more than I needed to get laid. Mostly. Before I let the balance slide in the other direction, I motioned for her to sit. Across from me. Half-naked lap dancer ground in closer and purred her protest. I patted the tiny patch of cloth allegedly covering her ass and urged her off me. "Sorry, I have some business to attend to. Maybe later?" I offered this last only to combat her fast-forming pout.

She glanced at Moreno, shrugged, and crawled out of my lap, but before she left, she kissed me big and wet. As she walked away, she tossed back, "Thanks for nothing, Ronnie."

"No problem, Star."

Ronnie. Ice woman had a nickname. Nice.

I didn't watch Star leave. I was too busy comparing Moreno, make that Ronnie, to the stripper. She wore way more clothes than Star, but was exponentially more sexy. Ronnie's suit was all business, sharp lines and expensive cloth. Her voice was polished and smooth, with only a trace of her Latin heritage. I wondered if she went full-on fiery Latina when she was riled.

She repeated a version of her early comment. "You seem to be quite at home here."

"Actually, I've never been to this *particular* club. And I don't think the strippers know *me* by name."

She nodded, impassive, signaling I wasn't going to get a rise so easily. Fine. I could be all business, even when a half-naked woman was shaking her business a few feet from my face. Curiosity beat out my attempt at nonchalance.

"Miguel said you have some work for me."

"Yes, but first I have a question." She paused. "What exactly is it that you do?"

"I find people."

"Really? You make it sound so simple, so innocuous. That isn't all you do, is it?"

Why the questions? Didn't she work for Miguel? Shouldn't she know what it was they were hiring me to do? Or was she just playing me, inviting me to a strip club, asking inane questions? If she was playing me, I didn't have a clue what the game was, let alone what rules applied. I took the offensive with a question of my own.

"Are you Miguel's wife?"

A person couldn't fake the shocked expression she wore. Her calm, cool poise briefly shattered and she sputtered her response. "Where the hell did you get that idea?"

"Same last name. He sent you to do the unpleasant part of the job while he does the real legal work."

"I'm half his age." I caught a hint of the fiery woman I'd imagined. Wonder what she was like fully riled.

"Maybe he likes younger women. Hot, younger women." My sideways compliment settled over her. Her continued bristling showed she didn't take it well. Was it because she didn't think she was hot or because I was the one delivering the compliment? She passed for straight, but how many straight women would select a gentleman's strip club for a business meeting?

"Miguel Moreno is my uncle." She let the declaration lie for a moment, then added. "I'm an attorney and I work with him. I have a client who has disappeared and I need you to find him. Do you want the work or not?"

This wasn't the way I usually got work. Her vocabulary, *client*, didn't match the lingo bondsmen like Hardin used—jumper, runner, even the more formal, fugitive. I didn't bother correcting her or asking more questions to root out the logic behind her terminology.

"I want the work." I'd settle on terms once I knew more.

"Good. Do you know Jed Quitman?"

"Not personally, but everyone knows who he is." Jed Quitman was king of the late night commercial. His payday and car title loan shops ran thirty second spots on every channel at every break long after respectable folks had gone to bed. He focused his business sights on the low of budget, promising extra funds to anyone with a paycheck or a car to put up as collateral. What his commercials didn't say was that once you got on the Quitman debt treadmill, you would never be able to get off since interest on the loans ran two to three hundred percent.

"Did you know he owns this place?"

I didn't, but I didn't want to start out this relationship with her thinking she knew more than me. Not my style, at least not with strangers. "I may have heard that somewhere."

Her quick smile told me she knew I was fudging. I attempted to wrest control of the conversation. "I haven't seen you around before. Are you new in town?"

"Do you know everyone in town?"

"Do you always answer a question with a question?"

"No." She didn't offer anything else, and I knew this was the make-or-break. I could continue to play this game, dancing around my attraction to her, or I could be all business and earn enough to eat on for a while. Either way, hunger was in control. Reluctantly, I chose business and repeated my earlier opening statement.

"Miguel said you had work for me. I assume it has something to do with Jed. Did one of his dancers get in trouble, skip bail?"

"No. He did."

My jaw dropped and she watched me take the surprising declaration in, seemingly pleased my poker face had vanished. I couldn't help it; Jed Quitman was the last person in the world I'd expect to be a jumper. I knew he'd had some light brushes with the law, most recently something having to do with tax filings or some other equally boring white collar crime, but his mug was plastered all over town. Just where did he think he was going to run to?

"So, Ronnie, you're telling me you guys secured a bond on Jed Quitman and he's skipped out?"

The question was meant to get a rise, but only a small flicker of discomfort appeared before she responded calmly. "You may call me Veronica, and yes, that's about the size of it. We'd like him found. Quickly." She placed a file folder in front of me, the crisp office supply at odds with the ashtray and glass rings shadowing the tiny topped cocktail table. Tapping the outside, she said, "There should be enough information in here to get you started, but you can call me if you have questions." She pulled a slip of paper from an enormous leather bag I imagined cost more than my monthly rent. She scrawled a number on the back and hesitated for only a moment before handing it over. "But I don't want you to turn him in to the sheriff's department. I want you to call me when you find him."

Where I turned him in shouldn't matter to me, since I would collect my fee from Moreno's office, not the sheriff, but what she was asking was something I'd never been asked to do before. Bondsmen were generally an unforgiving folk. Once a defendant jumped bail, they didn't give second chances. They almost immediately filed paperwork with the court to back the hell out of the deal. Besides, turning a fugitive over to anyone but the authorities was against the law, not to mention an infraction of my license. I ducked the legalities; she was the lawyer after all, and simply said, "That's not how I usually do things."

Again she flashed a smile, followed by a grave look. "I chose you because you have a reputation for being creative. Find Jed and we'll have lots of other work for you."

I met her eyes. They were bright, fierce, and deep, dark brown. Rich chocolate. I licked my lips, trying not to care my desire was plain to see. She knew me, or about me anyway. I knew nothing about her. If I turned down this job, I'd probably never see those eyes again, at least not this way—urging me to give in. And despite all the warning signs, I wanted to give in to whatever she asked. Not because I needed the work or the money. What I needed was to figure out this spell she cast, a powerful mix of indifference and intimacy. An intoxicating combination.

I gave her my answer, pretending it was my decision and that I was in control. "I'll do it. *Veronica.*"

She didn't hesitate. "I knew you would."

So much for my control.

❖

Morning always came way earlier than it should. I glanced at the clock. I had fifteen minutes until Chance showed up with coffee. Despite the early hour, the heat and humidity were already cloaking everything in a suffocating haze. It would only get worse, but I jumped in the shower anyway, mostly to let a cold stream of water wake me up.

As I stepped out of the shower, I heard movement. I grabbed a towel and wrapped it around my waist without bothering to dry off. My holster hung on the hook where most folks keep a robe. I drew out the Colt and leaned over the threshold. I called out, "Don't do anything stupid. I've got a clear shot."

Chance stuck her head around the corner, impervious to my threats. "Put the beast away, or I'll pour your coffee down the sink."

Her threat was scarier than mine. I dripped my way over to the kitchen and set my gun on the counter, replacing it with the steaming hot, extra large cup of coffee she'd brought. "You'll make someone a good wife," I murmured between sips.

"As if." She crossed her arms and lifted a chin in the direction of my terrycloth ensemble. "You're going to distract the infielders in this outfit. And you might skin a knee. Wouldn't want to scuff up those picture perfect legs now, wouldya?"

I mock laughed at the joke. My body was a fugitive recovery agent's wet dream. I had so many distinguishing scars, they'd have to add an extra page to the Wanted notice. Most of the marks were the result of harmless play, careless risks—falling from a roof, getting too close to a knife. Only one held a story worth telling, but one I seldom told. Chance knew, but only because she was there when it happened. We didn't talk about it. Not directly.

Time to change the subject. "How the hell did you get in?" I'm not the type who leaves a key hidden over the doorjamb or under a flowerpot. I break into too many other people's houses that way. Anyway, it's against my nature to even have a flowerpot.

She pulled an enormous muffin from a paper bag and answered between bites. "Landlord. Flashed my badge." She wiped a crumb from her lips and grinned. "I may have mentioned something about a warrant."

"Great. Make sure you show up for the eviction hearing." Old Man Withers would love a reason to kick my sorry ass to the curb. I only paid on time occasionally, but I still viewed myself as a worthy tenant. I didn't make noise, I didn't have any pesky pets, and I owned enough guns to arm the entire complex in the event of a siege. He overlooked my good qualities in favor of constant harassment about the rent. The price was reasonable, but I hated to part with cash. I liked to stay liquid, keep my money available for special opportunities.

"Come on, Bennett. We need to get going. Go put your clothes on." She tossed me a team shirt and waved me out of the room. I dressed quickly. Shorts, socks, shoes, T-shirt. I don't spend money on clothes. The women on the team would be decked out in the best sports gear around. Chance would have a glove and bat for me in the car. My usual exercise involved running around the lake in a tattered shirt, old gym shorts, and well-worn sneakers. Free, flexible, easy.

The softball fields were full of athletic dykes showing off for their peers. Chance's team consisted of a dozen or so law enforcement types with a couple of women from the local crime lab sprinkled in to keep it from being an official police team. As much as things had changed over the years, the department wasn't going to sponsor a team in a lesbian softball league. Unlike their competitors, Chance's Champions sprang for the cost of their own uniforms and entry fees.

While Chance went to do official sporty things, I plucked a bottle of water from the team cooler and settled into the dugout. My presence was insurance against a possible forfeit, and I wouldn't be expected to perform unless there was an emergency. Fine by me. Except for my ability to round the bases faster than anyone else out here, I wasn't gifted with much in the way of athleticism.

Officer Nancy Walters, a sturdy blonde, reached across me and grabbed a Gatorade. Cold drips trailed across my bare leg and she reached to wipe them off. She grinned when I froze her hand in a steely grasp mere inches from my thigh.

"Sorry, Luca. Didn't mean to get you wet."

She didn't mean anything personal by it. Walters was a shameless flirt and would have made the same comment to any living, breathing female in the vicinity. Doubtless I was one of a rare few who hadn't succumbed to her persistent charm. One cop in my bed, ever, was plenty. "No problem, Walters. Didn't know you'd exhausted your supply of willing victims."

"There'll always be a spot for you. Say the word and I'll swear off the rest."

"I'm too shady for you law-and-order types. You should stick with women who share your sense of morality. It'll keep you out of trouble." I actually enjoyed the banter. As much as I preferred being on my own, there was a certain appeal in the camaraderie. I may not like to work in a group, but every now and again, I didn't mind the feeling of being included. These women shared life and death and all the mundane details in between. I couldn't stomach such closeness every day, but an occasional injection gave me a boost. And there was another benefit to being part of the in-crowd. Information.

"Hey, Walters, what do you know about Jed Quitman?"

"What don't I know?" She puffed up. "He's a piece of work, that one."

A tall, lanky brunette punched Nancy's shoulder then slid beside her onto the bench. Gail Laramore retired from the force last year when she'd hit her twenty. Now she ran her own security firm. Her last position with the department had been as a detective in organized, aka white collar crime. She retorted, "Don't listen to a word she says. She merely fancies herself as the 'pulse of the city,' but if you want real intel, I'm your gal."

"Shut up, Gail. You don't know shit. Once you turned in your shield, you officially became not in the know. Besides, running a desk doesn't compare to patrol. The real action happens in the open, on the street, when the tough broads like me are on guard." Nancy delivered the banter with an easy grin.

I held up both hands and signaled time-out. "I imagine both of you know everything there is to know about Quitman. Mind sharing?"

Gail answered first. "I hear he skipped out on his bond. You looking for him? I think they only got him on some white collar thing."

"Yeah, I'm on it. As of yesterday. Care to share what you know?"

"Sorry, kiddo. I don't know anything about his pending case." Interpretation—she knew something else, not about his pending case.

"Okay. Anything else you'd care to share?"

She gave Nancy a pointed look and shook her head. Nancy didn't miss a beat. "Talk, Gail. I can keep a secret."

Gail sighed. "Okay, okay. I don't really know anything. I hear rumors, though." She shot me a pointed look. "You know about the strip clubs?"

I nodded, not wanting to let on that I only knew about strip club, singular.

"The department's had an eye on him for a while. Something about other non legitimate business activities. Rumor is the clubs are a cover."

"If there are other, non legitimate businesses, why not run them from the payday loan shops? Give them an air of legitimacy."

"No one said the guy is smart." Gail reached across me to get into the cooler. "Although come to think of it, I did get the impression we were encouraged to look elsewhere when we started to get close to him."

Finally, a real revelation. "Who did the encouraging?"

Gail shrugged. "When I got waved off one case, there were dozens more to take its place. He's connected. When it's time for him to take his fall, it'll be for more than a simple fraud case."

Nancy piped up. "He's a real charmer. I hear he's having an affair with Caroline Randolf." As soon as she delivered the declaration, she made a show of zipping her mouth shut and shooting a glance behind me. "Hi, Perez, what's up?"

Damn. Teresa Perez had a way of interrupting important moments in my life. I wanted to ask Nancy more about what was certainly only a rumor. No way was the uptight, do-gooding, conservative, and extremely wealthy patron of popular Senator Dick Lively slumming it with the likes of Jed Quitman, but I didn't want to have the discussion in front of Perez. I especially didn't want to let Perez know Nancy had been so free with intel on a former mark. I didn't have time to do more than file the subject away for future consideration before Perez slid onto the bench beside me and dwarfed me in her shadow.

She was full of questions. "Who let Bennett back on the team and who's having an affair with Caroline Randolf?"

I immediately blew off Nancy's rumor. Perez, a homicide detective, had been around city politics long enough to confirm or deny the dirt on local bigwigs. If there were any truth to the rumor, the tell would have come in the form of a smug grin.

Teresa didn't sit beside me because she liked me. She did it to prove she was bigger, that she'd always be there, looking over my shoulder. My occasional appearance with her fellow cops always pissed Teresa off. It wasn't playing on the team that got under her skin, it was that playing on the softball team was the closest I ever got to what she considered the right side of the law anymore. Teresa had never forgiven me for how and why I left the force in the first place. I didn't talk to her about anything, personal or business, so I was relieved when Walters, the flirt, called out, "Who's that babe?"

As one, we swung our heads in the direction of her pointing finger. Walters was not a subtle sort. Veronica Moreno was suddenly in our sights. Tall, dark, and lovely. So much for avoiding the personal or business. I didn't volunteer my insider knowledge to my teammates, but a growl of possessiveness simmered inside.

Perez's growl was loud, visceral, and full of her usual bravado. "Leave the Latin ladies to me. None of you gringas has what she needs."

I half rose out of my chair, but Nancy beat me to the punch. "Keep your seat, Perez. She looks like she's otherwise engaged."

Again, we all swung back toward Moreno who was now pressed against a well-muscled guy dressed in a baseball uniform.

Perez grunted. "Damn, that's disappointing." I silently agreed. None of my fantasies featured Ronnie playing for the other team.

"I hope you guys are talking about how you're going to win this game." I swung around at the sound of Chance's voice. For some reason I couldn't explain, I didn't want her to know I was pumping her friends for information. Maybe it was because she was my usual source and I didn't want her to feel like she wasn't special. No, that wasn't it. I didn't want her to think I was taking advantage of our friendship more than I already did. I sensed that while it was okay for me to take advantage of her, she wouldn't appreciate me taking advantage of her friends.

Nancy saved me. "Us girls are just gossiping. Gail can't stop talking about the boring cases she used to work in Organized. She should spend a night on the streets with me. I could show her a good time." She laughed hard at her own joke.

Chance shrugged. "She's welcome to join me over a dead body sometime." She consulted her clipboard and hollered for the rest of the team to join us in the dugout. As she read out the lineup, I considered what Nancy and Gail had said. Quitman was probably involved in all kinds of illegal activities, but none of that was my concern. All I needed to do, wanted to do, was find him and collect my fee. Nothing they told me was important if it didn't help me track him down.

Chance barked. "Perez, Laramore, Bennett, Walters, Chavez, Yancy."

I shot to attention. Chance didn't usually bother reading my name since it was always the last one on the list. "What's up, Chance?"

"The other team's regular pitcher is out. Don't swing at anything. You'll get walked and Walters will bat you in. You can run faster than anyone on the team. It's time for you to step up."

Right. Step up. I didn't bother reminding her this wasn't my team. Gail and Nancy grinned at my obvious discomfort. I mouthed "you owe me" and strode out of the dugout to select a bat I wouldn't swing.

I waited out the sorry pitches and strode to first base. Walters swung a few practice swings, and while I waited for the big hit to signal the start of the race, I glanced around at the other fields, hoping to catch a glimpse of Moreno. After what I'd seen earlier, I needed to get over it. Figures she'd be straight. She was probably sitting in the nearby stands, doing something domestic like knitting, while she watched her man win one with the fellas. Straight women didn't usually put me off, but I didn't want to think about, let alone see, Moreno in anyone else's arms.

Chance's plan worked, but I nearly wasn't fast enough to outrun the bionic arm of the other team's second baseman, baseperson, whatever. As I streaked to home plate, the whoosh of the speeding ball spurred my dormant competitive streak. I launched off the ground and dove toward the plate, stretching my arms in front of me like an Olympic diver. My fingers clawed the dirt and found purchase as the rest of my body hurled its weight forward, unable to stop before slamming into the desperately reaching catcher.

"Safe!"

I lay on my back and watched the exuberant umpire wave his arms and do his little officiating dance. I uncurled my fingers from around the base and felt my face, which was coated in cinder and pain. As I rubbed away the debris, a shadow loomed followed by an arm extended toward me.

"Need some help?"

Of all the scenarios I'd imagined for my next meeting with Ronnie Moreno, this had never factored into the mix. I could only imagine how I looked, coated in dirt, sweat, and surprise. She wore tall sandals, flowing tan linen pants, and a bright yellow blouse. Expensive, designer. Not a wrinkle in sight. Her long black hair was pulled back and her sharp features were softened by a welcoming smile. I grabbed her hand and let her help me to my feet.

"Nice play."

"Thanks." I struggled to stand upright and act more suave than I felt. "We should clear the plate. My teammates are a serious bunch. No citizens on the field." As I waved her to lead the way off the field, I saw Chance watching us from behind first base. She raised her eyebrows. I shook my head and raised my hands to signal I had no idea why Ronnie had shown up here. Chance answered with a smirk. I focused my attention on Ronnie. "Have you been watching long?" What a line. I was a regular Casanova.

She pointed across the park. "Actually, I've been watching my cousin play, over there. His team finished up a few minutes ago." She grinned. "Just in time for me to catch your swan dive."

Cousin. Well, that was promising. I bantered with renewed hope. "About as graceful as I ever get. It worked though."

"It did." Her tone told me my grab for home base did more than merely score a point for the team.

I signaled her to follow me to the bleachers. "I'd invite you to sit down, but you're likely to get your nice outfit dirty. You always dress up for ninety degree outdoor activities?"

"It is definitely hot." She slid onto the bench, deftly ignoring my question. "I didn't think about how hot it could get when I got dressed this morning. I'm not used to it."

I settled in next to her and inhaled the scent of citrus and ginger wafting from her warm skin. I hadn't thought about how hot it could get today either. Was it possible we both no longer referred to the weather? I searched for safe topics. "Not from around here?"

Her eyes shaded over and where I'd read invitation a moment earlier, I could no longer read anything. "How about you? You from around here?"

Two unanswered questions equaled two strikes. Normally, at this point, I would toss out another pitch and if I got more of the same, game over. I purposely avoided asking another question. We all have secrets. Why should Ronnie Moreno be any different? Frankly, I wasn't ready for the game to be over. I could find the answers to my questions some other way. In the meantime, it wasn't killing me to have a gorgeous raven-haired beauty at my side. Not everyone agreed.

"Bennett, you're wanted back in the dugout." Perez loomed over us. I didn't move. She flashed a big smile at Ronnie and waved me away. "I'll take care of your friend here." Again, I didn't budge.

Ronnie inched closer and patted the space on her other side. "You're welcome to join us."

I watched the scowl form on Perez's face and I smothered a smug grin. Teresa didn't share. I didn't either. Only one of the many reasons we didn't get along.

"As soon as Bennett heads back, maybe I will." She stayed in place, waiting.

I pick my fights carefully. Teresa Perez wasn't worthy of my ire. Not today anyway. And what she didn't know was that I'd see Ronnie again, probably soon when I delivered Jed Quitman on a silver platter. I started to get up, but Ronnie's hand on my arm stopped me. She spoke to Teresa. "You won't mind if I keep her a bit longer. We have a couple of private matters to discuss. Attorney client matters. I'm sure you understand."

She didn't, but she quickly covered the shade of anger and disappointment that crossed her face. As she stalked down the bleachers, I stood. "I do need to get back."

"Sure, I get it. I suppose it's too soon for any word on Quitman?"

"A little." I gestured toward the field. "I've been busy."

"You'll let me know, right? Like we discussed?"

"Business that bad? Miguel can't afford the fee?" I referred to the money he'd owe the county if Jed's bond was forfeited. I was only partly teasing. Her anxious tone belied mere professional concern. I reflected back on Walter's comments about Jed Quitman's loverboy ways. Was it possible Veronica Moreno had fallen victim to his seedy charms?

"Not funny. Just find him. Promise?"

Her entreaty was more command than question and I surprised myself at how willing I was to obey orders. "I'll find him." What was it with me lately and all my grand promises?

This one got me a quick hand squeeze and a whispered, "It'll be worth your time." Her breath was sweet, her words were silk. Talk about promises.

❖

Five games later, we accepted our championship trophy. I agreed to join the group for a celebratory beer at Sue Ellen's. I hoped my attempt at civility would keep Chance from interrogating me about Ronnie on the ride home. Not like I had much to tell other than Ronnie was an attorney who was way more interested in a fugitive than circumstances suggested she should be. I could also tell her I knew nothing about Ronnie other than she was a knockout and the subject of several inappropriate personal fantasies.

I opted out of both, the latter primarily because it would've been weird. Chance and I exchanged sexual favors as a way of bartering balm for our respective aches, but we didn't talk about sex, love, or relationships with each other or anyone else. Well, at least until now. Chance's first words once we got in the car were, "Watch out for that one."

"You know her?"

"Her? No. I haven't seen her around before. Her uncle, Miguel? He's a piece of work. Runs a mill practice. When he does go to trial, he's a tricky bastard. I wouldn't put it past him to screw you over. If she's working with him, she can't be much better."

I chose a neutral tone. "She seems okay."

"Whatever." She pulled into my parking lot, but didn't park. A clear signal I was on my own for the rest of the night. Fine by me. I was tired, sweaty, and buzzed. A shower and sleep were higher on my list than sex. Still, our bond spurred me to say, "I had fun today."

"You're a good sport, Luca. Thanks."

As she drove away, I considered the fun we could have had.

CHAPTER FOUR

Monday morning I woke up tired and way more sore than a pinch hitter should've been. I considered digging back under the covers, but I knew a run would work out the kinks. I cut my usual route in half, but the sweat and motion did the trick. I regained the ability to move my limbs without wanting to scream.

After a quick shower, I fled my coffeeless apartment. The tiny convenience store at the corner served a watered down version of the black brew for fifty cents a cup. Perfect for the budget-conscious professional. Java in hand, I climbed into my car and considered my next step.

I do most of my work in my car. She's a simple black Ford Bronco, circa nineteen ninety-one. I love her because she's paid for and she doesn't demand a lot of attention. Also, in a city full of flashy cars, she doesn't draw a lot of attention. I spend a lot of time sneaking up on fugitives, trailing them until I figure out the best way to make a grab, haul them in, and collect my fee. As much as I would love a tricked out ride, my Bronco is a better tool for my line of work. The outside may be nothing to look at, but the interior has most of the creature comforts I need: a cooler, a secret compartment for my gear, and about a half dozen weapons, including a Taser I purloined from the few minutes that I was a cop. I didn't get much else out of that occupational foray; I figured the weapon was my exit bonus. I rarely use it because it leaves marks, but sometimes firing it in the general range of a jumper who's weighing his options is a convincing tool.

After I collected my last big fee, I bought an iPhone, and I'm still getting used to the idea of having the Internet in my pocket. I suspect the old-fashioned way of finding stuff, nose to the ground, poking around, is still better, but I can't argue with the fact that some searches are a lot faster with the blazing speed of online research. The ability to look things up on the fly is a big plus. The monthly bill is one of the few items I consider a necessity.

I leafed through the folder Veronica, make that Ronnie, had provided. She was certainly thorough. Not only had she included all the paperwork Quitman had filled out for the bond, but she'd also slipped in additional documents—county tax information on his home and a list of businesses he owned and storefront locations. I noticed Quitman was the surety on his own bond. Odd. Most bondsmen don't allow defendants to guarantee their own bond, since their interest in escaping the long arm of the law was usually greater than their regret about losing whatever money or property they pledged to secure their own release.

His home address wasn't far. I decided to start there. Amazingly, many bail jumpers hunker down in their houses like ostriches, thinking if they don't come out, no one will come looking. I plugged the address into the phone and let a soft female voice lead me to Jed Quitman's house.

Strip club owners and payday lenders weren't supposed to live among the Dallas elite, but Jed Quitman was a rule breaker of the first order. His gaudy McMansion was a poor attempt to simulate a life of wealth, and I'm sure his neighbors longed for him to lose his ill-gotten gains and flee their stodgy settlement.

I looked down at my own outfit. I didn't fit in much better than Quitman. My Bronco was the only car parked on the street, though I was certain lots of Mercedes, BMWs, and Lexuses lurked in secure garages nearby. I slipped a backup pistol into my boot, stepped out of the car, and strode to the front door. The doorbell played a symphony while I waited for someone to answer.

I expected a servant, but what I got was a curvy blonde barely wearing a swimsuit, a towel over her arm. She probably served all right, but I was willing to bet she didn't do windows.

"Yes," she said, part question, part declaration, delivered between smacks of chewing gum.

"I'm here to check out the space for the delivery." The lie rolled off my tongue with ease. I'm not a fan of telling the truth upfront. It's usually more valuable to start with a story more likely to bend as needed, and fiction works well for me in that regard. I wanted in the door, and leading with "I'm looking to take the man of the house to the pokey" wasn't likely to get me over the threshold.

Her puzzled look quickly dissolved into excitement. Clapping her hands together, she squealed and bounced in place. "I can't believe it. I can't believe it!"

I tore my eyes away from her bouncing breasts, which was difficult. They were clearly the largest model money could buy. Jed had probably purchased them, which made her all the more willing to accept my implication that I was there to do the groundwork for his latest gift. I smothered a grin and replied, "Oh, you can believe it all right."

"I've been wanting one forever. I dropped a thousand hints and he always pretends he isn't listening when I talk about it."

Lying is a two way street. The liar, in this instance me, needs to get a good read off the lied to in order to keep up the appearance of authenticity. Right now, I had her believing what I needed to gain entry, but unless she gave me another hint, my cover wouldn't last. I probably had about two minutes to figure out what "it" was. A pole? A tanning bed? A pool boy? Looking at her well sculpted yet voluptuous bod, I could only imagine the perfect gift for a stripper, turned society dame.

I looked around as if "he" was somewhere close by and whispered in her ear. "I'm not supposed to ask, but if you have a particular place you'd like it, I could probably arrange to have it placed there."

She turned and her lips breathed her words across mine. "I know just the place." She grabbed my hand, and next thing I knew, I was scrambling to keep up as we ascended the *Gone with the Wind* staircase to the second floor. She held on to me the whole way. I have to admit, her excitement was contagious and I was more than a little bit turned on. I attributed the rush between my legs to too much time spent in one weekend with women who take their clothes off for other people's pleasure. An image of Ronnie flashed in my head. Sleek, tailored, triple hot. I supposed strippers weren't the only catalysts for my arousal.

She led me directly to the master suite. Of course. It was a wretched place. A cross between the gaudiest Vegas playroom and a bordello. All that was missing was the heart-shaped bed to sit below the ornately framed ceiling mirror. Seriously, if you're going to decorate in porn star vogue, go all out.

"Jed says the bedroom shouldn't be for anything but fun, but I love this room and I hang out in here even when he's away. It will be more convenient for me here and it is a gift for me, right?"

Yes, dear, the imaginary gift is all for you. I still didn't have a clue where to go from here, but I figured the bedroom was the perfect place to pick up some personal information about the elusive Jed Quitman. Most interesting was the fact she acted as if he was merely at work, not skipping out on pending doom. Second most interesting fact was that whatever the gift was, it wasn't intended for fun. I ventured a question.

"Tell me what you have in mind."

"Well, first I need you to answer a question for me."

Great. "I'll try."

"Is it the fold out kind?"

Couch? Ironing Board? I still wasn't sure, but I took a wild guess. "Why yes, it is."

"Perfect!" She pointed to a far corner wall, lined with mirrors. "It should fit there, right?"

"I can measure, but what do you think?"

"If it's the one I've been hinting about, it should be perfect. Once it's delivered, I'll be spending all my time up here. Girl's got to stay in shape you know."

I didn't know about that. My only foray into the world of fitness are my morning runs, but those were more about waking up than staying in shape. What I did know now, or at least assumed I knew, was that whatever fictional gift Jed had purchased for his woman of the week, was a piece of exercise equipment, likely a treadmill since it folded. Well, it would if it were real, which it wasn't. Now I needed to figure out a way to get rid of the little woman while I sniffed around the house.

She was directly behind me, so close I could hear the slight hitch in her breath when I backed up and brushed her thigh. Maybe getting rid of her wasn't the answer. I reached an arm around her waist, lowered it and cupped her ass in my hand. "Seems to me you're in pretty good shape already."

She giggled. I ignored my aversion to gigglers and asked, "What?" in a husky voice.

She pulled me closer and placed my other hand on one of her ginormous breasts. "I want my ass to feel this tight. You like that?"

I didn't. Well, they would do in a pinch, but watermelon boobs installed by surgeons weren't really my thing. Neither were airy blondes who live off the largess of their bottom feeder boyfriends. But I was horny and I could use some more time in the house, so I forced myself to play along.

Forty-five minutes later, she was naked and sated, and I was still clothed, mostly, and still horny. I couldn't bring myself to let my skin touch the sheets where she and Jed had done God knows what. I rolled out of the bed and pulled on my boots. Her arm was like a lasso, circling me around the waist.

"Wait, it's your turn."

I forced a smile. "Company policy. No fraternizing on the job."

She pouted. "What do you call what just happened?"

"Excellent customer service. Do you agree?"

She smiled, a lazy, sleepy, post orgasm smile. I pulled the sheet up to her chin and kissed her on the forehead. "You rest. I need to check out the circuit breakers to make sure the outlets up here can handle the machine. It's very powerful." I no longer cared that my words carried a double entendre. I was restless and figured I had very little time before some servant came along and interrupted the charade.

Part of the Barbie doll's charm was her ability to sleep through anything. She snored like a freight train while I riffled through the built-ins in Jed's closet. If any clothes were missing, I wouldn't have been able to tell considering the large racks were loaded down with enough gaudy garments to clothe the entire homeless population of Dallas, some with tags still attached. I had the feeling even the coldest, most desperate homeless man might reject Jed's hand-me-downs. Even someone like me whose standard fare consisted of T-shirts and jeans could tell the entire collection lacked taste no matter what the price.

I glanced back out at the bed. Freight train was still fast asleep, but I had no idea how long her power naps usually lasted. I pushed my way through the clothes looking for something relevant buried in the back where people assumed no one would look. Jed's secret space was surprisingly barren, which made the crumpled cardboard box stick out all the more.

The box was plain, not a word written on the outside, no postage label. The clear packing tape had been peeled back and replaced several times judging by the mass of lint collected on the sticky side. I opened the box and uncovered another layer. A worn manila envelope. It held six DVDs in plain white sleeves. No labels. I flashed back to the fifty-five inch plasma TV in the "fun" only bedroom and recalled an intricate electronic system with row upon row of brightly labeled DVDs on the adjoining shelves. I doubted that whatever was on these hidden, unlabeled DVDs was meant for whatever fun Jed and Barbie had in mind. I shoved the box under my arm and walked out of the closet.

"Hey, babe, whatcha' doin'?"

She was propped up on her shoulder giving me her best sex appeal stay and play look.

I shrugged at the closest. "Just checking the circuit breaker to make sure I don't need to make any adjustments." Hefting the box, I added, "I'm going to go put my equipment back in the truck and call the office to check in. I should also check the power access in the garage, but that won't take too long. Are you too tired to go over some other details with me when I'm done with all that?"

She scooted across the massive bed like a snake slithering toward its prey. When she reached the edge, she looped her hand around my leg and pulled me toward her. I leaned down to let her deliver her answer and her tongue directly into my ear. "I'll wait here. Hurry back."

I descended the stairs and found the door to the garage. I knew from searching the department of public safety website that Quitman owned two cars, and I was surprised to find them both sitting right in front of me. A Jag and a Corvette. Both were unlocked, but they didn't contain a single clue. I'd hoped for a GPS, but the only stray item I found was a condom wrapper under the front seat. Not exactly a clue to Quitman's whereabouts. I strode back through the house ready with another lie should I run into a household employee, but Barbie's ready posture upstairs made me wonder if maybe they were off for the day. I hunted around the downstairs, but didn't see anything else of interest. Time to go before my luck ran out. I quietly let myself out the front door, feeling a slight tinge of guilt for the naked woman waiting on my return.

I'd spent more time at Jed's house than I realized. I was hungry and I wanted to look at the DVDs. Home was the best place for a private viewing. I still had a few staples from Sara Johnson's grocery cart. Surely I could manage to throw an edible meal together.

A half hour later, I settled in with a plate of Nacho Cheese Doritos and pickles. I'd have ice cream for dessert. If anyone saw my feast, they'd think I was pregnant. As if. Just one more reason to live alone. No explaining necessary.

My TV was the huge old clunky kind with a big antennae of its own and rabbit ears to help it find the most basic connection available. I did have a remote—wouldn't want to get too much exercise bobbing up and down to change the channel, but DVD player wasn't on my list of essentials. I fired up my laptop and pushed one of the disks into the side slot.

DVD number one was boring at first. A local newscast. Looked like someone had taped the entire broadcast without regard to a specific segment. I watched and rewound, trying to catch the date in case it turned out to be significant. The weather pinned it down for me. We'd had several bad storms a few weeks ago, complete with tornadoes touching down around the metroplex. I was pretty sure what I was watching was from that night.

Except for the breaking weather bulletins, the broadcast was plain vanilla. Why would Jed have saved a DVD of the news? The broadcast ended and I started to pop the DVD out, but before I could hit the eject button, the moments of static faded into a new scene, definitely not the evening news, but newsworthy nonetheless.

The picture was grainy. Thank God. Otherwise the sight of Jed's naked body might have scarred me forever.

There he was in all his glory, spread-eagle on a bed, arms restrained to the bedposts with what appeared to be silken scarves. Even with the sketchy picture I could tell he remained in place of his own volition. Moments later I saw what motivated him to stay in place. Dressed in only a thong and a black leather bustier, she wielded a cat-o'-nine-tails like a pro. I'm not big into punishment as play, but for the likes of this beauty I'd be willing to give it a go.

I set down my trashy meal and replayed the video. As much as I dreaded witnessing Jed's humiliation, I was intrigued by the dominatrix. I imagined she had a face to match the rest of her good looks, and I had to imagine since it was partially covered by the cat-eye mask she wore. Piercing blues shone through, and I was certain those sapphire gems were only a hint of hidden treasure. A flicker of familiarity sparked, then faded. Several plays later, I still couldn't figure out the significance of what I was seeing.

The other DVDs in the box featured homemade porn, pretty much the same flavor. Cateye woman starred in all but one. The one of these things is not like the others video featured a young, curvaceous, nude blonde punishing some bad boy other than Jed Quitman. In a fun twist, this time the masochist wore the mask, so details about him were limited to his salt and pepper hair and muscular body. Oh, and based on what I remembered from a few unfortunate high school dates, a smallish penis. I could imagine why Jed had the other tapes in his closet, but this one? Maybe Jed had more than one closet.

I opened the file Ronnie had given me. I'd reviewed it earlier, but more with an eye toward pinpointing Quitman's location. The DVD had piqued my curiosity, and now I wanted to know everything I could about Jedidiah Quitman.

He'd skipped out on a simple fraud charge. With no prior felonies, he'd likely get probation. Odd. Bail jumpers usually skip out for one of two reasons. Risk or stupidity. Not much at risk here, and Jed didn't strike me as a stupid person. He had some other reason for his no-show, and I suspected Ronnie Moreno had a clue she hadn't bothered to share. I probably wouldn't reach her at eleven o'clock at night, but I wanted her to start her day tomorrow knowing I was smarter than she gave me credit for, so I left a voice message on her office phone.

After the call, I put the first DVD back in and watched Jed the bail jumper enjoying a personal dose of punishment one more time for good measure, and then I fired up Google. A simple search for Jed's name turned up dozens of hits, but nothing out of the ordinary. He wasn't the sole owner of the club I'd met Ronnie at earlier. In fact, the ownership was buried in circles of fancy LLCs and DBAs, but I finally located Jed's name among a crowd of others. I jotted down a list of his business partners and tucked it into my "file," aka wallet. Too soon to tell if any of this information was important, but I had a sneaking suspicion Jed's partial ownership of a strip club had more than a passing connection to the personal porno flick I'd found at his house.

I clicked on a few more websites, but my tired eyes made for fuzzy viewing. I turned off the computer and the one lamp in my living room slash office, and headed for bed. I was down to my Hanes when I heard a loud knock on the door. I didn't bother getting dressed. Only one person ever knocked this late.

I should have a peephole, but my landlord's cheap. His idea of safety is don't open the door. I took my forty-five long Colt just in case my instincts were off. Holding the gun in one hand, I cracked the door and leaned away from the opening.

"Dammit, Bennett, put the gun down." Jessica Chance held a hand out, palm up, and leaned away from me.

I lowered the gun. "Sorry, Jess. Come on in."

As she strode through my doorway, I set the Colt on the kitchen counter. Everything in my apartment was pretty much in arm's reach. Hands free, I grabbed her by the arm and she whirled toward me. Her eyes were tired, but not enough to mute her need. She wasn't here about a case, wasn't here to chat. She was here for the one thing we could always rely on each other for.

I barely waited for her to remove her jacket and shoulder holster before I shoved her to the wall and pinned her with my weight. Inch for inch, we were well matched. She could beat my grasp, but she wouldn't since to do so would defeat the purpose for her visit. Five months was a long time to go between lovers, but we had never been lovers. Only friends who doubled as sex partners, taking what we needed in frenzied bouts of lust to hold us over until someone else came along. I hadn't been celibate since our last encounter. She probably hadn't either, but in this moment, I didn't think about who her in-between lovers might have been. I didn't think about anything but the fierce burn between my legs and the pounding of want I could feel from her chest beating against mine.

I kissed her. Rough and long. Tender nips and slow explorations were for slow seductions, not for us. She thrust her tongue into my mouth, hard and deep. She tasted of the beer she must've grabbed right before she came over. I finally pulled away, fighting for air. She was panting, her eyes glazed. She slid a hand up my bare thigh and cupped my ass. Her breath seared hot against my neck. My clit buzzed.

"Standing around in your underwear, waiting for me?"

I ignored the question. The only answer she wanted was for me to take her. Fast and hard. I grabbed her wrists and held them over her head while I tore at the buttons on her shirt. I knew she had just come straight from work because she was wearing a bra, a concession to comfort made in deference to the cold interrogation rooms down at the station. Vivid memory of the impersonal service I'd delivered to Jed Quitman's ladylove earlier in the day flashed in my mind. I'd left that encounter unsatisfied. I was about to service Jess, but it was decidedly different. Touching her, stroking her, fucking her—whatever she needed, whatever she craved—would leave me satisfied.

The bra wouldn't give and I ripped the clasp. Dragging the soft cotton over her breasts, I leaned in and licked my way around her small tight nipple. When she arched against my mouth I used my teeth until she moaned. I clamped down, sucking, biting, lost in her aroused cries as she writhed against me. I held her wrists tighter and slid my free hand down the flat plane of her stomach, groaning at the ripples of pleasure that trailed behind.

She dripped need and I thrust into her. I sank deeper and rolled my thumb against her swollen clit. She would come in seconds. She would come again later, slower, but right now she craved quick release and I would give her what she needed. As Jessica shivered away her pain in the throes of brutal orgasm, I held her close and quietly kissed away her torment.

CHAPTER FIVE

I rolled over and looked at the clock. Six a.m. Before I could process why I was even awake at the ungodly hour, I encountered another surprising development. Jess was still in my bed. Naked. Sleeping. I stared. Couldn't help myself. Tiny snores erupted at infrequent intervals. I knew if she opened her eyes and found me staring, our relationship would forever be altered, and not just because she wouldn't want me to know she snored.

We'd fucked half the night. I made her come again and again until I thought she was too exhausted to move, but she still managed to satisfy my needs. I can only give so many orgasms away without needing a little release myself.

She stirred and I glanced away, nestling back into the sheets. I feigned sleep until she fully rose from hers. When I heard her feet touch the floor, I rolled over. "Are you hungry?"

"Didn't you get enough, Bennett?"

She rarely called me Luca in the light of day. It wouldn't be comfortable for either of us. I hadn't been talking about sex and I felt the need to correct her assumption. "I meant breakfast. Isn't that what you people do when you get up this early?"

She waited until she tugged her shirt on before turning to face me. "You have food?" She watched my face closely. I couldn't hide my jumbled, half awake thought process. She probably wouldn't want a bowl of Doritos and a beer to start her day. Without waiting for me to answer, she shrugged and stepped into her pants. "Thanks, but I can grab something on the way in. Long day ahead."

I pulled up the sheet. Maybe her full dress was why I suddenly felt weird about being naked. I couldn't, wouldn't process beyond the idle thought. She walked to the door and paused with her hand on the knob. Then, without turning, she shook her head and left. Weird.

Weirder still that I noticed the change in the air between us.

❖

A quick shower and clothes and I was ready for the day. Earlier than I was accustomed to, but I hadn't been able to roll back over and go to sleep this morning. I attributed it to hunger. Of one kind or another. Determined to live large, I fired up the Bronco and headed to my favorite diner since Maggie's wasn't open for breakfast. Maggie's wasn't about the food anyway. Her place was close, she was a loyal friend, and she let me run a tab. My stomach can forgive a lot when it's filled for free, but I still had some bucks left from my last job, and eggs and bacon were high on my list of priorities.

The Market Diner was down the street from the courthouse. A middle-aged woman in a beehive hairdo served me several plates— eggs, bacon, hash browns, biscuits, pancakes, and topped off my coffee. Lots of folks in this joint were regulars and she called them all by name. She called me Sugar. Some might like that, but the moniker made me want to be a regular.

Twenty minutes later, stuffed and sleepy, despite five cups of coffee, I left the diner. I pulled a scrap of paper from my wallet and checked the name. Get Out Quick Bail Bonds. I'd never done any work for them, but they'd written the bond for Maggie's brother Billy on his last case. I figured they might have a better address than the one I'd checked out the day before. When folks are hot on getting out of jail, they sometimes slip up and tell the truth. Kind of like a vow to go straight. If I could get them to give up the info, it might make this non-paying side job go faster. I was still processing my next step in the hunt for Jed Quitman. An hour or two on the Billy hunt should clear my mind.

Like most bonding companies, this one had taken up residence in a building abandoned by some other business. This one used to be one of those quick oil change joints. I pulled the Bronco into one of the bays and found my way back to the front entrance. A strip of bells jangled as I walked through, the obvious alarm system. I knew what most fresh out of jail customers didn't. This place might be a dump, but it was probably wired up tighter than most banks. The inside was cramped and cluttered, stacks of paper lined the walls and a computer from another time sat on the counter in the tiny reception area. A scraggly brunette in jeans and a T-shirt tossed instructions my way.

"Grab a clipboard and start filling out the bottom half. We'll be with you in a minute." She resumed her conversation with her current customers.

I ignored her instruction and sank into one of the orange plastic chairs nearby and waited until she finished up with the elderly couple at her desk. When they left, I strode over. "I'm looking for a guy you posted surety on a while back. Want to see if you have his last known address." I pulled out my hardly ever used license and flashed it. "Professional courtesy."

I didn't know her and she wouldn't recognize my name. Her boss was one of Hardin's biggest rivals and Hardin hated his guts. I did work for plenty of bonding companies other than Hardin's, but not this one. Steering clear was a professional courtesy to him.

She stared me down. "He still on bond?"

I didn't think so, but I knew she wouldn't cave for a vague response. "Nope. Just need to talk to him about a separate matter."

She didn't have any motivation to keep Billy's information private, but she didn't have any motivation to help me out either. The scales were even and her expression made it clear it was up to me to tip things in my direction. I fished around in my pocket for one of the last fifties from the last job and reluctantly shoved it her way. I made a mental note that Maggie owed me another steak.

The address was in South Dallas. A perfect place for a crackhead like Billy to blend in with like-minded souls. Another drug deal was as close as the nearest convenience store. Back in my car, I took a minute to make sure my backup Sig had a full clip and I stuck a spare in my boot. The holster for the Colt barely qualified as concealed since anyone with half a brain could tell the big bad bulge in my jacket was a gun. Jacket weather had faded fast as the Texas summer approached. The start of summer on the calendar had little bearing on when heat started to break us down. I've seen temperatures in the high nineties as early as April. As long as I wore a big gun, I'd have the jacket on and it was already starting to suck.

The drive was short and boring. Every block in this area looked the same. Run-down, unkempt, plain. Billy's last address was a dive. Big surprise. I parked at a nearby Stop and Shop and waved to one of the hookers pretending to look like she was only stopping and shopping. I didn't have much cash left, but I cared about my car. As in I wanted the battery, tires, and other necessary parts to be attached when I returned.

She mistook my intentions, but I quickly pulled her hands away from my waist and set her straight. "I don't need an afternoon delight. I only want you to keep an eye on my ride."

She put her hands on her hips and raised her voice. "You a cop?"

I shushed her. "I am the exact opposite of cop." Not exactly true, but it's how I felt most of the time. I pulled a twenty from my pocket. "You want to make some money or not?"

She grabbed the twenty and didn't bitch. In this part of town, an Andrew Jackson would buy a blowjob. That I wasn't asking for contact was a big bonus in her world.

"You just bought yourself thirty minutes. I ain't cheap."

I left rather than argue the point. The apartment listed with the bonding company was really an old hotel, converted into week to week units. I'd picked up a jumper here before. Each unit was a single room with a tiny kitchenette. Most of the residents were transients who needed an address for a short period of time, until their probation or court settings were over. I wondered if Billy ever actually stayed here or whether one of his no-good friends provided him with the address for the court forms.

Apartment three nineteen. Accessible only by stairs. Apparently, disabled folks better be able to afford better digs than this. I huffed my way up. I run several times a week to stave off my bad eating habits and because it's free, but no matter how in shape I might be, stairs always kick my ass. By the time I reached the door, my quads burned and I wished for a paper bag to breathe into. While I thought of a plausible reason for showing up, I rested against what I thought was a closed door. I didn't have a chance to prepare a script since the door swung open at my touch. I pulled the Colt and braced for impact.

Nothing. I stepped over the threshold and let my eyes adjust to the dark room. All the blinds were pulled. Seconds after I regained my ability to breathe, I wished I hadn't. The iron stench of blood filled my nostrils and I fought to keep from spewing my big greasy breakfast all over the floor.

❖

One of the advantages of a small place is that it's easy to clean. In theory. This particular apartment would never be clean again. Long-empty fast food wrappers, heaping full ashtrays, and an assortment of handmade bongs and used syringes lined every surface. Besides the usual signs of a junkie in residence, chairs were on end, couch cushions ripped open, stuffing stuck to every surface because blood was streaked, splattered, and smeared everywhere. Walls, surfaces, floor. I'd already stepped in it and that fact fixed me firmly in place. I could tell the blood was dry, but the last thing I needed was to track my boot prints all over a crime scene. Besides, I didn't need to move around to see what had caused the mess.

She was well into death, but I could still tell she was young. Probably because I'd just seen her very much alive. She wasn't any older now than she had been when she'd starred in the homemade porno I'd pinched from Quitman's house the day before. Seeing her now, in real life—make that death—was beyond weird.

Amazingly, her face was the only part of her body untouched by the massive angry knife that lay beside her on the floor. Her clothes were torn, rent through with long cutting strokes. She lay in a heap on the floor. The only evidence of her energy, the bloody swath of fight splashed all around the room.

From where I stood, the only room I couldn't see was the bathroom. I supposed there was a chance the killer lurked in there, but I doubted it. She'd been dead for hours, and no way he would have dropped his knife en route to a hiding place. Everywhere I looked, his footprints were framed in blood. Just to be safe, I cocked the Colt and pointed it in the direction of the bathroom while I used my other hand to flip open my phone and hit speed dial.

"Chance here."

"Jess, it's Luca. I need your help." I hoped she got the point that I needed something personal. I didn't want to say a lot over a cell line.

"What's up?"

I gave her the address and apartment number and asked her to come alone. She grunted a response and hung up. I'd seriously tipped the scales in our ongoing favor exchange. When she saw what I was calling about, I'd owe her for life.

My phone call hadn't spurred any action from the bathroom. I fisted the end of my T-shirt and pulled it up over my face, but nothing could block the smell of death.

Jess arrived quickly, but she wasn't alone. When I saw her new partner standing over her shoulder, I stepped outside and shut the door behind me.

"What's going on here?"

This from the partner. Jess would never ask such a stupid question. I gave her new partner a once-over. He was a huge hulk of a man. She'd mentioned him, but I didn't remember his name. I mentally assigned him the title of Detective Dickhead. Her last partner, John Hayes, had been shot during a bust and was riding a desk indefinitely. John and I got along just fine. I'd never met this guy before, but these few seconds told me all I needed to know. In the foreground, she shrugged and I knew he'd pushed to ride along. She wasn't going to be able to do what I wanted with this guy standing watch. I directed my response to Jess and I stuck to bare facts.

"Dead body inside."

Dickhead snapped to attention, drew his weapon, and stepped in front of Jess. The patronizing gesture pissed me off. "Maybe you missed the important part of what I said. *Dead* body." I jerked my chin at his gun. "You need a body bag, not a loaded weapon."

He practically growled. Jess put a hand on his arm and he lowered his weapon. She was his superior and he'd do what she said whether he wanted to or not. She took over. "Talk to me, Bennett."

"I got here about two minutes before I called you. Door was open." Slight untruth. "Blood's everywhere. Knife on the floor. Twenty something female full of holes. No sign of anyone else in the place."

"What're you doing here?"

"A job. Bad tip." I felt a trace of guilt for lying to her, but no way was I going to tell her anything else in front of Dickhead. One mention of the videos starring dead girl, and they'd be all over me about handing them over and full of questions about where I'd gotten them. Plus I didn't want to betray Maggie's trust. If Billy had a warrant, the last thing he needed was the cops to make him for what had gone down inside. No way Billy was responsible for the carnage on the other side of that door. I hoped.

Jess pointed at my jacket. "Give me your gun."

"What the hell?"

Her expression begged me not to argue. Not in front of her partner. I pulled out the Colt, and handed it over, handle first. I didn't try to hide how pissed off it made me.

Jess shoved my baby into her waistband and did a stellar job of ignoring my anger. "Wait here." She tapped Dickhead on the shoulder. "Elton, cover me."

Elton. Dumb name. I watched Jess ease into the apartment with Elton practically standing on her heels. I stayed outside. A chore. I didn't want to go back inside the bloodfest, but I didn't want to stand outside waiting either. Our huddle outside the door had already collected an audience from the scary residents of the nearby apartments. With Jess and Elton inside, the gathering miscreants focused on me. I still had a gun, but I didn't want to risk flashing it in case Jess reappeared and decided to confiscate it too.

I rapped on the door. "Hey, you two, we're attracting a crowd."

Jess came to the door and waved me in. "Stand exactly where you were when you were in here before." Once I was in place, she asked, "Is everything exactly how you found it?"

"I didn't move from this spot. Walked in. Saw what you see now. Called you."

Elton chimed in. "Why didn't you call nine one one?"

I ignored him. Jess looked hard into my eyes. "You sure she wasn't who you were looking for?"

"Absolutely. Clearly, my tip was bad." I shifted in place. "Jess, do you really need me to stay here? It's not like you don't know where to find me."

She glanced at Elton's back and frowned at the familiar reference. I hadn't meant anything by using her first name, but obviously I needed to be more careful in front of the new guy. I raised my hands in surrender. She finally gave in. "Go, but we'll need you to come in later to give a statement."

"Thanks, Chance." I shifted in place for a minute, unsure how to ask for the other thing I wanted, especially with Elton standing a few feet away.

As if she could read my mind, she said, "You can have your gun back when we get your statement."

I knew there was no point arguing. I stalked back to the Stop and Shop in search of the hooker guarding my car.

She tangled with me about the extra time. I bought her cigarettes and she left me alone.

I considered taking the rest of the day off. Take a little drive up I-35 and see if my luck held out at the tables better than on the streets. By the time I got home I realized I was too tired to make the drive. Finding dead bodies is a sobering, bone-weary activity. I don't know how Jess did it on a regular basis.

When I started my day, I had intended to go by the courthouse after I checked out the apartment for Billy. I had wanted to track down Ronnie Moreno and get some more details about Jed Quitman. Right now, I cared more about a nap than either of the men I was supposed to find.

The bed was a wreck from last night's play. My sheets still smelled like Jess, and I pillowed myself in the comfort of the familiar, falling quickly into deep, welcome sleep.

CHAPTER SIX

The pounding on my door was impossible to ignore. I don't own an alarm clock for this very reason. I hate rude awakenings. I work for myself so I can come and go as I please. The time I spent as a cop cured me of ever wanting to punch a clock or answer calls at odd hours.

Maybe the pounding was Old Man Withers, my landlord. I'd just given him a down payment on the rent that was due two weeks ago. Surely he knew me better than to think I'd have come up with the rest of the money by now. I burrowed under the covers.

My stalker didn't quit, adding to the heavy knocks with a growling, "Police, open up."

Now I wished it was Withers. I dragged on a pair of jeans and T-shirt and stood on my side of the door. "What do you want?"

"Open the door."

Yeah, right. "Not until you tell me what you want."

"Okay, Bennett. We'll have this conversation in front of God and everyone."

I recognized the voice, but didn't bother telling Teresa Perez that God wasn't likely to be hanging out in front of my doorway now or ever. "Tell me what you want or get the hell away from my door."

"I want to talk to you about the dead woman you were hanging out with this afternoon."

I cracked the door. She wasn't alone. I assumed the guy with her was her partner. A skinny guy with slumped shoulders. I imagined he'd become beat down about a week into working with Perez. "Who was she?"

They exchanged glances before Perez spoke. "Maybe you should tell us."

Why were they here? I'd expected Jess to call me to come in for a statement, not send a goon squad, especially not Perez, to harass me. I flashed on the image of the now dead, naked girl, who'd been very much alive during her video performance. Perez would not be the first one I told about this tidbit of information. I struck a reasonable tone. "I'm sure you know I've already talked to Chance."

If I'd thought invoking Jess's name would get me anywhere, I was mistaken.

"*Detective* Chance doesn't get to cherry pick her cases. You'll be dealing with us. You can tell us what you know about Emily Foster here or we'll haul you in."

That wasn't going to happen. I knew I'd have to answer their questions at some point, but I'd do it on my terms. Not seconds after an REM-rich nap. I needed to buy some time to figure out what was going on. I suddenly thought of a perfect delay tactic. I pulled a card out of my back pocket. Yes, I'd worn the same pair of jeans as the day before. The business card was wrinkled, but usable. I tossed it into the hallway. "You want to talk? Call my attorney." I shut the door on Perez's face and waited out the fade of their footsteps before I picked up my cell phone and dialed a number from memory.

Jess didn't answer. I didn't leave a message because I didn't want to record for all posterity the choice words that came to mind. How dare she sic Perez on me? We often disagreed, but it never occurred to me she wouldn't trust me. She should've at least had the balls to tip me off about who was handling the case.

I wandered into the kitchen in search of water. The clock on the stove read four p.m. I pulled a semi clean glass from the sink, then put it back. Water wouldn't quench this thirst. I pulled a long neck beer from the fridge and sucked it down. I nursed the second one while running searches on my computer.

My first find was golden. Jed Quitman, or at least Quitman Enterprises, owned the seedy apartment complex where Emily

Foster was cut to ribbons. A fact curiously absent from the list of Quitman's businesses Ronnie had given me. That he owned the complex was interesting, but not surprising. Strip clubs, low-budget housing, high interest check cashing. All of his enterprises catered to a similar clientele. No small wonder Billy would live in Quitman's slum, but a pretty big coincidence that I'd be on the job looking for both Jed and Billy at the same time and find such a close connection.

And what about the girl? I was certain Perez hadn't meant to slip and give me a name, but having one wasn't proving to be very helpful. Searches for Emily Foster didn't yield much. No driver's license for any Emily Foster in what I thought was the dead girl's age range. No property ownership either. I did find a misdemeanor criminal record for someone who might be her, but I couldn't know for sure without a date of birth. Lost in beer and Google, when the phone rang I answered the call without checking the caller ID.

"Thanks a lot, Chance."

"Luca?"

The gravelly tone came from a familiar voice, but it wasn't Chance.

"Hey, Dad. Look, I can't talk now. I'm waiting for a call to come through."

"Yeah, okay. That's fine. I didn't have anything much to say anyway."

His sad growls were laced with sloppy slurs, designed for one purpose. I fell for it every time. "What's up?"

"Nothing much. I've got a great lead, but I'm a bit short. End of the month and all. Thought I'd let you in on it. Someone should benefit."

I knew the code. We'd developed our own language years ago. After Mom left, we no longer needed our special speak, but it was easier to keep up the pretense. I sighed. "I'll be over in about an hour."

In an hour it would be after five and then I'd be able to pretend that his drunk slurs were socially acceptable. Not that I really cared about being acceptable, but I would at least be relieved of the nagging feeling I should intervene. The time for intervention had passed. Way before my mother had ever walked out. I couldn't do anything about his situation then, and all I could do now was soothe his aching soul with the medicine he liked best. Bets and alcohol.

I picked up a twelve pack of Pabst. I didn't care for the swill, which was precisely the point. He didn't answer my first few knocks, but the extra key was under the same dead plant that had been sitting on the porch of my childhood home for as long as I could remember.

"Dad, you in here?" I called out the words as I walked through the house. The place had the same sour musty odor I'd come to expect, but would never get used to. As I made my way through the cluttered rooms, my pace quickened. He'd sounded pretty sloshed on the phone, but he'd sounded worse. Plenty of times. I set the beer on the kitchen counter. A fleeting wave of guilt washed over me for contributing to his demise.

I heard the sliding glass door of the patio and glanced up. He was wearing his Kiss the Cook apron and wielding a spatula. His eyes blinked from the change in light. "Luca, that you?"

Who else would it be? I should be used to his haze. "Yeah, Dad. It's me. What're you grilling?"

He stoked the coals of his ancient Weber. "I got some sausages from Jimmy's. Mrs. Teeter brought them over. Thought I'd grill those up for you. Don't have much to go with them though."

I was pretty sure Widow Teeter planned on sharing said sausages with dear old dad, and she would have been happy to provide side dishes, including a little personal dessert if he would only invite her over. He had no problem accepting her handouts, but their relationship never seemed to go further than a few words exchanged while she unloaded the extra groceries she used as bait. Good thing the attraction wasn't mutual. She had no idea what she was likely to catch if Dad ever did bite. I'd witnessed enough of his slow deterioration to believe he would never have a fulfilling relationship again. If he'd ever even had one in the first place.

Sausage from Jimmy's, an authentic Italian deli, sounded great, but eating them in this depressing house, with all its smells, sights, and memories while my father drank himself beyond oblivion was not what I was in the mood for tonight. Now that I was awake, I was keyed up. My skin was too tight. I needed to flex. Normally, I'd seek out Jess when I felt this way. Work off some of this nervous energy with mindless sex. But I was here now, and as much as I might resent it, the man who raised me needed attention. I knew exactly what would make us both feel better. I felt in my left pocket, where I'd stuffed the money I'd set aside to pay the rest of the rent. Not big on leaving cash under a door, I'd planned to pay up whenever I ran into my landlord.

"How about you save those sausages for another day and we take a trip up I-35?"

His eyes lit up, then dimmed. "I'm a bit short. You can go on without me."

"Naw, it'll be more fun with the both of us. I can spot you. Let's go." I envisioned my landlord's red face when I informed him I'd spent the rent on vice-riddled entertainment for my father. Maybe it wouldn't go down that way. Maybe he'd be all smiles when I paid several months in advance instead. I spent a moment enjoying the image before my rational self shelved the fiction. Fiction or not, it was time to forget a little, and who better to do that with than the man who'd forgotten most of his life in the bottom of a glass of whiskey.

❖

Dad liked to talk. I let him do all of it, which made the ninety minute ride seem like days. By the time we rolled into the huge parking lot of the Winstar Casino, steps from the Texas-Oklahoma border, I'd heard every last detail of his unemployed life. I longed for the loud clanging noises of the machines inside.

"What'll it be? Paris, New York, Rome?" I pointed at the various façades that made the Winstar Casino "world class." I didn't give a damn where we ended up. I had money in my pocket and it would spend as well in the Big Apple as it would under a fake Eiffel Tower.

"Let's go to Rome. I could use a good toga party."

"Sounds good." I parked the car near the fake coliseum. Dad stumbled out of the car while I pushed away the vision of his beer-slackened body wrapped in only a sheet.

I considered leaving my window slightly cracked. The heat was unbearable even this late. I'd emptied most of the guns out before we'd hit the road, but I hated to risk a break-in. I rolled the window up tight and pressed both door locks. I shoved a hand in my jacket. The Sig was okay, but I missed the reassuring weight of the long Colt. I didn't leave the Sig in the car. Texas law didn't allow even permit holders to carry where alcohol was sold, but we weren't in Texas anymore.

The electric doors to the casino slid open and the rush of refrigerated air caressed me like a lover. The racing lights, the clinking glasses, the beeps and whirs of thousands of blinking machines signaled I was in heaven. I vowed I'd never leave.

"What'll it be?"

I'd almost forgotten he was with me. "Whatever you want." I knew where he was headed. Dad loved poker. He sucked at it, but the big stakes games on TV had him convinced it could be a viable way to make a living. It might be. But not for him. He drank too much to manage a decent poker face or keep up with the cards. I was a passable player, but blackjack was my real game. The simple act of counting to twenty-one was a meditation. Right now I craved its simple, rhythmic, hypnotizing release.

I'd get what I wanted soon enough. I steered Dad to a five card table and set him up with a stack of chips and a wad of ones to tip the waitress I knew he would abuse with increasingly leering stares and suggestive comments as the night progressed. I started to walk away, but he held onto my arm. "Stay. Play a round with your dear old dad."

I don't know if I ever would've walked into my first casino if it wasn't for my dear old dad. I was fifteen. About as big as I am now. By his side, no one asked any questions. Roulette, craps, blackjack, and poker. We blew the monthly mortgage payment on my introduction to the world of high stakes. I loved it. Until Mom found out what we had done. I hadn't yet learned Dad's methods of hiding the fun behind "helping out a friend at work" or other random, acceptable ways to blow money. Not the first crack in the relationship between my parents, but a substantial wedge in an already shaky foundation.

I slid into the seat next to him. One round. Then I'd leave him to his drinks and losses.

As the dealer tossed out the cards, Dad started running the table. "My daughter and me, we've played the tables together for years." He draped an arm around my shoulders. "She's a better player of course. And better looking for sure."

I ducked out from under his shoulder, hitched my shoulders at our fellow players. He laughed and announced, "She's embarrassed." I was. I always was. Didn't matter. He would keep it up until I gave in, laughed at his jokes, belted back drinks, and punched him in the shoulder like we were pals. We were pals. Except sometimes I was the parent.

"You heard from your mom lately?"

He always asked. I suppose he imagined a day when the answer would be, "Yes, she called and wants to come home. Can you meet her with a moving truck at the corner of..." I kept it simple. "Not lately."

"I heard she got married again." He feigned nonchalance, but I knew better. I wondered if he knew details. I didn't want to know. I did want to know. I couldn't decide.

"That so?" I tossed out a noncommittal response and let him take it from there.

"Good one this time. A banker. Lives in Southlake."

I resisted the urge to laugh. The last two had been good ones too, according to my mother. A car dealer and a judge. If you heard her tell it, my dad had been the only bad decision she'd ever made, my brother and me close on its heels by association. How Dad found out her current doings was a mystery. Why he still cared was another mystery, but I couldn't fault him for a trait I shared. I didn't have to encourage him though. I tried to change the subject. "How's Mrs. Teeter doing?"

"She's good. You don't act surprised to hear your mom's moving back to town. Did you already know?"

I shook my head. Not paying attention to my mother's life was my personal payback for all the years she didn't pay attention to mine. I only knew that she'd moved out of state because of Dad's incredible network of gossip. I suppose that's what happens when you're the only bachelor in a neighborhood of little old ladies. Even the married ones treated him like a second husband. Only their version of nurturing involved nursing his obsession with what went wrong with the only relationship he'd ever had.

While he checked out his cards, I sized him up. Sprouts of gray hair lined the edges of his mostly balding scalp. He was a good six months of nutrition and exercise away from being the shell of his former self. I had a hard time imagining the handsome young quarterback who'd escorted the homecoming queen to all the big dances in the tiny west Texas town where they'd grown up. I'd seen the pictures so I knew the fairy tale had once been true.

My memories of the reality were bleaker. Not enough money and not enough love to overcome the dark hole that appears when the fake lights of youth fade away. Torn rotator cuff meant no more football. Rough economy meant no more job. The homecoming queen who'd grown up wanting for nothing lost patience with her king. She wasted no time finding a new one. The woman formerly known as Jackie Bennett was apparently on to her fourth marriage, while Dad still lived in the same house, slept in the same old recliner, cursed at the same old television, and relived memories that had never really been real.

"Check out this hand."

He leaned close. I could tell he was trying to get a look at my hand. I shoved him away. "You're going to get us kicked out. Play your own cards."

He raised his beer and took a deep swallow, then tossed out some chips. "Fine, fine. I'll buy you a steak with my winnings. Then you'll respect your old man."

A steak wasn't going to do it. I placed my own bet. Small. I had a lousy hand. I didn't care. I wasn't sitting here for fun. Respect? Maybe never, but someone had to keep tabs on him. Since my brother had escaped halfway across the country, I was all he had.

Apparently, he didn't need me for the moment. I watched the dealer rake away my chips and double Dad's stack. I ventured back into our stilted conversation. "Maybe you should buy that steak for Mrs. Teeter."

He shrugged. I gave up. If he ever decided to make a move with the widow, it wasn't going to be because I pushed him. I eased my chair back. "You good?"

He waved me off. "Go, get some faces and aces. I'm fine."

I strode over to Paris and scouted out the blackjack table with the best looking dealer. I wasn't in the mood to care if I won or lost, but at least I could have a hot woman to look at while I threw my money away. Didn't take long before I found more than I was looking for.

She was a petite version of Ronnie Moreno. Olive skin, deep, dark brown eyes. Her crisp tuxedo shirt and creased black pants reminded me of Ronnie's sharply tailored suit. I settled in and placed the minimum ten dollar bet. I hoped she didn't mind being stared at for the next couple of hours.

Our relationship started out well. I pretended she was the elusive Ronnie and she pretended she didn't notice I was entranced. While she shuffled the deck, I looked away only long enough to order a drink. When I turned back to the table, she smiled. The difference struck me at once. Her smile was pleasant, friendly, easy. Ronnie's smiles were dazzling, passionate, layered. They made me want to swim into the depth and discover hidden treasures.

I looked up at the sound of a clearing throat and met the dealer's patient gaze with a smile of my own. Easy would do for tonight. After a couple of hands I settled into the rhythm. Winning, losing. Betting again.

CHAPTER SEVEN

A hangover magnified everything. The sound of my upstairs neighbor clomping across the floor, the barking of the dog next door, the growl of the lawn mower outside my window. Oh, and the shouts of an angry woman just outside my door.

I'd expected Chance to show up at some point. She owed me an explanation and I imagine she thought I owed her one as well. I wish she'd waited. I didn't even know what day it was let alone remember the source of my lingering anger. The last image in my foggy memory was my old man weeping over a two thousand dollar win at the poker table. I couldn't recall if the win ended our father daughter bonding on a happy note, or if the story played out as it usually did. I wanted to sleep more than I wanted to relive.

"Go away. I'm sleeping." I pulled the covers over my head and prayed for mercy. No such luck.

"Luca Bennett, answer this door or I'll leave you to face the cops on your own."

Despite my stupor, I recognized the voice. Out of place here, but forever fixed in my mind. Fiery, confident, and pissed off.

I stumbled to the door, at once dismayed and thankful I was still wearing my clothes from the night before. I reeked of smoke and beer, but at least I was dressed.

She was dressed too, sans smoke odor and remnants of alcohol. White linen shorts and a chili red blouse set off her dark Latin coloring perfectly. She was taller than I remembered, but as sexy in her casual daywear as she was in tightly tailored lawyer drag.

"Are you going to stop leering and invite me in?"

I shook off the trance. As hot as she was, she'd shown up unannounced, and I was too tired to take advantage of whatever she had to offer. I'm not big on hospitality anyway, and her tone drove the last vestiges of welcome out of me. "Actually, no. I was sleeping. I only answered to tell you to keep it down." I started to shut the door, but a surprisingly strong push from the other side kept it open.

"You think I want to spend my Saturday morning visiting your dive? Think again." She glared her next point. "Trust me, Bennett. You want to let me in."

I didn't trust anyone, and I started to say it, but curiosity about why she was here, how she even knew where I lived, won out. I swung the door wide and swept an arm to invite her in. She barely hid her distaste as she searched for a place to sit. I use surfaces as storage places and undeveloped real estate was scarce at the moment. I shoved a pile of newspapers to the floor and pointed to the now empty chair. She sat, but didn't settle in. I briefly considered offering her a drink, but I wasn't confident I had anything besides beer, and I was certain I didn't have a clean glass in the place. Hospitality would only prolong whatever bad news she was here to deliver.

"Okay, Moreno. What's the story?"

She looked amused at my use of her last name, presumably after my last attempt at using the casual Ronnie, but she only hesitated a moment before answering. "Seems you need a lawyer, and word is I'm it."

"What?"

She pulled a leather bound notepad from her oversized purse and consulted the pages. "Detective Perez wants to question you regarding the death, make that homicide, of Emily Foster."

I smiled at the memory of the cops' faces when I'd flung Ronnie's card their way. The act was nothing more than a delay tactic. I hadn't even considered they would actually call Ronnie, figuring instead that Chance would have called them off by now.

I was equal parts pissed that Chance hadn't stood up for me and pleased that Ronnie had taken their call when I'd not given her a heads up or, for that matter, a retainer.

"Oh, that. Yeah, sorry. I only wanted to put them off for a bit. I can clear this up on my own. "

"Is that so? Are you the same Luca Bennett whose private investigator's license was reinstated just months ago? Are you the same Luca Bennett who has a penchant for breaking and entering? Are you the same Luca Bennett who regularly carries a loaded weapon when she apprehends fugitives?"

The truth hurts, especially when it's delivered in an accusing tone from a hot babe who should be naked and moaning rather than delivering a litany of my faults. I'd had enough. I pointed at the door. "Like I said, I'm sorry I put you out. I don't need any legal services and I'd appreciate it if you would get the hell out of my apartment. Now." I walked to the door, expecting my harsh tone to spur her to follow.

She stayed seated in the chair. "Sit down, Luca. I'm not going anywhere."

I don't know why I did what she asked. It was another in an ongoing series of inexplicable actions on my part. She barely waited until my butt hit the chair before she started in. "What progress have you made on finding Jed Quitman?"

I was too sleep-deprived for non sequiturs, but my blinking response did nothing to keep the questions at bay.

"Do you have any leads at all?"

I held up a hand. "I thought you were here about something else."

"I'm here about a lot of things. You need a lawyer, whether you think you do or not. We're settling your fee. You answer my questions and I'll represent you. Seems like a good deal to me."

"I don't even know you, and I know all the good criminal defense attorneys in town. If I needed a lawyer, which I'm not saying I do, then I could have my pick."

She laughed and gave the interior of my place a pointed, judgmental look. "Fine, Bennett. Hire the best. What are you going to pay them with? Empty beer cans? Pizza boxes and Big Mac wrappers?" She let the comment settle, then added, "Besides, I might be better than you think."

She had a point, one I didn't want to concede, but a good one nevertheless. I wanted to know where she'd come by her inside intel, but I would die before asking. I made a silent vow to learn as much about her as she seemed to know about me. In the meantime, I could use some lawyerly advice. I gave up my reluctant façade and told her I'd been to Jed's house and his playmate of the month seemed to have no idea he'd skipped out.

"What's your next step?"

Information is a precious commodity and one I don't share unless it buys me something of value. "I've got a few ideas." The first one was figuring out the connection between Billy Flynn and Emily Foster. Since that didn't have anything to do with the case she'd hired me on, I decided to keep it to myself.

"I want things done by the book." This from the woman who wanted to bypass the cops when I found her jumper. I let it pass. Apparently, we both had secrets. What she didn't realize was there was no book in my line of business. Once we took our tests and got our license, all bets were off. Bring in the jumper and collect the bounty. Two steps. No rules. If I wanted to pretend to play by the rules, I'd still be a cop. I didn't bother filling her in. She didn't need her pristine world shattered. "I'll take care of things. Now, about my situation?"

"Why don't you start by telling me what happened. Unvarnished version."

I explained how I'd come upon the dead body of the young woman the day before. When I finished my summary, conveniently leaving out the name of the jumper I'd been searching for, she settled back in her chair and tapped the arm with thinking fingers. Those fingers were long, slender, and well manicured. I imagined them raking my back, leaving a trail of marks. She clenched them into a fist, and I wondered if she was reading my mind. My bravado dissolved and I struggled to think of practical things, like my freedom, which spurred me to ask, "What now?"

"You promised Detective Chance you would give a statement, right?"

I nodded.

"Well, it shouldn't be a problem to give one to her colleagues. I'll go with you. I'll call and let you know when I've got a time set up." She stood and affected a nonchalant expression. "Is Detective Chance the woman who was with you at the courthouse when we first met?"

"Matter of fact, she was." I hid my surprise at her memory and I stifled a jealous surge that she knew enough about Chance to single her out for attention. I didn't reflect on the exact source of my jealousy, but I did ask, "You work a lot of cases with her?"

"No. I haven't been…I haven't been in court with her at all."

Her pause was a quick blip, but I caught it. What had she planned to say? "I haven't been…?" Ronnie Moreno had something to hide and I found myself liking her even more because of it.

❖

I hoped my dad was home, sleeping off his share of the hangover. I almost called him, but it was way too early still. I did riffle through my own jean pockets and discovered we'd had a successful night. I did anyway. I shoved five twenties in my wallet and put the rest in a coffee can in the cabinet. Banks are for people who can afford to lose money. At least now I'd have enough to pay the rent and eat until I found Quitman. And I would find Quitman.

After her early morning visit, I was more curious than ever about Ronnie, but the imminent police interview focused my attention on Billy and the late Emily Foster. Emily, such a plain name for a whip-wielding beauty. As much as I wanted to laser focus on the mystery of Ronnie Moreno, I figured the only way I was going to get close to her was with some intel on her client slash jumper. I'd have to find a way to combine my efforts or leave Billy for later. My stomach growled an idea my way.

Maggie's place may not be open for breakfast to the general public, but I wasn't general public. Besides, I reasoned, her grill was just as good for eggs and bacon as it was for burgers and steaks. Time to pump her for information. Maybe Billy's last known address and Quitman's slumlord holdings were more than a coincidence.

I took a shower to rinse last night's smoke away and found a ragged, but clean pair of Levi's and a T-shirt, only slightly wrinkled. When I pulled up to the bar, Big Harry, Maggies's cook, dishwasher, and jack-of-all-trades was tossing the contents of a sixty gallon trash can into the Dumpster. He held the can with one hand and waved with the other. I hopped out, in a hurry to catch him before he went back inside.

"How's Maggie this morning?"

"Good morning, Luca. Nice to see you this fine day."

I caught my breath and started over. "Good morning, Harry. You doing okay?"

"Can't complain. Got a roof over my head and food to eat."

Simple needs. Simple satisfaction. Harry and I weren't much different. "Glad to hear it, Harry, glad to hear it."

He gave me a once-over. Apparently satisfied I'd settled down, he answered my original question. "Maggie's inside. She hasn't been herself lately. You know anything about that?"

"I might."

"You gonna fix things for her?"

"I'll do my best."

"She's countin' on you." He started toward the door. With his hand on the handle, he looked over his shoulder. "You comin'? You look hungry." Astute guy, that Harry. I followed closely as he entered the building.

I sat at the bar and waited impatiently for Maggie to show. Ten minutes later, when she finally appeared, she didn't seem different. She tossed a full plate of bacon and eggs on the bar and settled in next to me. "What's shaking, Luca?"

I could tell she wanted to ask about Billy, but didn't want to push. That was different. I eased into the subject with a bit of what Maggie liked best. Gossip. "I got a paying gig. You know Jed Quitman?"

"Quick Cash Quitman? Sure. Who doesn't?"

"He skipped out on a court date. I'm looking for him."

"That so? Should be easy to find him. His mug's plastered all over town."

"You'd think so, but even his main squeeze doesn't seem to know he's gone. She's sunning herself by the pool at his fancy mansion."

Maggie had firsthand knowledge about my voracious appetite for beautiful women. Her disapproving look spurred me to change the subject. "I have a lead on Billy."

She reached for my arm midflight. My eggs would be cold and rock hard by the time she finished with me. I cared about missing a meal, but I cared about Maggie more. As gruff as she acted, she'd give me her last dime if I was in need. "You ever been to his old apartment?"

She shook her head. "He hasn't had a place of his own for a while. If you found a place, it probably belongs to one of his worthless jailhouse pals. I used to let him bunk with me, but not after the time he hocked my new television. You think I'm a bad sister?"

Since when did Maggie care what I thought? "Not my place." I quickly corrected my non answer. "Look, you can't fix people like Billy. I've seen plenty like him. He's got to change on his own, make better decisions about who to hang out with." Especially after what I'd seen the day before.

She nodded. "You say you have a lead?" She affected nonchalance, but I knew better. She was dying to get into my business, but no way was I going to talk about the dead body I'd found in my hunt for Billy. "It's not solid yet, but I swear I'll find him." Now that I'd committed myself, I moved on to other subjects. "Tell me more about Quitman."

"Billy used to do some work for Quitman."

"Really? What kind of work?"

"Odd jobs and the like."

"How long ago?"

"It's been a while. Billy's not so good at holding a job."

Big Harry strode over to the counter. "Maggie, I got a guy out back saying you ordered fourteen cases of champagne. You celebrating something you didn't bother telling me about?"

Maggie huffed off the barstool. "Luca, I got to take care of this."

I took the interruption as an opportunity to exit. Maggie would keep me cornered all day if I let her. Besides, she'd given me the connection I was looking for. If Billy had worked for Quitman, then the fact he'd lived in one of Quitman's slums wasn't much of a coincidence after all. Maybe finding Billy would lead to Quitman or vice versa. Probably too optimistic, but now I had a good excuse to combine my work on the gratis job with the one that could actually keep a roof over my head.

CHAPTER EIGHT

B ack at my apartment, I fired up my laptop. Before I dug back into the search for Quitman, I needed to know more about the elusive woman who'd hired me. I began my search for all things Ronnie Moreno.

The State Bar of Texas website had no listing for a Veronica Moreno, but Google listed dozens of entries for the woman named as one of the top lawyers under forty in the nation. Princeton undergrad, Harvard law. She'd clerked for a federal court of appeals judge before taking a high-dollar position in the litigation department at Sacking, Bird, and Wise, a go-to Manhattan firm. The list of representative clients and cases on Ronnie's bio page boasted big names, both individuals and corporations. I didn't know a lot about the legal profession, but I knew enough to know that Veronica Moreno had an impressive list of credentials. As if I wasn't already impressed.

About six months ago, the information trail hit a dead end. She was listed as one of the key players in a big win by Blanco Corporation against a huge plaintiff class action lawsuit. Then nothing. No more press releases, no more bio at SB & W. Her listing with the New York State Bar Association merely said "not currently registered." I poked around a little more only to find out New York protected their own. If an attorney had any sanctions in her record, that fact didn't show up online. You had to send a written request to the courts.

Maybe her departure from the big law firm simply meant she'd scored a big bonus on the Blanco case and packed in the high pressure legal scene. If so, then what was she doing hustling criminal cases with her slick uncle, Miguel Moreno?

Next I searched for property. She owned a house in North Dallas. An expensive one. Far as I could tell, she didn't own anything else the state was required to know about. If she had a nest egg, she wasn't flashing it around. I'd seen all I needed to. The key to Moreno wasn't in the pages of the Internet. I'd have to do some old-fashioned stalking to figure out her story. Why her story mattered so much I couldn't say. I should spend all my time on Quitman, but since I had enough in the coffee can to pay for rent, food, and gas, I could afford to squander some of my time. I vowed to spend the rest of the morning finding out what I could and then let it go. I wouldn't let my curiosity burn a potentially lucrative contact. The contents of my coffee can would only go so far.

Miguel's office was steps from the courthouse, in the same strip of buildings as all the bonding companies. Appropriate. A large billboard, strategically placed for newly released inmates to see, featured a well-suited Miguel Moreno with an appropriately serious expression. Larger than life Miguel promised aggressive defense for a long list of crimes, affordable payment plans, and bonding services twenty-four seven. I wondered if he sent Ronnie out in the middle of the night to bond clients out of jail and if so, did she look as much of a fashion diva in the wee hours as she did in daylight.

As I idled in the parking lot, I considered whether to wait for a while, see if she came out and then follow her or whether I should go on in and announce I was there to see her. The Bronco's struggling A/C decided the matter. I decided to go in. After all, she was my lawyer.

The reception area was a poorly disguised security gate designed to keep out the Commerce Street riffraff who had no money to hire an attorney. Based on what I'd learned at the softball tournament, Moreno & Associates' services were priced to capture the last dollars of low income folks. The strip of leftover Christmas bells hanging from the door proved frugality was an office theme. If someone couldn't hire Miguel, they were truly indigent. Again, I wondered what six hundred dollar an hour Ronnie Moreno was doing in this dump.

"May I help you?"

I glanced at the receptionist. She had to have been the one to speak, but based on the diligent filing of her nails, you'd never know she'd noticed me walk in the door. Her hair was swept up in an Aqua Net wave, poised high above her forehead and her makeup featured a full color palette. Hours spent on appearance, even if in this case it was to no avail, was obviously very important here at Moreno & Associates.

"I'm here to see Ron—I mean, Veronica Moreno."

She narrowed her eyes. I stood stock-still and waited. "You're not a client."

"No, I'm not." Not entirely true, but I wasn't in the mood to explain. "It's a personal matter." I didn't feel like explaining that I was a bounty hunter either. I didn't make a habit of telling many people what I did. Seemed counterintuitive.

"You don't say." She leaned way back in her chair and gave me a once-over. "Didn't know Ronnie had been in town long enough to establish *personal* matters." Uh-oh. My attempt at avoiding questions had train wrecked. She rocked her chair forward and wheeled as close to the front counter as she could get. "You know her from back East?"

Ah, the gatekeeper was a gossip. I nodded and leaned in close to give my lies the aura of authenticity. "I was surprised as anyone when she came back."

The wave bobbed agreement. "No one knows why. At least not for sure." She looked around the room and lowered her voice. "I have my ideas."

I affected a look of great interest and waited patiently.

"Bad break up." She nodded solemnly, agreeing with her own conclusion. I joined in to encourage her along. Didn't take much. "She's been pretty bitchy since she showed up and she argues with Miguel. A lot."

Interesting. I wasn't sure what to make of it. I didn't have much time to process the information before we were interrupted by the jangle of bells on the door and the subject of our conversation strode through the door.

Ronnie didn't look happy to see me, but she hid her frown as soon as she noticed the watchful gaze of the receptionist. "Maria, stop gossiping and get back to work. Luca, come with me."

She charged through the inner doors without waiting for me to acknowledge the order. I shot a look of surprise at Maria who mouthed "See what I mean?"

Ronnie's office was the size of a closet, furnished with a miniature desk and two tiny chairs. She didn't invite me to sit, but I did. She settled into the chair behind the desk and made a good show of acting like she didn't have to pretzel herself into the space. She didn't waste any time getting down to business.

"You found Quitman?"

"No."

"I thought you were the best."

"I am. You want to tell me why you care so much about a bond jumper?"

"Why are you here if not to tell me you found Quitman?"

Again with the answering a question with a question. Two could play this game. "What's a legal eagle like you doing in a two-bit firm like this?"

She sprang to her feet. "I apparently have enough expertise to represent two-bit bounty hunters who need a defense against a murder charge."

Zing. "Tone it down. I'm not wanted on a murder charge and if I was, I think I could hire myself a lawyer with a bigger office."

She looked from my T-shirt down to my boots and shrugged. Okay, so maybe she was right. I couldn't afford an attorney with a bigger office, but if I was really in trouble, I would definitely find someone who'd been around the block at the criminal courthouse a few more times than she had. She looked at her watch. "We have an appointment at three to meet with Detectives Perez and Dalton. Do you need more time to retain other counsel?"

"I thought you were supposed to call me to let me know when you scheduled the interview."

"It was going to be the first thing I did when I got to the office, but here you are."

Yep, here I was. I could choose to go it on my own, hire someone else, or accept the services of Ronnie not quite knowing what strings were attached. I decided to follow the strings to see where they led.

❖

I declined Ronnie's offer to ride to police headquarters together. I had a particular errand I wanted to run and I wanted to do it alone.

Quitman's Quick Cash, store number one, lacked the tender loving care of its owner's house. The storefront's battered exterior and wrought iron protection bars signaled the temperament of the south Dallas neighborhood, mere blocks from an area city leaders touted as the next frontier of urban renewal. Battle zone was a more accurate description. Despite the heat, I shrugged into a jacket and slid an extra clip into the pocket. Despite the sign warning it was illegal to carry, no way was I wandering around here unarmed.

I'd never had cause to darken the door of such a place. Probably because I operated a cash only business. I didn't expect to find Quitman in residence, but I figured I might get a feel for the business side of my target by checking out the foundation of his financial empire.

I spied four security cameras and wondered if any of them actually worked. Most likely the majority of them were for show. Pretty obvious Quitman didn't spend any money he didn't have to on this rat trap of a business. I made my way to the counter and waited behind a tattered young woman with a baby on her hip and two more little kids in tow. I watched as she handed over a wrinkled slip of paper, a paycheck stub, symbolizing forty hours work at a fast food joint at poverty level pay.

The kid behind the counter examined the stub, then pushed a form at her. "Initial here, here, and here. Sign here." He pointed as she signed, and when she finished the last scrawl of her signature, he snatched back the form and wandered through a door behind the counter. Within moments he was back with a small stack of bills. She barely waited for him to count them out before she grabbed them and stuffed them into the pocket of her stained jeans. She readjusted the child on her hip and urged her brood toward the door. Based on what I'd read online, I figured she'd just committed her entire family to an infinite cycle of debt hell. Interest on Quitman's payday loans ran about average. Average was around three hundred percent. Unlikely little mother of three was ever going to get enough raises at the burger joint to allow her to come close to paying off the loan. She'd wind up recycling the debt, week after week until she was crushed under the load. And then Quitman would sue her for payment in the municipal court. I wanted to find the guy if only to steal his wallet and ask him how he liked being fucked.

"Can I help you?"

I looked up at the guy and stifled my anger. After all, he probably didn't make much more than burger flipping mom of three, and he certainly wasn't the brains behind this outfit.

"I need to speak to Mr. Quitman. Any chance you know the best way for me to reach him?"

He looked at me like I was crazy, like did I really expect to find Jed Quitman, swinging social player wannabe, in this dump? He had a point. I wondered if he'd ever even met Quitman. "He doesn't come around here much, I imagine."

He glanced around before answering. "I only met the guy once. He doesn't make a habit of setting foot in this dump."

Wow. I hadn't expected such a visceral response. Now I knew the cameras weren't functioning. Either that or counter guy totally forgot his little tirade was being videotaped. I decided the former was more likely and I took advantage of the opening. "I guess you know all the fuss about his case."

I hoped he would know what I was talking about since I would lose ground if I had to spell it out. I wasn't disappointed. "Oh, he'll be fine. The people whose palms he greases think an indictment is a badge of honor."

My furrowed brow reflected real confusion and he took pity on me. "You know, politicians. Randolf, Lively. That whole group."

I didn't know. Not much anyway. I knew the names. Everyone did. Senator Lively was a powerful politician, but even more powerful than him, Caroline Randolf and her circle ruled parts of the city crucial to the election of any politician seeking office. Plus, I remembered the conversation at the softball game and how Nancy had mentioned a connection between Randolf and Quitman. Another recollection tickled my memory, but it slipped away before I could hone in the details.

"What's your name?"

"Henry. Henry Charleston."

"Henry, how long have you worked here?"

"A couple of years. Working my way through school at UNT. You're not here to cash a check are you?"

"Nope."

"Need a payday loan?"

"Nope."

He waited patiently for me to state my real business. I didn't have any. Just wanted to see Quitman's business side. I considered asking about Billy, but decided this guy wouldn't have any reason to know who he was. Better I stick with questions about Quitman. The kid was sharp and I could use a lead. I plunged ahead, deputizing Henry Charleston, honorary bounty hunter. "If you were Mr. Quitman and you wanted to disappear, where would you go?"

"Disappear disappear, or just lay low for a while?"

"Either."

"If I wanted to disappear, I'd go to Madagascar. No extradition treaty, lot of natural resources, and the dollar goes pretty far there."

I didn't ask him why he was so well-versed in escape plans. "And if you wanted to lay low?"

"I wouldn't even have to leave town. There are plenty of people right here in the city who owe him big time. All he has to do is call in some favors and wait until the dust settles."

From the mouths of college students straight to my ears. Jed Quitman had the resources, the connections to hide in plain sight.

Now, if I could figure out why he was hiding, maybe the where would follow.

❖

The lobby of the Jack Evans building, Dallas police headquarters, was open, airy, and featured unique artwork. The goal—to make it seem like an inviting place. Might work for most folks, but the whole building made my skin crawl.

I'd arrived ahead of Ronnie and stalked a path along the floor-to-ceiling windows, watching for her arrival. It occurred to me she might not know where she was supposed to go. Maybe I should have paid real money for an attorney, rather than trading favors and future promises for legal representation.

I'd rattled both the windows and the nerves of the guards on duty by the time Ronnie finally appeared, looking as if she was headed to a day of shopping at Neiman's rather than a homicide interrogation. I don't know designers, but I'd bet she'd contributed to the summer homes of several with her purchases.

"You're late."

She ignored me and reached into her fancy handbag and extracted her wallet. She pulled out her ID and bar card and held out her hand. "Your ID?"

I noted her bar card was issued here in Texas. Interesting. I doubted she'd had time to take the Texas bar exam since she'd left New York. I pulled my too-thin wallet out of my back pocket and fished out my driver's license. She plucked it from my grasp and strode over to the security gate that led to the inner sanctum. She handed the stack of credentials to the guard and flashed a winning smile. "We have an appointment with Detective Perez. Please let her know we're here."

We moved to the other side of the lobby while he made the call.

Five minutes later, Perez's sidekick, Dalton, showed up to collect us. He shook Ronnie's hand and motioned for us to follow him. We walked down a couple of long hallways before he stopped outside a slightly open door. He opened the door wide to reveal

Perez waiting within, practically salivating. She sat in a plain steel chair at a plain steel desk with no drawers, the only furnishings in the room.

I took a deep breath and started to walk in, but Ronnie grabbed my arm. She ignored Perez and addressed her partner. "Detective Dalton, do you have an arrest warrant for my client?"

Thanks for the suggestion, Counselor. I forced my facial muscles into a poker face. Dalton didn't hide his surprise as well as I did. "No, ma'am."

"Then we'd like the courtesy of conducting this meeting in a real office instead of one of your perp interview rooms." Ronnie delivered her declaration without a hint of animosity. She added a smile at the end, designed to defy him from calling her disagreeable.

He stammered for a moment and shot a look at Perez. I knew her well enough to detect she was seething underneath her cool demeanor, but no way was she going to let Ronnie see her unhinged. She'd probably gone ape-shit when she learned the hot woman she'd flirted with at the softball game worked for the dark side. In Perez's world, there was only black and white. Cops were good, defense attorneys were evil. She was a rare breed. Thank God.

Perez saved the fight for another day. She stood, bowed slightly at the waist, and threw her partner under the bus. "See, Dalton, I told you we should've used the conference room. Grab us some waters and meet us there."

Once we were settled in the conference room, Perez didn't wait for the water bearer to show up before she fired her first shot. "What business did you have with one of Quitman's strippers?"

I didn't bother telling her that Emily Foster's role in Quitman's business was way more than mere stripper. I did wonder if the masked woman in Quitman's videos was one of the strippers at the club as well. If so, why the mask? Wasn't like porn star was something to be ashamed of if you regularly shed your clothes for cash.

Ronnie saved me the trouble of responding to Perez's question. "Detective, before we get started, let's lay some ground rules. First, we're here voluntarily. I assume this interview is not being videotaped." She gave the ceiling a pointed look and waited for confirmation. Perez nodded and Ronnie started up again. "Ms. Bennett will be happy to share with you the details of what she found at the apartment, but as for the exact circumstances of how she came to be there, those details may be privileged, and I will need to consult with her after I hear your specific questions." She waited for a reaction. She got none. "Now, this will go a lot more smoothly if you don't treat Ms. Bennett like a hostile witness. When you refer to 'one of Quitman's strippers' who are you referring to?"

Perez stared holes into Ronnie. Detective Water Bearer wasn't back yet, and I imagine that was the only thing that saved Ronnie from an eruption of the famous Perez temper. She clenched her fists, then shook out her fingers before she responded. When she spoke, her voice was icy calm. "Bennett knows how the game is played. She doesn't need a well-dressed, fancy New York lawyer to hold her hand. But since you're new around here, I'll cut you some slack.

"Your client was at the scene of a brutal murder. She didn't have a key and the only person who could've invited her in didn't live to tell about it. The victim was a twenty-two-year-old stripper, Emily Foster aka Missy Bloom, formerly employed at the Foxy Lady, which is owned by one of your other clients, Jed Quitman." She made a show of scratching her head. "Hey, counselor, think you might have a little conflict?"

Ronnie didn't hesitate. "Oh, I don't know, Detective. We fancy New York lawyers don't really know much about the law."

I did my best to keep up. How did Perez know Ronnie was licensed in New York? Stupid question. I'd found the same information with a few keystrokes. The real question was why Perez cared enough to do the research. I didn't have much time to wonder before Perez refocused her ire in my direction.

"You got an answer, Bennett?"

I didn't have to say a word. I knew Ronnie would caution me against talking, but the situation had gotten crazy. What had been a simple favor for a friend had morphed into an unfortunate coincidence. My curiosity overcame my caution. I figured the only way I'd get any info from Perez was to flash some of my own. I ignored Ronnie's glare and spoke. "Back off, Perez. I'll tell you what I know."

She waited, not a clue that what I knew would be no more than a paragraph in her notes.

I cleared my throat and offered up a blend of truth and fiction. "I went to the apartment looking for a bail jumper." Close. If Billy could afford to post bail, he would probably never make it back to court.

"The door was open, not wide open, but cracked. I didn't notice until I went to knock and it swung open. I stepped in and I saw her. Right away. Didn't need to get up close to know she was dead. Had been for a while. I know the drill at a crime scene. I didn't move, but I'd already stepped in the evidence. I called it in. You know the rest."

Perez started to speak, but stopped when the door opened. Her partner juggled four bottles of water and Ronnie stood to help him.

"Sorry. I had to get these from the machine and I couldn't find the right change." He slumped in a chair on the far side of the table. Perez rolled her eyes. No doubt she thought she was the unfortunate one in their relationship. I knew better. She adjusted her attention back to me.

"Any particular reason you thought you'd find Quitman at that dump?"

I spent a minute parsing the question before I answered. Perez was a bulldog. No way she didn't know Quitman owned the apartment complex. Was she trying to trip me up? If I corrected her assumption, said I was looking for Billy rather than Quitman, she'd set her sights on him as the killer. Billy was a lowlife, but no way was he a killer. *He's wanted for aggravated robbery.* I shoved the thought aside. A person could wave a Coke bottle during a robbery and get it bumped up to aggravated. Prosecutors had a tendency to charge high and plead low. I'd assumed that had been the case with Billy, but I couldn't be certain. Anyway, I'd find out on my own if he was involved. I owed it to Maggie not to sic the cops on him, especially not a charge hungry cop like Perez. I shrugged. "Just working my way through the list."

"Yeah, I heard you already swung by the Foxy Lady. Or were you there looking for something a little more personal?"

Bitch. "Unlike you, I don't need a stack of dollar bills to get my needs fulfilled. Don't you have citizens to protect? Or is tracking me how you get off, Perez?"

Ronnie put a hand on my thigh and tamped down hard. I'm sure she meant to calm me down, but the blaze that shuddered through me only made me more agitated. Only now I wasn't gunning for Perez. I was wishing she and her lump of a partner would disappear and leave me to exercise my rights with the sexy attorney at my side.

"Watch yourself, Bennett."

If she only knew. "Look, I'm happy to help, but I've told you everything I know. Ask Chance. She'll confirm I was standing right inside the door when she got to the scene. There was blood everywhere. If I'd been walking around inside, there's no way I could have hidden it."

"You know that's the thing that I find the most questionable."

"What are you talking about?"

"You said earlier that you 'called it in.' You didn't call it in; you called Detective Chance. I can't think of a reason you'd do that unless you were hoping your girlfriend would help you out of a bad situation."

I felt Ronnie stiffen beside me at the word "girlfriend." I didn't take the time to analyze why since I was busy bowing up myself. First off, Chance wasn't my girlfriend under any possible definition of the term. Second, whatever she was, whatever intimacy we shared beyond friendship, was a carefully guarded secret. At least I thought it was.

My mind whirred through the scenes of the last few days. I hadn't heard from Chance since she sent me on my way at the murder scene. I'd been so pissed for what I thought was her betrayal, I hadn't given a second thought to whatever hell she might be facing. I'd put her in a bad position, calling her out to a murder scene, asking her to come alone. I remembered the way her new partner had reacted. Chance didn't have any backup for her decision to help me out. I'd repaid her by being pissed off and slinging her name around like a get out of jail free card. What price had she paid for bailing me out? Again.

I shot a look at Ronnie, willed her to see I was done talking and to save me from Perez. Save me from myself. She stared deep into my eyes and I caught a glimpse of something, but before I could name it, her disconcerted expression morphed into steely resolve. Transformed, she did what lawyers do best.

"Detective Perez, my client hasn't done anything wrong. The unfortunate girl was murdered long before Ms. Bennett ever arrived at that apartment. You know it. I know it. You're wasting time when you could be out finding the real killer. We're going to leave now. If you need anything further, you will contact me directly. You are not to talk to Ms. Bennett unless I'm present."

She stood and waited for me to follow suit. I couldn't get out of there fast enough. I had a lot to do. Figure out why Billy had been at an apartment owned by Quitman. Figure out why one of Quitman's strippers was dead and whether Quitman had anything to do with the murder. Or Billy, for that matter. But above all, I needed to find Jess. Make things right.

CHAPTER NINE

I ignored Ronnie's suggestion that we go somewhere to talk. I had a lot to say, but not to her. I broke a few traffic laws on my way across town.

I'd been to Jess's place only a handful of times, but mostly in the dark. My prior trips had a singular focus, and I'd never really paid attention to the difference between our homes. Her yellow nineteen fifties bungalow home with red trim and its cascading rows of colorful landscaping made my unkempt gray apartment building, surrounded by yards of cement parking spaces, seem like a dump. Which it was.

I'd never stopped to wonder if Jess owned or rented. She must own. No renter took such good care of a place they didn't own. She'd lived in the house for as long as I'd known her. I knew her parents were no longer alive. Had she inherited it from them? Was this her childhood home, now hers? Did she plan on meeting the love of her life, moving her in, and living out her days in the coziness of familiarity?

I shook my head. I'd gone our whole relationship without knowing the answers to any of these questions, without ever knowing I wanted to know. Why did I care now? I rang the doorbell, ready to face the Jessica I knew rather than ruminate about the one I'd never bothered to get to know.

I could tell by the noises within, she was there, but she kept me waiting for several minutes. For a brief, jealous instant, I wondered if she was alone. Before I started to wallow in the thought, she opened the door.

"Go away, Bennett. It's been a long day."

I held up a bag. "I brought dinner." My gesture wasn't entirely altruistic. I hadn't eaten since breakfast at Maggie's and I was starving. I'd picked up a sack of barbecue from Dickey's. Jessica's favorite. I hoped the sweet spicy smell would grant me entry.

She grabbed the sack from my hand and peered inside. She opened the door all the way, turned, and walked back into the house. I took her action as an invitation and followed.

She led me to the kitchen where she motioned for me to sit at the table. She began pulling plates out of cabinets. Matching plates, without any chips and cracks. Her kitchen featured items like pots and pans hung from hooks in the ceiling. A chrome spice rack and a crock filled with fancy utensils made it look as if someone actually cooked here. The contrast between her place and mine was stark. I kind of liked it here.

She set a couple of cold beers on the table and unpacked the bag. We ate in silence. She didn't seem to have much to say to me, and I didn't know how to open the conversation about Perez's veiled accusations. When our quiet meal was over, she threw away the wrappers and fetched two more beers. She drank half hers down while I fiddled with the label on mine, desperately seeking an opening, but finding none in the silence between us.

Jess was one of the few people with whom I felt comfortable in complete quiet. We'd never used words to console each other, but for the first time I felt like she needed more than I had to offer. Or maybe what she needed had to come from someone other than me. Our relationship had been a series of scattered encounters. She'd been at my side when I lost hope of having a respectable profession. The last thing I wanted was for her to lose what she valued the most because of me.

❖

Chance and I graduated in the same class at the academy. Each of us was assigned to a cop a few years our senior during our post graduation probationary period. Chance was assigned to Teresa Perez. My mentor was Perez's partner, Larry Brewster. Perez and Brewster were part of a trial program, partners temporarily assigned apart to train the rookies. Larry was a career guy, had his sights on working his way up the ladder. Years in uniform, detective's exam, maybe even a cush desk job on the cusp of retirement. Larry was a cop's cop. While he tried to sell me on the same, I was already looking for a way out.

It took me less than a month on the job to realize it wasn't for me. Everything about it was too black and white. The cars, the rules, the money. The jeans, boots, and T-shirts I wear now may be a uniform of sorts, but it's one of my own choosing. My desire to leave might have eclipsed my judgment that night. Official reports say no, but Perez will go to her grave believing I messed up. She might be right.

The call over the radio signaled a domestic dispute. No weapons reported. First such call from this residence. Protocol didn't require more than one car respond in such instances. At the time.

Larry took the call and assured dispatch we were en route. On the way in, he walked me through the rules. Assess the immediate danger. Separate the parties. Get their statements. Make a decision about arrest. He made clear that last action would be entirely within his discretion. Whatever. I wasn't bucking for a medal. He could make all the arrests he wanted. Then he'd be the one to testify in court, get ripped up by some slick defense attorney as a reward for putting himself in harm's way.

The minute we saw the open door the rules were our enemy.

The entryway was pitch-black and neither Larry nor I could see a thing. He drew his weapon, motioned me to move behind him, and ducked into the house. I practically walked on his heels, excited about the prospect of real police work. Finally, something besides rousting drunk college students from Lower Greenville and taking statements from drivers in pile-ups on Central Expressway.

The whole house was dark. Dispatch had reported a nine one one call from a female at the residence. She stated her drunk boyfriend had slapped her around and he wouldn't leave. The call had been disconnected before the operator could get any additional information. Typical. Drunk boyfriends who slapped their girlfriends around often pulled the plug on calls to the police, racking up interference with an emergency call charges in addition to assault. More paperwork for us, but more potential jail time for boyfriend. I was occupied thinking about the hours we'd spend writing this up when I heard the first gunshot.

Larry pulled up short and I balanced on the balls of my feet to keep from running into him. I yanked my gun from its holster and struggled with the safety. Back then my only experience with firearms was the training I received at the academy. Paper targets, plywood cutouts. The pressure to pass the class didn't compare to the sharp sting of hearing real shots fired on a real call. I was more excited than scared. Should've been my first clue things were about to go seriously wrong.

Larry spoke quietly into his handheld. "Unit two fourteen to dispatch. On scene. Shots fired. Request priority backup." He waited for acknowledgment then added, "Proceed with caution. We're in the house. No contact with residents yet. Keep this channel clear."

I inched forward, but Larry pushed me back. We began a heated, though whispered exchange. "We're backing down. We'll wait outside until backup arrives."

"We're already in. Shouldn't we make sure no one's getting hurt in there?"

"Gunshot changed all that. Out, Bennett. Now." Larry turned to lead the way out. He took a step toward me, the firm set of jaw made it clear. We weren't taking any further action until backup was on the scene. Arguing was pointless. I nodded and turned to lead the way back out of the house. The sound of the second gunshot pushed me to move faster. What I heard next stopped me cold.

"I'm hit."

I'd barely turned before Larry pitched into my arms. I staggered under his weight, almost dropping my gun. Blood poured from his shirt. Neither of us were wearing vests. Department rules didn't require us to, and hot Texas summers made the decision between sweat and the risk of a rare firefight an easy one. I fumbled the buttons on his shirt open and tore the already blood-soaked T-shirt beneath. I was no longer concerned about other victims. One of our own was down. For a brief moment, I understood the blue line. Someone in this house had crossed it. They would pay dearly for the transgression.

First, I needed to make sure we were out of the line of fire. I had only the vague notion the shot had come from the back of the house. I glanced around. The entry we'd walked through had another exit, leading to another part of the house. I reasoned the shot probably hadn't come from that direction and decided the gamble was worth the risk.

"Larry, we've got to move. We're too exposed right here. I'll be as gentle as I can." I rolled him onto one of the rugs lining the entry and eased him along the cool marble tiles. The door I'd seen led to a study. I kept moving until Larry was tucked under a massive oak desk. Finally satisfied we were safe for a moment, I used the radio to update dispatch on our situation.

"This is unit two fourteen. Officer down. I repeat, officer down at twenty-nine Santa Maria Lane. Shots fired. Shooter believed to be still on premises."

"Unit two fourteen, this is dispatch. Backup en route. Where are you in relation to the house?"

I described where we were, explained that I couldn't move Larry out of the house, and acknowledged the instruction to stay put and take no further action until backup arrived. No doubt the news that a rookie was the only able gun at a shoot-out had the higher-ups twisted in knots. I did everything I could to make Larry comfortable. I knew nothing about gunshot wounds at the time, but random thoughts, like apply pressure, floated through my reeling brain. I balled up his shirt and kept it pressed against the wound. The shirt turned red fast. Help had better come soon.

We waited. The quiet house almost lulled us into a sense of safety. I raised the radio to risk another transmission, and then I heard the high-pitched, desperate scream. Surprise, fear, horror. The noise conveyed all of that, mirroring my own emotions. Larry's eyes went wide. He jerked his head in the direction of the door. I knew what he was saying, but I hesitated. He jerked again, adding a grunt this time. The rules dictated I stay by my downed partner, but Mr. Protocol was telling me to go help the screamer, go do our job. I wanted to. Bad. Took me only a minute to decide duty be damned.

I propped Larry's gun in his right hand, not sure he'd have the strength to fire, but I wanted him to at least have the guise of protection. I squeezed his free hand and left the relative safety of the room, shutting the door behind me.

The house was two stories. I heard faint whimpering, but I couldn't tell which floor it was coming from. I crept from room to room downstairs, sweeping my gun from side to side like I'd seen cops do on television. Pretty sure I was a poor caricature of the real thing. When I was sure the ground floor was clear, I hunkered down in the kitchen, peering at the staircase. I'd already deduced whoever I was looking for was somewhere up there. I'd also already figured out that's where the shots had come from. I was supposed to wait for backup. Survival echoed the same sentiment. My own anyway. The survival of whoever had screamed hung in the balance. I'd always liked to gamble.

Shout "police" was what I was supposed to do, but I knew all it would get me was a target on my head. I hoped the boyfriend was distracted with whatever he was doing to make screams fill the air. I moved as quickly as I could, thankful the steps were carpeted to cover the sound of my approach. Seemed like hours later when I finally reached the landing. I glanced down once before I took the last step. No movement below. I looked at the radio on my hip. Nothing. Larry was safe downstairs. I couldn't use the radio without raising a ruckus. Rules be damned. I was going in.

I led with my gun and took small, careful steps down the hallway. The first door I came too was cracked slightly. I eased it open. A closet. The next door was open wide and I quickly identified it as the source of the screams I'd heard earlier. Bodies huddled together in a corner. A woman in her twenties. Her right eye was swelling fast. She clutched the hands of two little kids, a boy and a girl. Their wide child eyes tracked my movement and I placed a finger over my lips to signal them to silence. They didn't say a word.

Their mother wasn't so well behaved. She screamed again, but this time she wasn't screaming in pain, she was screaming for her life.

"Help us! He's crazy!"

I dropped back into the shadows and hid in the closet next door, determined her cries were not going to get us all killed.

He stepped into sight, a large revolver trained out into the hallway. His head scraped the ceiling and his bulk filled the doorway. This man didn't need a gun to enforce his will on the weak cluster of family huddled behind him. He probably didn't need a gun to enforce his will on anyone. The gun only sped up his fury. He looked around, but I was out of his sightline. Ideas ricocheted through my head until finally I had a plan. Lure him out of the room, away from the stairway. Give the woman and kids a chance at getting out. I drug my hand along the width of the bulky equipment belt around my waist. Handcuffs, baton, Taser, flashlight. I decided my flashlight was disposable and quietly pulled it loose. I cracked the door and slung it hard, far down the hallway, far from the room where boyfriend stood waiting.

I got lucky. The loud crash sounded like the flashlight had made contact with something big and breakable. Whatever it was, it was enough to send boyfriend on a hunt. I heard him stumble past. I smelled him too. Booze, sweat, the sour stink of aggression. His shadow lumbered away down the hall, and I saw him enter a door at the far end of the hall. I slipped out of the closet and moved quickly to the room I'd entered earlier. The three souls were still in the corner, rocking catatonically. The woman moaned in an eerie rhythm while the children wept silent tears. With long, sure strides, I crossed the room and placed my hand roughly on her mouth. I needed to scare her into silence or she would get us all killed. I leaned in close to deliver my message.

"You have to get out of here. Take the kids. Fast. Quiet. No screaming, no talking. Do you understand?"

She nodded. I gave a gentler warning to the kids. "Go with your mom. Fast and quiet. He's not going to hurt you anymore. Okay?"

As they ran out of the room, I stood in the doorway and covered their escape. I considered myself lucky that I didn't accidentally shoot one of them. The escapees were fast, but noisy. Their loud footfalls on the stairs brought boyfriend running back down the hall. He took one look at my uniform and roared for me to get the hell out of his house. I risked a glance at the stairs. The little ones were having a hard time, but they were almost at the bottom. I raised my gun and pointed it square at his chest. "Police! Don't move another inch."

For a few seconds I was impressed with my ability to keep a madman at bay with the flash of a pistol and a few simple words. But my amazement was short-lived. He started down the hallway, slowly at first, but quickly gaining speed. I yelled for him to stop again, but his entire focus was on his escaping family of victims. I pulled the trigger and hoped for contact.

Nothing. No loud bang. No slowing down. He kept coming as if he didn't even notice I'd aimed a bullet at his heart. I looked down at the worthless weapon in my hand. I'd experienced this once before, at the range. Where it didn't matter. The damn gun was jammed. I knew how to fix it, but it would take time. Time I didn't have. Boyfriend was a force and he was headed my way, gun drawn, eyes lasered in on his family.

I had only one skill that would be useful in this situation. I could run. I could run fast. I bent my knees and dug in for a strong start. I took a deep breath and pushed off. Now *I* was a force and he could reckon with me. I channeled every anger I'd ever felt and barreled toward him full speed, fueled with fury.

Now he noticed me. He didn't stop, but he did slow down. I didn't, but in my blur I saw him raise the gun, point it toward the bottom of the stairs. I didn't follow the direction of his focus. I knew without looking, the last kid was probably just reaching the final steps. I was steps away. Steps would take too long. I launched into the air and missiled myself into his chest.

I'm no petite flower. The force of my broad, warp speed self shook his forward progress. He teetered to keep his balance and I kicked and clawed to fight him down. He pushed me away, but I hugged him like an endangered tree. Our bodies nearly silenced the sound of the next shot he fired.

Nearly.

I felt the crack of gunfire in my side and staggered back, clutching my side.

With me no longer clinging on, he started toward the stairs, resuming his original intent. I summoned reserves of adrenaline and launched again. As we crashed through the banister and fell through the air, I heard shouts of *Police* echoing through the air. I hoped they weren't too late.

Weeks passed before I remembered anything else that happened that night. The days I spent in the hospital recovering from the through and through gunshot wound and the broken arm were crowded with visits from fellow cops. Chance came by every night before she went on duty. She didn't say much, but her presence was solid, comforting, real. She never talked about that night, but her visits jogged my memory. I felt the warmth of her embrace, holding my broken body, almost refusing to let go until the paramedics finally pried her away. She'd been whispering a few phrases over and over. "She doesn't mean it. You did good. Don't pay attention to her." Didn't make sense at the time. Didn't make sense until her mentor, Teresa Perez, paid me a visit the night before I was scheduled to be released.

She came to the room alone and in uniform. Not a regular patrol uniform, but the dress one with all the extra ribbons and pins. I knew her from the academy, but didn't know her well. She'd always been standoffish, as if teaching rookies was beneath her. And I know she resented the new training program, having to split off from her regular partner and ride around with newbies.

I invited her to sit.

"No. I'm not staying long." She shut the door behind her but stood as close as possible to the exit. I didn't have anything to say to this virtual stranger, so I waited. She obviously had something to say to me.

"Larry's funeral was today." Her tone was flat, her expression conveyed no emotion.

He'd died at the scene. Bled out. Chance had told me when I'd woken up from surgery. I'd shed my tears then for the waste.

Larry wasn't my idol, but he was a good guy, a good cop. He left behind a wife and kids. People who'd loved him. His partner stood in my hospital room wanting something from me. She stared and I searched my brain. Finally, a memory came flooding back.

"What the hell were you thinking, Bennett?"

I didn't know what she meant, but the breath of her whispered words, spoken directly into my ear, was excruciating. I was consumed with pain, wishing desperately for a quick death, sure I wasn't going to survive both the gunshot and the fall. Apparently, I wasn't alone in my wishes.

"You should've been the one to die. Not him. I knew you'd never amount to anything, but to drag him down with you? I'd kill you myself if—"

"Leave her alone, Perez." I knew this voice. It was friendly. My pain-twisted mind couldn't come up with a name, but I knew she shouldn't be talking to Perez that way. She cradled my head. "She doesn't mean it. You did good."

"Shut up, Chance. Your pal will pay for this. A good man died tonight because she thinks she's above the rules."

I clawed at the floor, trying to sit up. "What is she talking about? I need to get up. Help me get up." Jessica held me in place. Her whispered words a chant against the pain, "Don't pay attention to her. She didn't mean it. You did good."

Perez had lost her partner. I cut her some slack. "I'm sorry, Perez."

She was ice. "You're not sorry for the right reason. He wouldn't be dead if you hadn't gone off half-cocked. Wait for backup. That's all you had to do. Then he'd be alive and you could get yourself shot some other time, on someone else's watch. You'll never make it. You suck as a cop. We have rules for a reason." She glared as she delivered the crux of her message. "I will do everything in my power to make sure you never make it further than patrolling a lonely traffic beat."

Perez's power didn't have the reach she thought. The day I was released from the hospital, I received a letter notifying me my presence was requested at a ceremony. Department wanted to pin a medal of valor on my chest. Rookie cop saves family in distress. Dress uniform, lots of brass, press, and flowery words. I threw the letter in the trash and penned one of my own.

❖

I told Chance everything that had happened since we'd parted ways at the crime scene, and ended with, "I didn't mean to get you in trouble."

Chance took the beer bottle from my hand and scooped up the tattered label I'd scraped from its side. "Don't worry about me. I'll be fine. Perez will never change. You need to steer clear of her."

Her words were gentle, but the warning strong. Now I knew for sure Jess hadn't willingly given up the murdered stripper case. It had been ripped from her, because of me, because of my past and her connection to it. All these years later, Perez had never forgiven her for sticking up for me. Jess wouldn't care so much about the case, but the symbol was another matter altogether.

"Jess, I don't care about Perez. At least not for myself. I'm sorry for you though."

"Yeah, me too, Luca. Me too."

CHAPTER TEN

After I left Jess, I sat in my car for a while. I knew what I needed. After a few minutes of internal debate, I fished my phone from the console where I'd left it. Three missed calls, all from Ronnie Moreno. If I thought she was calling about something other than business, I wouldn't hesitate to call her back, but I couldn't deal with her laser focus on Quitman after the day I'd had. I needed release of a different kind. I bypassed her voice mails and dialed a familiar number, a surefire way to combine work and pleasure. Late on a weekday, I prayed I could get what I needed.

"Bingo here."

I reflected, not for the first time, on what a stupid name he had. "It's Bennett. I need a game."

"Kind of late."

"Thanks for stating the obvious. You got something or not?"

"I'm about done for the night, but I'll see if I can throw something together."

"Good." I mentally calculated the time it would take me to run home and make a withdrawal from the coffee can. "I'll be there in thirty minutes."

Bingo's place was a duplex near the SMU campus. I left the Bronco a block away and walked through the eclectic neighborhood to the modest brick house. Low-key, high-dollar. I offered the password to the pseudo bouncer at the door and grabbed a beer from the fridge. Bingo joined me in the kitchen.

I towered over him, but he never let his short stature interfere with his cocksure attitude. Bingo ran the best underground poker game in town and he considered himself as mildly famous as the local B-list celebrities that flashed their cash at his place. He dressed like a Vegas nightclub act, wearing a blue velvet smoking jacket with shiny satin lapels, and he never seemed to mind that his reddish brown toupee always hung at an unnatural angle. I didn't mind either. Bingo was more than a late night way for me to wager my hard-earned cash. He was a reliable source for some of the juiciest gossip in Dallas.

"Hey, Luca, I haven't seen you for a while. I thought you were tapped out."

I'm constantly annoyed at how many people seem to know too much about my personal life. I reached into my pocket and pulled out a wad of cash. I laid it on the counter. "Count me in." I nodded at the pile. "That should be plenty unless you raised your game when I wasn't looking."

He grabbed the bills and counted out chips to exchange. "You're good." He motioned toward the dining room table. "They'll deal you in next round."

I watched the last round play out. Bingo's crowd was small tonight, but colorful. Two preppie college students battled it out against a blinged out, has-been pro NFL player and some random white guy I'd never seen before. I trusted Bingo to screen his customers. He used a layered reference system. No one crossed the door without multiple references from long time players. My only reference was my dad, but he and his former work buddies had played at Bingo's since I was a child. To this day, I don't know how Dad made the cut, but I had early memories of bringing him bottles of beer from the fridge while he gambled away our monthly house payment in a high stakes game. Memories.

One of the preppy guys finally reached his limit. On his way out, he made a show of telling his pal he was going to visit the Alpha house where he had a better chance of getting lucky. I almost felt sorry for the sorority girls whose choices were limited to these affected boys in their sharp pressed chinos, collared shirts with horses and alligators, and loafers with no socks, flashing Daddy's money, but then I remembered they lived in an all girls house and my pity vanished.

I slid into the empty seat and did what I do best—take risks.

"Looking for anyone interesting?"

Bingo always asked about my work. Maybe his fascination was fueled by his love of gossip, but I chose to believe that, unlike my dad, he admired me for pursuing a profession a little on the edge. In the past, I'd traded tidbits of information about my pursuits for the closest thing to parental approval I'd ever get. Tonight I'd be trading for whatever intel Bingo could provide. "Not sure he's interesting, but curious for sure. Seems Jed Quitman's gone missing."

"Seriously? He get one of those strippers pregnant again? Last time, he sent her away instead of the other way around. Maybe they're ganging up on him. Decided to turn the tables."

"You think?" I tapped my cards, signaling for two more. "He's up on felony charges for fraud. Maybe he just wants to avoid a pen trip."

Bingo laughed. "How many white collar boys you know wind up in the pen?"

He was right. Most of those cases worked out with some kind of probation and heavy restitution payments. While victims of fraud fantasized about the thieves that stole their money spending time behind bars, the reality of getting paid back usually took preference. I remembered my conversation at the softball field and floated an idea. "You know of any connection between Caroline Randolf and Quitman?"

"Other than the fact Jed provides a steady flow of funds to Dick's campaign, just like Randolf?" Bingo finished dealing. I organized my cards and my thoughts. The idea that Jed Quitman, sleazy as he might be, would be having an affair with a society bigwig like Caroline Randolf was almost too incomprehensible to put into words, but I did it anyway.

"I heard Quitman and Randolf might have more in common than donations to Lively's reelection bid." A little vague, but I could feel the rest of the table listening in. Bingo shook his head and jerked his chin toward the kitchen. I ditched the subject until the round was over, then made some noise about getting another beer. Bingo followed me into the kitchen and motioned for me to talk quietly.

"Where'd you hear about Quitman and Randolf?"

The question took me by surprise. The way Nancy had been talking at the softball game, I didn't get the impression the Quitman-Randolf rumor was some big secret. Still, I guarded my source. "Several places. Why, is it true?" His face contorted and I recognized his discomfort for what it was. "It is true! Wow. Okay, I get it's creepy, but why the big secret?"

"I'd leave Quitman to the cops if I were you."

Talk about a non answer. Bingo knew me better than that. "You know how I feel about cops. Besides, I can't live off my winnings." Since I'd lost big on the last hand, he knew that was true.

He shuffled from one foot to the other, seemingly unsure about what to say next. "I hear you, Luca, but word is Quitman was into some really kinky shit."

That much I knew from the DVDs, but I acted surprised to draw him out. "Like what?"

"I don't know details, but he had something going on at that strip club he owns. I've heard rumors about a private back room, tapes, and blackmail. Let's just say he has more reasons than a stupid fraud charge for ducking out, and you're probably not the only one looking for him."

Interesting. No answers and lots more questions, which led me back to wondering what Jed was hiding from. I was becoming more and more convinced it wasn't the law. I played the next few hands distractedly, thinking about Ronnie and the answers she probably had.

I placed a big bet and hoped my good hand foreshadowed more good fortune.

❖

The next morning I rolled out of bed and fumbled my way to the kitchen, praying for a cup of coffee. When I finally woke up, I remembered where I lived and that I was my only caretaker. Coffee came in a plain white ceramic mug, poured from a glass pot, by a waitress in a greasy diner.

I wasn't about to impose on Maggie another time this week, and not just because I hadn't made any progress on finding her brother. I spied my old Nikes where I'd left them by the door after the softball tournament. I hadn't been running since last Saturday. Coffee or run. I decided to kill two birds with one stone. I found a T-shirt and a pair of shorts from the top of the pile and hoped they wouldn't be too ripe out in the open air. I walked past my shoulder holster, a rare move for me. I usually didn't leave the guns at home, but I figured I could outrun any attempts on my life, though I couldn't imagine anyone thinking my raggedy self would have anything worth stealing. I shoved a few stray one dollar bills in my waist band and headed out the door.

I'd slept too late. Eight thirty a.m. And the heat was already oppressive. As I picked up speed, sweat poured down my back and coffee cravings receded to the back of my mind. I slipped into the groove of each pounding step and plotted out my day. Ronnie Moreno was definitely on the to do list. She was probably in court by now. I needed to corner her when no one else was around and pin her down on the real story behind Jed Quitman. I hadn't called her on it, but what she'd asked me to do—bring Jed directly to her instead of the authorities—would be a violation of the law, an infraction of my license. I didn't care so much about committing a transgression now and again, but maybe I could leverage the shady ethics of her request to get her to talk. If that didn't work, I could always pretend I wanted to talk to her as one of her clients.

Which led me back to the dead girl. She was connected to Jed two ways: she starred in one of the videos I'd found at his house and she was living, and or at least she'd died, at an apartment building he owned. An apartment Billy had listed on a bond application. And Billy had worked for Jed. Lots of connections, but none of them led me to closer to finding Jed or Billy.

Looking for missing people was normally an easy task. People were generally simple creatures. They like the same restaurants, gas stations, stores. They loved home, and amazingly, most of them simply came and went as if ignoring court orders and warrants would make them impervious to apprehension. I relied on people's habits to get my job done. If I wanted complexity in my life, I would've accepted the medal, stayed on the job, and joined the ranks of folks like Perez and Chance. Perez with the chip on her shoulder and Chance with her tortured nightmares. I needed no part of that kind of life. If Ronnie didn't have some answers, I was off this case, no matter how much money I'd lost the night before.

❖

I figured it was still too early for Ronnie to be out of court, so I decided to do a little hunting for Billy while I waited for the perfect time to confront Ronnie.

Homeless addicts are harder to find than respectable folks. They don't pay rent, mortgage, utilities. They don't have credit cards, driver's licenses, or places of employment. Unlike the rest of us, they are invisible on Google. Fine by me. I like a good hunt, the old-fashioned way.

After showing his mug shot around South Dallas without success, I figured enough time had passed that the cops weren't still hanging around the apartment building Quitman owned. Perhaps it was a little brazen of me, as a "suspect" to snoop around, but I craved the adrenaline of a solid risk.

The same hooker charged me twice as much to watch the Bronco since I'd taken three times as long as I said I would on my last visit. A bargain.

I avoided the crime scene and instead went straight to the manager's office. He was a slovenly guy, slumped over a plate smeared with unrecognizable globs of food. I'd been starving since my run, but I immediately lost my appetite. "I need to look at your records."

He answered with his mouth full. "Who the hell are you?"

"Investigator. Following up on the incident in three nineteen. You locate the rental records yet?" I hoped Perez had asked him to look, but hadn't had time to follow up. My bluff paid off. He set down his fork and pawed through a box full of stuffed plastic grocery sacks. Finally, he handed me one. "All the receipts for the last year are in there."

I took the bag and looked at the jumble of paper inside. "I only need the receipts for the one room."

"That's them. We get a lot of travelers stopping through."

Travelers. Yeah, right. By grabbing this bag before Perez, I was probably saving this guy a lot of questions about his business. I closed the bag and ventured a question. "How long has Quitman owned this place?"

"Quitman?" He wore a puzzled expression.

"Jed Quitman. Quick Cash Quitman?"

Still nothing. Either he didn't know the owner or he was covering for some reason. I wasn't sure it mattered, but I knew it wasn't worth pressing with this guy. I considered showing him Billy's picture, but I had mixed feelings. When Perez returned for what I'd just taken, I didn't want her to know I was showing Billy's mug around. I decided to save the picture for the transients in the hallways.

"Never mind." I held up the bag of receipts. "This is all we need. Thanks." He'd already resumed slurping his meal before I edged out the door.

I put the receipts in the Bronco and spent about thirty minutes talking to whomever I could find. One woman recognized Billy's picture. Said she thought he'd done some odd jobs around the place, had seen him recently, but she didn't know much else. I considered talking to the manager again, but decided to let some time pass between the murder investigation and my questions. No one seemed to know anything about a connection between Quitman and the apartment building, which didn't surprise me. Junkies aren't always up on the latest business ventures.

After I'd exhausted the pool of willing bystanders, I still had some time to kill. May as well put in a little time on the paying gig. A quick Internet search garnered me Caroline Randolf's address. Since I'd already been up close and personal with one of Quitman's playmates, I should probably check Randolf off the list too.

When I pulled up to the address, I realized I wasn't going to get easy access like I had at Quitman's place. Quitman was rich, but Randolf was super duper rich. Her palatial gated mansion, set deep into a spacious football field sized lot, made Quitman's house look like servant's quarters. I shifted the Bronco into park and reached around to the backseat. I fished around for a minute, but finally came up with a clipboard, which I occasionally used for the role of survey taker or whatever it took to get in the door. With a place like this, Randolf could probably afford help smart enough not to fall for my ruse, but maybe I'd at least get a glimpse in the door.

I boldly strode to the front gate, ignoring a sign that directed working visitors to the servant's entrance. A real survey taker would want to talk to the principals, not the help. I pressed the intercom button and waited. A screen above the button came to life and I was face-to-face with a snarly faced elderly gent in a too tight suit.

"May I help you?"

I waved the clipboard in front of the screen and ad-libbed the purpose for my visit. "I've been retained by the Friends of Love and Light, a nonprofit seeking to build a new homeless shelter near the downtown area." I pretended to consult the clipboard. "Ms. Randolf is listed as a person of interest based on her generous philanthropy to the citizens of Dallas."

"You don't have an appointment."

Not a question, so I didn't bother answering. "Her input would be vital to the project."

"Call her secretary and make an appointment." His abrupt response was accentuated by a burst of loud white noise followed by a silent black screen. So much for getting an inside look at Randolf. I glanced at my watch. Almost noon. Maybe I could get a little inside look at Ronnie Moreno. And some lunch.

When I arrived at the Moreno Law Firm. Maria told me Ronnie had already left for lunch, and she tried to shoo me away when I pressed her for details. I leaned across the counter and flashed my best smile. "I'm not looking for state secrets. I just want to know where she eats lunch."

Maria batted eyelashes my way. "She's not your type."

Oh, she was my type all right, but I doubted I was hers. "That may be. Maybe after I give her an update on the work I'm doing for her, I could come back here and we could discuss my type." I flashed my best smile.

She gave me a long look of appraisal before she shot me down. "Sorry, my boyfriend Hector gets really pissed when I flirt with anyone else." She left unsaid that Hector would likely come unglued to find out his lady was flirting with a dyke. Which brought me back to my original quest.

"Too bad. Hector's one lucky guy. Now, care to tell me where I can find Ronnie?"

"She let you call her that?"

I shrugged, and she shook her head. "Okay, if you rat me out, you're on my shit list. She's at Herrera's." She looked at the clock on her desk. "Probably just got there."

I barely took the time to throw her a kiss. Herrera's wasn't far. Geography likely explained the uncharacteristic choice of establishment. Ronnie struck me as more the Capital Grill type, steak and salads, one martini, maybe two if she'd had a good morning at the courthouse. Of course, nothing I learned about Ronnie so far jibed with the image I had in my head. Bright, successful big city lawyer. She dressed like a model and carried herself with poise. Based on the online chats about New York salaries—yes, I'd checked—she had been pulling down somewhere around four hundred grand a year, not including bonuses, before she cut ties and moved to Dallas to handle shit cases for her uncle, the guy who got clients through a one eight hundred number posted on tacky billboards all over the city. Why I presumed to know the kind of place she liked to dine was a mystery.

Herrera's was a bit of a dive, but the good kind where all the attention went into the food, not the furnishings. And I was starving. My brain was occupied with fantasies of dragging warm, crisp tortilla chips through butter and homemade salsa, and I didn't notice Ronnie's booth already contained two other occupants. Miguel, I recognized. The other guy, brown, buff, and handsome, with his arm around Ronnie, I didn't have a clue. I stood at the edge of the booth, grabbed a handful of chips and jumped into the conversation.

"Hi, Ronnie. Thought I might find you here. Can we talk business or are you on a date?"

She waved to the empty space beside Miguel. "Have a seat, Luca. You want something to drink to go with those chips?"

She was seriously the most unflappable woman I'd ever met. My choices weren't really choices at all. I could stand there eating chips out of my hand or take advantage of her offer of hospitality. I sat. She wasted no time in making introductions. "You've already met my uncle, Miguel." I nodded and grabbed more chips to feign disinterest as she turned to handsome guy. "And this is my brother, Jorge."

Jorge stuck his hand out and I reached for it with an awkward left since my right hand was still full of chips. I said the first thing that came to me. "Are you a lawyer too?"

His grin was infectious, but his words were infection. "Lawyer? No way. I'm a cop."

Perfect. As if I didn't feel awkward enough already. Why had I thought Ronnie would be dining alone? Truth was I hadn't thought past finding her, seeing her, getting some answers. The chance I'd be getting any answers in front of her brother was slim. I wondered if Miguel knew the specifics of what she'd asked me to do about Quitman. I sensed Quitman was Ronnie's special project and I felt strangely protective. But as hungry as I was, no way was I going to sit and make small talk for the next hour. I would make arrangements to meet with Ronnie later and make a quick getaway now. Head for a restaurant with more food than lawyers.

I set the chips on a napkin and pushed it to the edge of the table. "Nice to meet you, Jorge. I stopped by to ask your sister a couple of questions, but I don't want to disturb a family lunch. Ronnie, I'll call you later." I started to slide out of the booth, but Miguel's hand on my arm stopped me. Only the presence of a cop at the table kept me from pulling out my gun and demonstrating how little I liked having my personal space invaded.

"Don't leave. Jorge's on his way to work. He just stopped by to say hello."

I ignored Miguel's entreaty and looked to Ronnie. She nodded. "Stay, Luca. We have some things to discuss." Indeed we did, but I hadn't planned on talking about any of it in front of Miguel. A waitress walked by with a plate of steaming enchiladas. I ached for a bite. Hunger made the decision for me. "Okay." Jorge slid out of the booth and I took his place.

Miguel decided to lead the conversation. "Do you have a habit of running afoul of the law, Ms. Bennett?"

Jeez. And here I thought I'd have to make small talk. I chanced a look at Ronnie who subtly shook her head. I ignored her attempt to ward off the conversation and jumped full in. "I have a habit of doing what I need to do to meet my client's needs. Like a good lawyer would do."

"Ah, but there's the difference. I have a license and standards to uphold."

Billboard guy lecturing me on standards was a bit much. Give me a break. "I have a license too, *Mr.* Moreno."

"One that's been suspended before, I hear."

Not correct. I'd never had my license suspended. I had, however, been placed on probation, just last year. And I regularly broke the rules, but I rarely got caught. As for the time I had, if the fugitive's brother hadn't unloaded a shotgun in my direction, I doubt anyone would have ever known I'd broken into their house. While I tried to think of a snappy comeback, Ronnie intervened on my behalf.

"Miguel, we discussed this. Luca comes highly recommended. You left this to me and either you trust me or you don't."

I attempted to ignore the way her use of my first name warmed my insides. To cover, I glared at Miguel who finally caved.

"Fine, mija." He pushed his menu away. "I really should get back to the office." We both slid out of the booth. He threw a couple of twenties on the table, enough for a party of six, and leaned down to give Ronnie a hug. "I'll see you later this afternoon."

I stood in the aisle, unsure of my next move. I wanted answers, but pride told me to leave before I had to give some of my own. Ronnie intervened again. "Sit." She gestured at the cash on the table. "We may as well use his money since he likes to throw it around." She picked up a menu and began running her finger down the page.

I noted the hint of disdain and filed it away. Ronnie's respect for her uncle seemed to be limited to family ties alone. Again I wondered why she was working for him, in such a dive, after experiencing the fancy trappings of a wealthy New York law firm. I sat and stopped wondering.

"Why do you work for Miguel?"

She didn't look up from the menu. "Who says I work *for* Miguel?"

The inflection was slight, but I wasn't in the mood for splitting hairs. And I wasn't in the mood for her non answers. I pressed. "Okay then, why do you let him push you around?"

She closed the menu and slowly set it on the table. She took a moment to move around a few pieces of silverware and take a drink of water. When she finally met my eyes, I could tell her mundane actions covered a fierce and fiery anger, one her eyes couldn't hide. "Do you have family, Ms. Bennett?" And just like that we were no longer on a first name basis.

"Why, yes, Ms. Moreno, I have family. I have a father who drinks too much when he hasn't lost all his money gambling. I have a mother who I barely know because she got tired of always looking for the brighter side and went off to find it with a man half her age. Oh, and I have a brother who acts like neither one of them is off their rocker, by blowing through life without attachments of any kind."

"Yes, I have family."

"Then surely you understand that people sometimes do things for the sake of family without readily apparent reasons."

I did and I didn't. I snuck beer to my dad and drove him to Oklahoma on a weeknight to gamble away my rent. Once a year, I listened to my mother talk about the trivialities of her life with all the passion of a person whose life actually made a difference. But I didn't let anyone push me around. "I can understand a lot of things, but family ties don't explain why you would take a job that's beneath you, working in a two-bit law firm, representing scum of the earth."

"You don't know anything about me, about the firm I work for and why, and you definitely don't know anything about my clients. I suggest you stick to doing what you do best, which so far doesn't seem to be much." She didn't try to hide her anger.

Her voice rose with every word and I caught the edge of an accent in her snapped words. I felt like pushing, so I decided to impress her with a combination of knowledge and theory. "Does Caroline Randolf know her lover, Jed, likes it rough or is that one of his well kept secrets?"

Surprise flooded her features. She tried to cover it by jabbing a finger my way as she emphasized her earlier point. "You don't know what you're talking about. Find him. That's all I asked. Leave the rest to me."

I wasn't hungry anymore. For food, for money, or for this woman. She could find her own damn client aka bail jumper. I was done. I was furious, but I feigned nonchalance. "Find him yourself," I said before I stalked out of the restaurant.

CHAPTER ELEVEN

For all my big talk, I wasn't ready to give up looking for Quitman, especially since finding him might net some information about Billy.

I couldn't shake my own reference to Caroline Randolf, and while I couldn't wrap my head around the idea that the grand dame of Dallas society would have anything to do with the likes of Quitman, I was willing to concede it didn't hurt to look a little closer. When I pulled up at the Foxy Lady, I spent a few minutes searching the Internet for a photo of Randolf to show around. Thankfully, even strip clubs have free wi-fi. Despite the dicey connection, I finally managed to locate a decent, recent photo. Damn if she didn't have the bluest eyes I'd ever seen. I'd seen those eyes before, or ones exactly like them. Could Caroline Randolf be the masked dom who'd starred in Jed's little production? No freaking way. I believed that about as much as I believed they were sleeping together in the first place. Still, my gut churned with anticipation. I was on to something.

Once the photo downloaded, I climbed out of the Bronco. It was around two o'clock, and I hoped the business crowd had left to spend an afternoon at the office, sated and slightly buzzed. When I pushed through the doors of the dark club, I resolved to pay more attention to the environment than the people in it. If Jed Quitman had a private studio for making videos like the ones I'd seen, the strip club was the perfect place for it. Based on what I could tell from the size of the building, the main stage and seating area only took about half of the place. I was willing to bet the door to the side of the bar led to private rooms, perfect locations for homemade movie productions.

The stripper I'd met on the first trip, Star, was working a pole in the center of the stage for the entertainment of the three other patrons seated at the tables. Maybe when her set was over, I could get her to take me someplace private. I settled in at the bar and ordered a beer from the bald, hulking bartender. He looked bored. I suppose constant exposure made even eye candy like Star lose appeal. I decided to chat him up. Maybe he was bored enough to share some back of the house secrets. I led off with what I hoped was enough inside information to get him to open up. "You seen Ronnie around?"

His glazed over expression didn't waver. "Don't know any Ronnie."

I didn't believe him. Pretty unlikely Star knew Jed's attorney, and this guy, who I had pegged as more enforcer than mixologist, didn't. I pushed the point. "Sorry, I thought you'd probably know Jed's attorney. She and I met here the other day."

"Latin chick? Sharp dressed?" I nodded. "Yeah, I seen her around. Doesn't look like most attorneys I know."

Okay, so he did know her, and it wasn't a stretch to believe he probably thought she serviced Jed in some way other than legal representation. For a fraction of a second, I wondered whether Ronnie played a bigger role in Quitman's life than attorney and counselor at law. If she did, it would explain her clandestine "bring him directly to me" order. The very idea made me nauseous until I remembered the bimbo who kept Jed's home fires burning. No way was Ronnie one of the many in Jed's stable.

But what about Caroline Randolf? If Jed was screwing around with the likes of her, then apparently no one was immune to his questionable charms. Yet nothing I'd seen so far explained why anyone would be attracted to this guy for anything other than his money. Randolf didn't need money. Did Ronnie?

While I was thinking of another question to ask big, bald bartender, I felt a soft, warm whisper on the back of my neck. "I figured you'd be back."

Star. I turned and invited her onto my lap. She'd probably be more forthcoming than Mr. Stoic behind the bar. "Good luck for me you're working today."

"Buy me a drink?"

"Sure." She took over from there, shouting out her order for a cosmo to the bartender. All I had to do was fork over fifteen dollars. I didn't resent the expense since I knew getting customers to buy high-priced drinks was part of her job description. Somehow, before I left, she'd pay me back in spades.

After the bartender handed her the fancy drink and she took a healthy swig, I leaned in close. "Any chance we could get some privacy?" She grinned and took my hand. Seconds later, we were in a tiny room, furnished in early American boudoir. The ancient looking red velvet chaise lounge was the only piece of furniture in the room. Scared about the many predecessors who'd likely been here before me, I chose to stand. I didn't see any cameras, but that didn't mean they weren't there. I took Star's glass from her hand and set it on the floor. Then I pulled her close and whispered in her ear. "I had something else in mind. Maybe you have a room with a little more equipment?"

Her head snapped up and she jerked away from me, fear in her eyes. I was definitely on the right track. I glanced up at the ceiling, and then took a step toward her. "Are there cameras in here?" I whispered. She shook her head and I sighed in relief. "Tell me about the other room."

"Nothing to tell. I don't know what you're talking about."

But she did. I was certain. "You know your boss, Quitman, is missing, right?"

"That's what you and Ronnie were talking about."

Since she mentioned Ronnie's name, I decided to veer off course. "Maybe I'll just ask Ronnie about the other room."

Star shook her head wildly and dug her nails into my arm. "Don't. Please. She doesn't know anything about it. If you talk to her now, Hugo will know I told you something." I quickly deduced Hugo was the bartender out front. Now I had some leverage. "No problem. I don't have to talk to Ronnie if you're willing to tell me what I need to know."

"You can't tell anyone I told you."

"Deal." Could it really be this easy?

"This place has a couple of rooms off-limits to anyone except special customers."

"What's a special customer?"

"Someone Mr. Quitman brings in, you know, personally."

"Have you ever been in one of the rooms?"

"No."

"Then how did you know what I meant when I said 'equipment'?"

"'Cause a girl who used to work here told me about them. She was the only one of the girls who ever got to work back there. She said the money was out of this world. Made her not mind a little kink."

"Her name?" I feared I knew the answer before she managed to get it out. She scrunched her brow. "I don't know her given name. Name she used here was Missy Bloom. She hasn't been here in a while. I don't know where she is." I didn't have the heart to tell her Missy Bloom's performance days were over. Instead I pulled Billy's picture from my back pocket. "You know this guy?"

"Sure, that's Billy. He does odd jobs around here. Come to think of it, I haven't seen him in a while either. He was sweet on Missy. You don't think they ran off together do you?" Her dreamy smile signaled she thought the possibility was sweet and hopeful.

I shrugged. I wasn't about to burst her fantasy of the handyman and the stripper, running off to find a better future together. I put the information in a mental file for later inspection. Pretty big coincidence, Billy and Missy dropping out of sight around the same time.

"Have you seen this woman around here?" I showed her the photo of Caroline Randolf on my phone.

"She looks familiar, but I don't think I've seen her here before."

She looked me right in the eye when she answered, her demeanor was relaxed and calm. I decided she was telling the truth. Star had probably seen Randolf's picture in the paper, not this dive. No surprise there. I switched topics. "Any idea where Quitman is hiding out?"

She shook her head. "Haven't seen him for a while." Again, she passed my informal polygraph.

"Any chance you could show me the special room?"

"You trying to get me fired?"

"Guess that means no."

"You're a smart one. I can show you some other things if you have the cash to pay."

I had the cash, but I didn't want to pay to play. Not today anyway. I needed to get home and figure out the significance of what I'd learned. "I gotta run." I pulled a fifty from the wad in my pocket. A pretty awesome tip for talking instead of touching. I pressed it in her hand. "I trust you'll keep this conversation to yourself. Now, go out there and tell everyone you showed me a great time."

After a long day with no lunch, all I wanted was a cold beer, easy food, and a soft bed. I headed straight home. I grabbed the bag of receipts I'd hustled from Quitman's apartment manager, and walked toward my apartment. As I came around the corner, I saw my landlord, Ernest Withers, with his hand on my doorknob, a key in his hand. My attempt to duck out of sight was futile.

"Luca Bennett, get your ass back out here. You think you can ignore me forever?"

I could only hope. I willed him away to no avail. Didn't matter how many guns I had on me, this guy made me want to run like a school girl. I silently ciphered the contents of my coffee can. I could cover what I owed, and it was time to get him off my back. I looked at his hand, still on my door handle. I didn't want him in my place. I rented for the convenience. For the lack of commitment, I was willing to trade privacy and solitude. A little anyway, but I didn't want him in my place.

"Give me five minutes and I'll bring it to you."

He let a few beats pass before he dropped his hand. He walked past me muttering. "Five minutes. If you're not there in five minutes, I'll beat your door down." I ignored his ramblings and walked to my apartment. I turned the knob, opened the door, and stepped across the threshold. Just before I shut the door behind me I heard him toss out, "'Course, I won't have to beat it down, since you can't be bothered locking it in the first place." I shook my head. Crazy old man. I always locked my door. He'd already forgotten he'd just unlocked it himself. Or had he? I turned back, intending to ask him what the hell he meant, but the door clicked shut and a large weight crashed on the back of my head. I blacked out.

❖

No hangover had ever felt like this. No matter how much I'd had to drink, I'd never woken up to Old Man Withers gripping my shoulders, begging me to wake up. His unshaven face, rank breath, and bleary eyes loomed large in my face. I pushed him away. Scratch that. I tried to push him away. And failed. All those times I told myself I could take him and here I was, flat on my back, held in place by two frail, arthritic hands. What the hell?

"Quit struggling, you damn fool."

I shook my head and was instantly sorry. I wriggled a hand loose and gingerly felt my head. Wet. I held my hand in front of my head. Red. The combination vaguely registered as not good. My head shouldn't be wet and red. Forever later, it came to me. I was bleeding.

"I called nine one one. That bastard clocked you. And good."

I finally summoned the strength to push his arms off mine and rolled over on my side. I swallowed the wave of nausea that surged into my throat. "What happened?"

"Not rightly sure. You were going to get the rent. I came to check on you and right when I put my hand up to knock, this monster of a guy practically flew out of your place. Knocked me down, and left the door wide open. You were laying in the entryway for everyone to see. Naturally, I had to come on in."

Memory trickled back. Withers had hassled me about the rent. I was on the way to the coffee can when blam! I couldn't remember anything after that. Old coot probably scavenged around for the rent before he called for an ambulance. I struggled to my feet but had to lean against the kitchen counter to balance. The bag of receipts I'd had with me still lay in the doorway. I leaned down to pick them up and nearly passed out when I straightened up again. I shoved them into a drawer and grabbed a roll of paper towels to mop up the mess that was my head. "I don't need an ambulance. Call them off."

He opened his mouth, but before he could answer, two women in uniforms appeared rolling a stretcher between them. I may have hated wearing one, but I had to admit, uniforms are hot. Guess the blow to my head didn't knock me completely senseless.

Withers finally found his voice and proudly announced his diagnosis. "She got smacked on the head. The cops should be here any minute."

The short brunette one came to my rescue. "Dispatch said a patrol car's on the way, but we can check you out in the meantime." She didn't waste any time putting her hands on me. She looked deep into my eyes, traced her fingers along my face, patting, probing. I squinted at her name tag, thinking I should at least know her name before we went any further, but the letters swam in the air, made me nauseous again. I gave up and closed my eyes. Reveled in the attention. Briefly.

Her partner waded in and ruined the moment by barking, "Ma'am, we need to take you in. You should have a CT scan to make sure you don't have any permanent injury."

Attraction is fleeting. Suddenly the uniforms weren't so hot. Not hot enough to convince me to leave with them anyway. I opened my eyes and fought to focus. "I'm fine. You can leave."

The paramedics exchanged looks. Withers, voyeur that he was, watched the whole exchange with rapt attention. Paramedic number two piped up, "Ma'am—"

I held up a hand to stop her. Ma'am, my ass. I wasn't going anywhere with these youngsters. "I'm good. Seriously, look at me." I walked a few steps, barely grasping the edge of the counter. I caught a glimpse of myself in the dull sheen of the ancient microwave I rarely used. I could've been an extra in a zombie movie. "Just leave a few bandages, maybe some gauze."

Both women eyed me, but I was certain now their intentions were pure. While they tried to figure out a way to get me on their stretcher, Withers offered his take on the situation. "She's stubborn, that one. If she's not going, she's not going."

Not exactly profound, but true. I wasn't about to spend hours and money I didn't have in a crowded emergency room. I nodded at Withers. "It's true. I'm not going."

The brunette shook her head. They made me sign a form I assured them I could read, but couldn't since the words fuzzed across the page. Then they were gone. I fumbled in the cabinet for a glass and filled it with water from the tap. That took all my energy, so I slumped into the nearest chair.

Withers watched from the doorway. "You should keep your door locked."

"You should get a job with the local news. Then you could get paid to state the obvious." Sharp pain dulled my senses, but something about what he said tickled them awake. "Wait a minute. *You're* the one who unlocked my door."

"Not me. I came to see you about the rent, but your door was not only not locked, it was open a tiny bit. I closed it to protect your privacy. I pulled it shut when I saw you coming."

I resisted the urge to point out that an open door might signal more than mere carelessness. I didn't have the energy to engage. All that mattered was someone had been in my place and they beat me over the head to avoid being caught. I glanced around the tiny entry. The intruder's weapon, a now dented and bloody, but previously unused toaster, lay on its side. A gift from my mother when I moved into this place, years ago. The irony of the gift then had been that she knew toasting bread was outside my cooking skill set. And now? Well, getting smashed in the head by a gift from my mother was as it should be.

If someone had been in my place, they'd been here for a reason. I don't have much worth stealing. Even the contents of my coffee can was running low. Shit. The rent. I pulled myself out of the chair and fumbled my way back to the kitchen over Withers's protests. He'd be cackling louder if he had any idea he might not get paid. I yanked open the cabinet. The can was on the shelf in the exact spot I'd left it. I peeled back the plastic lid and made a total withdrawal. I didn't make a habit of counting what I had on hand, but the wad felt right in my fist. I slid five hundred-dollar bills off the pile and shoved the rest in my pocket. I thrust the money at Withers. "Here. The rest of this month's and part of next."

His arthritis went into remission as he practically ran across the room to seize the cash from my hand. "Thanks, Luca. I'll be going now. Let me know if you need anything. The cops should be here any minute." He was gone like a shot. So much for concern over my safety.

Whoever had broken in hadn't wanted money, or was too stupid to look in the obvious places. Or I'd surprised him before he could finish looking for what he came for. I decided to have a look around. It only took a few minutes for me to conduct my search. None of my guns were missing. Those, the contents of the coffee can, and my computer were the only valuables I had. My laptop was smack in the middle of the coffee table, exactly where I'd left it. Confused, I slouched onto my ancient couch and contemplated my next move. As I did, something white under the coffee table caught my eye. I reached down and picked up a white sleeve that had held one of Jed's naughty DVDs. As I did, I remembered I'd left the DVD starring Jed and the blue-eyed beauty in my laptop. I should eject the DVD. Place it in the sleeve. Put it in the box with the others. I was in a trance and the empty sleeve signaled a message, slow and vague. DVDs. Box. Closet.

Suddenly, I had it. I stood up too fast and wobbled my way to the bedroom. I'd moved the box of Jed's DVDs back here. I wasn't sure why I did it. I hadn't been concerned about keeping them safe. After all, who would know I had them? Who would care? I threw open my closet doors and reached for the shelf. Disbelief fueled the futile action of running my hands along the surface, feeling for the thing that I knew wasn't there.

I slumped down on the bed, worn out from the sudden spurt of activity. My hand landed on a piece of paper with ragged edges. Someone had torn it carelessly from a notepad and scrawled the words *Stay Away from Quitman* in heavy black marker.

Who the hell had paid me this warning visit? I didn't have any answers, but someone had my DVDs. All but one, anyway. Someone who'd wanted them badly. I could only think of one person. I grabbed my car keys and made for the door before the cops arrived to slow me down.

❖

I still had her address from my earlier online search. She lived in Preston Hollow. Nice digs for a two-bit criminal defense lawyer. She must've squirreled away plenty of her six figure New York salary before she returned to the south.

I put the DVD in an envelope. I didn't put it in the mail with one of those "if you're watching this, you know by now I'm dead" notes. First off, I don't trust the postal service any more than I trust any other government agency. Second, I had a feeling I would need this DVD, and I wanted it where I would have ready access. I stopped at Hardin's place and asked him to put it in his safe. No one had the key but him. He glanced at the gauze I'd stuck to the side of my head, but didn't ask me any questions. He shrugged off my warning that someone had wanted the contents of the envelope enough to break into my place and thunk me on the head. Hardin's place was manned twenty-four seven. Anyone who tried to get into his safe would wind up at the wrong end of a twenty-gauge shotgun. I felt better already. Next stop, Ronnie's house.

The difference between her neighborhood and mine was night and day. My Bronco wasn't as old as these houses, but she lacked the same refinement. I didn't care. I would park on Ronnie's lawn if I had to in order to get her attention. I wanted answers and I wanted them now.

Her house was at the end of the street. As I pulled to the curb, I spotted a cute little red Mercedes behind me, stopping at the corner. Ronnie Moreno was behind the wheel. She turned left and headed in the opposite direction. I spun the Bronco and began chase. A slow, subtle chase through the residential section of North Dallas.

When we reached Central Expressway, I assumed she was heading downtown. Maybe a late night visit to the jail to bond out a client. Leaving the cherry Mercedes in the jail parking lot would be a foolish move. Someone should tell her she needed a less flashy ride for her evening slumming. Me? Well, I had a lot to say to her, but none of it had to do with her damn car. Concussion aside, my thoughts were clear on one thing: the goon who'd broken into my place was connected to Jed Quitman, and it was time for Ronnie to let me in on her little game. Coincidences are for fake psychics and fiction writers. Hours after I made a crack about Jed Quitman's sex life, someone wanted the evidence bad enough to break into my place and clock me for it. Coincidence my ass. Whenever Ronnie reached her destination, we were going to have a talk. I shot a look at my gas gauge and hoped she stopped soon.

She didn't get on the expressway. She crossed over to the east side. As we drove, the neighborhoods started looking less like hers and more like mine. When she turned off the main drag into a subdivision of tiny nineteen fifties bungalows, I gave up trying to second-guess. We could be going anywhere. Didn't matter. I kept one eye on her car and one on the gauge. When she finally stopped, I was on fumes. I used a last burst of energy and pulled in as close to her bumper as I could get without humping her fancy ride. She leaned out the window and shot an annoyed look in my direction. She reached my door before I found the door handle. I rolled down my window since I couldn't open the door without knocking her down. Her annoyed expression dissolved into surprise.

"Luca, you look terrible. What happened?"

No way she was going to set the tone of this confrontation. I waved her back. "I can't get out." She frowned, then finally shook her head and backed up. I opened the door and set one foot on the ground. The ground wasn't solid like it used to be. I eased my other leg out and faked a strong stance, one hand braced on the Bronco behind my back. She reached for my face. I jerked back and thunked my head on metal. "Shit."

My dazed condition rendered her reach unavoidable.

"You're hurt." Her tone was gentle. So was her touch. "You're bleeding." She reached an arm around my waist. Her slender arm was both strong and tender. My body betrayed me. I leaned in.

She misread my message. "Come inside. You need to sit down."

I pushed her arm away. "I'm fine. I want to talk. Now. Here." I struggled with an opening. "You're going to tell me what the hell's going on between you and Quitman, and I'm not leaving until you do."

If my accusation caught her off guard, she hid it like a champ. "You're not going anywhere in your condition. Come inside."

Before I could answer, a male voice called out, "Ronnie, everything all right out there?" He appeared at Ronnie's elbow. Her brother, the cop. He looked like he couldn't decide whether to cuff me or comfort me.

Ronnie put her arm back around my waist to signal the bleeding rogue posed no threat. "Everything's fine, Jorge. I'll be right there. Tell Mom plus one for dinner." She offered him a bright smile to emphasize the lack of danger, and waited until he reentered the house. The moment the door shut, she squared up with me. "You want to talk about Quitman? Fine. We'll talk later. Right now, you're coming with me." Her tone was tough, but her eyes were gentle.

I didn't budge at first. Even after seven p.m., the summer night was hot. The Bronco was hot. Probably overheated. I was hot. Probably fever. Ronnie was hot. My head swam. My thoughts were jumbled. I couldn't think of a way to douse the heat that came off her in waves. The prospect of cool air-conditioning was steps away. The prospect of more time with Ronnie's arm around me made those steps worth walking. I let her lead me to the house.

CHAPTER TWELVE

I was completely unprepared to greet a crowd. Ronnie guided me through a gauntlet of at least a dozen strangers. Each one offered a greeting mixed with genuine goodwill and strange looks. Maybe Ronnie didn't bring bloody strangers over for dinner all that often. I nodded in response. The only people I recognized were Miguel and Jorge. By the time we reached the apparent destination, the kitchen, my head throbbed so badly I couldn't enjoy the aroma of home-cooked, spicy cuisine. Ronnie pushed me into a chair and called out to the short, round woman at the stove. The apron-wearing woman turned, spatula in one hand, hot pad in the other, and flashed a dazzling smile. Until that very moment, nothing about her had seemed familiar. The smile did it.

"You're Ronnie's mother."

She flashed a questioning look at Ronnie before she answered. "Who else would I be? Spending the whole day cooking a feast for this crowd. Veronica didn't tell me she was bringing a guest to help celebrate her birthday, but she doesn't always keep her little mama informed, do you, mija?"

"Let it go, Mom. Luca is a business associate. I've invited her to stay for dinner since she drove all the way out here to deliver a message to me."

Mother Moreno shrugged as if she hadn't been the one to bring up the subject. "Your business associate is bleeding. You go take care of her, right now." She shooed us away. "Go now, out of my kitchen. I'll call you when it's ready."

And just like that, Ronnie was leading me back out of the kitchen to some other foreign destination. I'd watched the rapid exchange in the kitchen, barely keeping up. It was Ronnie's birthday. I was at her mother's house. Her mother was cooking birthday dinner to which I'd been abruptly invited. *Business associate.* Business. Yes, I was here for business. The DVDs. I needed to talk to Ronnie about the DVDs some asshole had broken into my apartment to take. I tugged her arm. She looked back, shook her head, and motioned me into a nearby room.

She pointed at a daybed covered in a lacy white spread. "Lie down while I get something for your head."

I would've laughed at her suggestion that I put my rumpled, bleeding self on the sweet, dainty bedding, but it would've hurt. I leaned against the wall instead. Unfazed, she disappeared for a moment and returned with a wet washcloth and a small basket full of supplies. I didn't say a word as she gently removed the gauze and wiped my wound. She was tall enough to meet my eyes, and they reflected compassion at my indignation. This whole encounter wasn't anything like the confrontation I'd planned, but I was paralyzed. By the head injury? By her soothing touch? I wasn't sure. I didn't like the uncertainty.

She placed the unused supplies in the basket and turned me toward the mirror. I still looked like shit, but I wasn't bleeding and my bandage no longer looked like a battlefield quickie. Satisfied I wouldn't leave behind bodily fluids, and fearful I couldn't stand much longer on my own, I accepted her re-invitation to sit on the bed. She joined me.

"You feel like talking about whatever it was that was so important for you to follow me out here with a bleeding head?"

"How do you know I followed you?"

"Don't answer a question with a question. It's rude. Besides, I saw you. Your car may suit this neighborhood, but in mine, it's kind of hard to miss." She leaned back. "Now, quit diverting. You're obviously angry, so I assume you haven't found Jed. What do you need?"

I considered responding with "what do you think I need?" but I was done playing around. I plunged in with what I hoped would shock an honest response. "If you wanted your client's property back, all you had to do was ask."

Her brow furrowed and eyes narrowed. After a moment she shook her head. "I give up. What the hell are you talking about?"

I'd bet the house she didn't know what I meant. I didn't have the energy to dissemble, so I gave up. "I had a box full of DVDs starring Jed Quitman. Sex DVDs. A thug broke into my place tonight, hit me over the head with my own toaster, and guess what he took? The DVDs. Nothing but the DVDs. Oh, and he left a note telling me to stop looking for Quitman." I paused as I considered whether to mention I still had one of the DVDs. I ruled against it and stated the reason without telling her why. "The only other person who knew I had the DVDs was you."

She jumped off the bed. "I didn't know any such thing."

"I told you at lunch."

"We didn't have lunch because you were rude. A condition that seems to be permanent."

"I alluded to them. I told you…" What exactly had I told her? My memory was as hazy as the rest of me. Oh yeah. "I said something about Jed liking it rough."

"Yes, you did." Her tone turned from incredulous to sarcastic. "I suppose your cryptic statement should have clearly pointed out to me that you had a box of sex DVDs that you got from God knows where." She paused, then squinted at me. "Planning to do a little blackmail, were you? Thug ruin your plans?"

Was it possible she didn't know anything about Jed's special hobby? On the drive over, I'd convinced myself she did, that her knowledge was a large part of the reason she wanted Jed handed over to her instead of cuffed and dropped at the sheriff's office like usual. Of course, it made more sense that the DVD thief was someone who didn't want Quitman found, considering the note warning me off the case, but I wasn't willing to let go of my preconceptions so easily. "You're seriously telling me you had no idea what Jed was into?"

Her shoulders ducked and her gaze flicked away. I knew she would lie before she even opened her mouth. "I didn't know he was into that. In fact, I mentioned what you said to Miguel, about Jed liking it rough, and he just laughed."

Okay, not a total lie. She was hedging. She knew something. Something important, but whatever it was, it wasn't about the DVDs. But who else would have known? Could my trip to the Foxy Lady have tipped someone off? I hadn't mentioned DVDs, but I had asked about the private room, equipment, and cameras. The only person at the club I could think of who wouldn't want Quitman found was Quitman. Had he gotten word I'd been snooping around?

Even if my visitor had been Quitman or one of his pals, there was a bigger picture. I just wasn't seeing it. Ronnie was too evasive and she'd acted cagey from the start. I now knew for sure this was no simple bail jumper case. My abrupt quit earlier in the day was the smartest thing I'd done in a while. Curiosity may have killed the cat, but it would never kill me. Ronnie could have her little mystery of the missing payday loan god. I'd scrape out a living sticking to the basics. Hell, if I found Billy, I bet Maggie would feed me for a month. I kept one hand on the bed, while I pushed myself to my feet.

"Where are you going?" She looked surprised that my visit would be cut short.

"Home."

"Why?"

"Because I'm done here."

"Are you sure? I'm not convinced you found what you were looking for."

"I didn't, but I've decided I'm no longer interested in looking."

"But we have a deal."

"*Had* a deal. The deal is over. I work for myself. I say when the deal's over." I moved slowly toward the door. Her hand circled my arm. The pressure was light but firm. I couldn't help it. I stopped and silently wished she'd keep holding me.

"How do you decide?"

She rasped the words and I almost forgot what we were talking about. Almost. "In this case? Well, when my client works against me, it's an easy call."

"I'm not working against you."

"My decision. I'm done."

She signaled her acceptance by dropping her hand. I had no excuse not to leave. I wanted to leave. I didn't need this shit. I've been clocked before, but because I decided to take a risk, not because someone decided to take one for me. I didn't like not being trusted. I'd said it twice. I was done.

She stood there looking hurt. Dejected. I didn't buy it. She was in on whatever there was to be in on. Whatever it was, a ten percent bounty wasn't a fair price.

Random thoughts cascaded through my head. I'd keep looking for Billy anyway and all signs pointed toward a connection. If I found Jed too, at least there would be a payday in my future. Wasn't like I would have to do much extra. May as well get paid for the work I'd done. The resolution didn't register with the rest of my body. I heard my voice, but my brain wasn't engaged enough to stop the words. "Fifty percent and I'll find him."

Ronnie's sad look vanished, replaced by a grin. "Deal."

I couldn't help thinking that she may be paying me more money, but I would be the one paying for that smile.

Dinner was strange. Lots of family, gathered to celebrate a birthday. Genuine camaraderie. Brightly wrapped presents. Good food. None of the elements added up to any of the deposits in my memory bank.

The last birthday I remember celebrating with my family was when I turned sixteen. When I got home that night, the smell of burnt food was my first clue about how the "celebration" would go. My mother was on the phone with the bakery, yelling about how they misspelled my name. My dad was well into his first six-pack, but he took a break to yell at my mother about how the hell she could spend that much on a cake to start with. She hung up with the bakery and lit into him. Her main point being if he weren't so much of a loser, she could have spent even more and gone to a bakery that damn sure would know how to spell. She slammed the door of their bedroom, probably before she heard his retort, something about how if she wasn't such a lousy cook…

I slipped into my room before they realized I was home. My little brother, Mark, the pacifist, was curled in a ball under my bed. I placed a finger over my lips and he nodded. I pried him out and we tiptoed toward the back of the house. I spied my mother's purse on the little table in the hall and I fished out a twenty to finance our expedition. We snuck out the back door and spent the next few hours at the local arcade. Casino for kids.

When we ran out of money, we went back home. The burnt smell still lingered. Mom was gone. Dad was passed out in his recliner. The illiterate cake was untouched. *Happy Birthday, Lupa.* Mark and I ate half of it. No plates, only forks. Sick with sugar, we left the uneaten portion of cake exactly where we found it and passed out a half hour later.

"Have some more tamales, Luca. You look hungry."

I zapped back to the present as Mrs. Moreno shoved a large platter my way. Took me a minute to process her words. I was a big girl. I wondered what hungry looked like to her. Must have been something in my eyes. I took four more tamales. I didn't want to be impolite. Oh, and they were amazing.

"Luca is probably always hungry, aren't you?" Miguel shouted down the table. "Your line of work is a bit sporadic, isn't it?"

Ronnie opened her mouth to say something, but her mother beat her to the punch. "Miguel, eat your dinner. No talk of business at my table."

I flashed her a big smile. "You're a wonderful cook, Mrs. Moreno."

"Mrs. Moreno, she called me." She shoved Ronnie in the side. "Polite and she loves my cooking. I like your friend. She can come back anytime."

The role of parental suck up was a new one for me. Apparently, it came with awesome benefits. I wasn't being polite. The food was incredible.

"She likes you," Ronnie whispered into my ear. "Watch out. She'll have you over every day to sample her cooking."

"And that would be bad because?"

"Next thing you know, you'll be mowing the lawn for a few enchiladas, trimming the shrubs for some tacos. It's an endless cycle."

I pointed at my almost empty plate. "Totally worth it. Did you eat like this growing up?"

"She cooked like this."

"Are you incapable of actually answering a question?"

"Yes. I ate like this growing up."

I couldn't comprehend her grimace. I shoveled the last bite of tamale into my mouth. Homemade Tex-Mex. Served by her mother. She'd grown up in paradise. I glanced around the table. The whir of introductions had left me with only scattered ideas of who was present. Ronnie's brother and his wife sat at the far end. Probably for the extra room. She was mucho pregnant. Mr. Moreno, Ronnie's dad, held court at the other end. I'd yet to see Mrs. Moreno's butt touch a chair.

The rest of the crowd was a blur. Aunts, uncles, and cousins. I didn't bother trying to remember names and faces. Despite Mrs. Moreno's invitation, I doubted Ronnie would bring me back. My goal right now was limited to getting her to tell me what I needed to know to find Jed. My motivation fueled by the prospect of a better payday. I leaned close and kept my voice to a whisper. "Can we go talk now?"

She shook her head and whispered back. "No. We have to stay for cake."

I rubbed my stomach. "Cake?"

"Tres leches. Homemade. Probably flan too."

I groaned. Seconds later, the bustling Mother Moreno emerged from the kitchen with an enormous cake. It looked great, except it was on fire.

Ronnie gasped. "Mom, candles are supposed to be symbolic!"

Her mother was not to be dissuaded. "So you say. Don't worry; you're still under two boxes. Now make a wish and blow."

I couldn't stop grinning. Ronnie shot me a look to let me know she didn't appreciate the humor of the moment, didn't appreciate me being there to watch the indignity of her puffed up cheeks preparing to be defeated by the wildfire atop her homemade birthday cake. I loved every minute of it. Especially the part where she doused the fire with one mighty breath.

I didn't have much time to enjoy the sights before the table's attention turned my way. During dinner, the only sounds had been the clank of plates and silverware. With the main food course out of the way, business conversation was apparently allowed. Ronnie's brother was the first to chime in. "Luca, what exactly is it you do for a living?"

As a rule, cops hate bounty hunters. We do what they do, but without all the rules. Sure, we're supposed to follow the law, but we don't and they know it. It drives them nuts. Plus, they think we make too much money for the type of work we do. Bullshit. I work hard for the money I make. Hell, my hourly rate for this particular case was probably somewhere around fifty cents. I started to answer his question, when I received a sharp poke in the side.

"She's a consultant. She's doing some work for our firm."

I pinched her on the thigh by way of payback, but she didn't flinch. Miguel had left the table to take a phone call and with no one to debate the point, I decided to go with it. I nodded at her brother and shoved a huge forkful of cake in my mouth to avoid further interrogation. Ronnie didn't get off so easy.

"Hey, Ronnie, when did it become 'our' firm? You actually planning to stick around? I thought you were already getting tired of putting crooks back on the street."

Ouch. Ronnie's wince signaled her brother's comment stung. I tried to look casual, but I was as interested in the answer as everyone else. Would she finally start offering up some real answers?

"Lay off, Jorge. Not everyone can have a cool job with a car and uniform like you."

About what I'd expected. I silently egged Jorge on. Someone had to be able to get her to reveal. He didn't need my encouragement.

"I'd give it all up for a car like yours. You won't make enough working for Miguel to replace that cherry baby when it's time."

"Are you trying to get rid of me?"

"No way." He patted his wife's enormous belly. "We want little Sophia to have all her tias around when she comes into this world. I just wondered how you were adjusting."

"She's adjusting fine." Mrs. Moreno snatched Jorge's cake plate away as if to punish him for his remarks. "You leave your sister alone. We are blessed that she's back with her family, where she belongs."

Ronnie stood and pulled at my arm. I shrugged loose. The conversation was getting good. I wasn't going anywhere. Mrs. Moreno pointed at her. "Sit. There are presents."

"In a minute, Mom. I have to talk to Luca. It's business." She stared her mother down.

Mrs. Moreno finally threw up her hands. She left the room speaking to no one in particular. "Business, business. What about family business? What about that?"

Ronnie shook her head and rolled her eyes. Then she led me back to the room where she'd duped me into continuing to work for her. She shut the door behind us. "I'm sorry about all that."

I wondered what all that was. All that food. All that family. All those questions. "Didn't bother me." It didn't. What did bother me was how far away she was standing. The room was small. Two steps and I was at her side. I took them and purred into her ear, "But if it would make you feel better, you can make it up to me."

"You're kidding, right?" She stared into my eyes. "You're hot, Luca Bennett. You know you are. But if I've inadvertently signaled interest, I apologize."

Inadvertently signaled? I knew instantly I'd been played. All the tender touches, playful smiles. Designed to get work out of me. I blew it off. I wasn't in this for a lay. I was in it for the rest of my essential needs. She wanted business. She'd get business. I stepped back. "If I'm going to keep working for you, I need some more information about Jed. When do you want to talk?"

She consulted her watch. "I should be done here in about an hour. You know where I live. Why don't you meet me there around ten?"

"Great. See you then." I walked toward the door. She didn't move as I brushed past. The connection crackled. I knew she felt it too, but I pretended to ignore it right along with her. When I reached the door a memory surfaced. I turned and caught her staring at my ass.

She covered with an annoyed, "What?"

"I have a little problem."

"Really, Luca. I can't."

"It doesn't have anything to do with you. My Bronco, it's out of gas. I barely made it here."

Relief flooded her features. "Oh, your car. Okay. Well, looks like I'll have to give you a ride."

Lady, I'm already on a ride with you.

Chapter Thirteen

When Mrs. Moreno heard of my plight, she made one of Ronnie's cousins go buy gas for the Bronco. I had mixed feelings about her kindness.

I followed Ronnie back to her house. I could tell she was holding back. In her SL Mercedes, she could have easily left me in the dust. Expensive house, expensive car. Again I wondered what she was doing working in a crummy law shop steps from the jail.

She pulled into the garage and signaled for me to park in the drive. I climbed out of the car and grabbed the several bags we'd placed in my backseat. Her family had loaded her up with presents. Lucky I'd come along. This haul never would have fit in Ronnie's roadster. I walked through the garage. Neat and tidy. No one did any work out here. The only eye-catcher was the presence of another car. A nineteen eighty Dodge Dart. I'd never even considered that she might not live alone. Poor relation? Deadbeat husband? She didn't wear a ring. Deadbeat boyfriend? Girlfriend?

"Are you coming in?"

She stood in her massive kitchen with its wide granite countertops, bright copper pots hanging from hooks in the ceiling, and gleaming stainless steel appliances. I strode in and set the bags down on the spacious table. By the looks of things, she hosted huge dinner parties when she wasn't springing lowlifes from jail. "Nice place."

"Thanks." She started pulling gifts out of the bags and arranging them in piles on the table.

"You live here alone?"

She looked up from her task and studied my face. "The car's mine." A slow smile slid across her face. "It was my first. You never forget your first."

True. I decided not to engage. "You ready to talk about Quitman?"

Disappointment flickered in her eyes. "If that's what you want."

"It's why I'm here."

"You needn't be so single-minded. You can have more than one reason for doing a particular thing."

Her tone was even, but she moved closer and her breath was so close I could feel it on my neck. She seemed to have a different set of rules for what she was willing to indulge in now that we were under her roof. I didn't like the contradiction. I wanted to walk across the room. Put distance between the way she made me feel and the way I wanted to. I couldn't move. She was breathtaking, sensuous. Everything anyone would want. She unnerved me. "I prefer to stay on track." I didn't mean the words, but I wanted to.

She acted as if she hadn't heard me. "How's your head?"

I reached for the bandage before I caught the irony of her question. Her knack for reading my mind, for getting me off track was uncanny. I didn't dislike it, but I wanted to regain control. "Let's talk."

She didn't reply, instead she uncorked a bottle of open white wine. She poured two glasses and handed me one. "It's too hot for red."

I wouldn't drink it, but asking for beer would encourage her avoidance. I took the glass. "Can we talk now?"

She walked off, speaking over her shoulder. "Okay, but in here."

I set the glass of wine on the counter and followed. She led us into a living area and motioned me onto a cool, tan leather couch. I waited before sitting, and she grinned to let me know she read my mind again. "Don't worry. I'll sit over here while we talk." She sank into an armchair inches away.

I relaxed into the couch. It was late. I was tired. The day had taken a toll. She drank half the glass before she started sharing. By that time I had to pull myself back from the hazy edge of sleep to catch her words.

"Jed's a regular client of Miguel's. At least his employees are."

I nodded. I didn't have to ask which ones. I doubted the clerks at the check cashing joints spent much time getting into trouble. The strippers were another story. Besides the usual violations taking place at the clubs, drugs were a regular deal. I didn't blame them for using. Pole dancing in a G-string for a herd of middle-class fat white guys required sedation.

"When he got arrested, it was a big deal, but Miguel doesn't usually handle big paper cases." In response to my raised eyebrows, she explained, "He's accused of fraud, purposefully avoiding tax payments, state and county. Representing him requires a lot of paper pushing, accounting, and math. More my thing than Miguel's."

"Gotcha. Your background made you the obvious choice." I settled back and watched her reaction. The heat flared, but just as quickly died back down. She obviously knew I'd checked her out and she hated it, but I'd have to try harder to get a rise. Or information.

She kept talking as if I hadn't spoken. "I'd barely dug into the case when I was contacted by the Feds."

"They taking over the case?"

"Not this case." She paused to drink from her wineglass. "No, they had a proposition involving a completely different matter."

I perked up, but waited without prompting. Ronnie's slow telling signaled she would set the pace. I didn't do a lot of work on federal cases. Federal judges usually released folks on their own recognizance if they released them at all. If there's no money at stake, there's no reason for me to get involved. And although I knew a ton of local cops, I had only one federal agent on my call list. She worked undercover in organized crime for the FBI. Could sleazy Jed Quitman be connected? I remembered the conversation at the softball game. Gail had mentioned Jed's payday loan shops might be a cover for something more sinister.

Ronnie cleared her throat and I focused on her next words. "They promised to talk to the DA's office if Jed would help them out in a corruption case they've been working."

They probably also threatened him with new charges if he didn't help. "Anyone I know?"

"I don't know if you know him, but you've mentioned his biggest contributor. Caroline Randolf."

I decided to come clean. "Stab in the dark. I heard a rumor Jed was diddling her."

"Maybe he was, is. I don't know. I do know the Feds think he's in bed with Dick Lively."

"I heard Quitman is one of his donors, but so are lots of people. Are you saying Lively's Mr. Clean reputation is overrated?"

"I don't know, but when I mentioned what the Feds wanted, Jed clammed up. Told me not to take their calls. He had his own ideas about how to get out of his state court mess. He gave me explicit instructions to take no further action until I heard from him."

"And what was his brilliant plan?"

"I don't know. The phone conversation where he told me he could handle things was the last one we had. I haven't seen or heard from him since."

"What's your theory?"

"He's in trouble."

"So? Isn't trouble your trade? He'll get arrested again. He can pay you again. Sounds like a perfect economy to me."

"Except he's in trouble because of me."

Her statement begged me to ask why. I wanted to as much as I didn't. Why would lead deeper. I didn't want to go there. Half the bond wasn't worth the investment she was asking me to make. But for the first time, the confident Ronnie Moreno was uncertain and her uncertainty bordered on fear. She didn't bother trying to hide it. I couldn't help but think her fear was rooted in more than worry over Jed Quitman's fate. I stood and walked to the kitchen. She didn't follow, but I could feel her questioning stare. Would I stay?

The giant fridge was like the rest of the kitchen, stuffed full of food I'd never seen before. Fancy jars with fancy names. Cheeses in all shapes and colors. I pushed several bottles around until I found the high-dollar beer I knew would be on hand for guests. I pulled two bottles, then went on a hunt for a bottle opener. I found several in one of the dozens of drawers. I popped the tops on both bottles and returned to the living room. I handed her a beer and she quickly drank the better part of it.

I liked her. More than the get in her pants feeling I'd experienced at first. I didn't want to, but I did. I'd already conceded a physical attraction, but like was more important. Deeper. Meaningful. I wasn't about to let on, but I could at least listen to her story about Quitman because I knew a deeper tale lay beneath. A personal revelation. Questions she wouldn't duck.

"Tell me."

Only took those two words to open the flood gates.

"One of the first things I did when I took over this case, before I got the call from the Feds, was place a call to Dick Lively's office. I wanted to line up potential character witnesses. People who would vouch for Quitman. With his general reputation in the community, we were going to need help painting him as an upstanding citizen."

"Quitman and Lively are friends?" I was skeptical. Clean-cut Dick Lively didn't strike me as the type to hang with the Jed Quitmans of the world.

"They don't run in the same circles, but they do have mutual business contacts. And Quitman has spent a lot of money to keep Lively in office."

"What's that about?"

"When you run businesses on the edge it doesn't hurt to have a powerful legislator in your pocket."

"I didn't think Lively could be bought."

"Apparently, he can't." She took another big swallow of beer. "He talked to me when I called. I mentioned Jed's name and was put right through. He was very polite, listened to everything I had to say. Said he'd be happy to help out. We agreed to meet and discuss how he could play a role in Jed's defense."

"I thought you said he couldn't be bought."

"Hear me out. Shortly after I talked to Lively, the Feds came calling. When Jed waived me off, I stopped working on the case until I could talk him down. I called Lively's office and indefinitely postponed our appointment. Lively himself called me back to find out why. I gave him some vague explanation about how I had gotten ahead of myself and wanted to wait to find out more about the state's case before I crafted a defense. And then Jed disappeared."

Her expression implied I was dense if I didn't get the connection. Maybe I was. "I don't get it. Do you think Lively is helping Jed skip out?"

She shook her head vigorously. Now I was certain she thought I was stupid. "No. I think Lively made Jed disappear."

My turn to think she was a bit off. I started gently. "The simplest explanation is usually the best. Couldn't it be that Jed decided taking off was better than going to jail and or being a witness for the Feds in a big corruption case?"

"Sure. If all things were even." She finished her beer. "Like you, I received a warning to stay away from the Quitman case."

I stiffened. "When?"

"Right before I hired you. A note stuck to the hood of my car at the courthouse, simple and to the point. *I don't need your help anymore. Thanks for everything. You can keep the retainer, but stop working on my case. Thanks, JQ.*"

Now I knew she was crazy. "Doesn't sound like much of a warning. Sounds like your client fired you."

She slammed her beer bottle on the table and anger flashed in her eyes. "Bullshit. Clients don't leave notes on their lawyers' cars. Besides, I've been in the process of reviewing all of his records, including his checkbooks. The handwriting on the note wasn't his. He disappeared and I've been told to let it go. Right after the Feds show up looking for help on a corruption case and I blow off the offer of assistance from one of the most powerful congressmen in the state. I don't believe in coincidences and I don't like being told what to do."

At last we had a couple of issues we could agree on, but I still didn't get why she gave a shit what happened to Quitman. He was her client, not her lover. *Cut her some slack, Bennett.* She'd finally shared the full story. Now I had a choice. I could keep looking for Quitman or I could bail.

I wondered how the DVDs I'd found at Quitman's house factored in. Enough to spur someone into breaking into my place and stealing them away. Or stealing them back. Could Jed have been the one who hit me over the head, to warn me away from trying to find him? I wanted to know the answer, but not just for myself. I wanted Ronnie to have the answers she was looking for. Knowing was important to her in a way I didn't yet understand, but I knew was essential. I couldn't give her the answers, but I could find Quitman and make him explain. I wanted to give her what I could, and finding him was what I could do. Insane as it was, I wanted to please her more than I wanted the money. The realization kicked me in the gut.

Chapter Fourteen

I rolled out of bed the next morning and groaned. Getting up early sucks. What sucks worse is not having any coffee in the house. The clock on my nightstand read six thirty a.m. I had an hour and a half before I was supposed to meet Ronnie at her office. Enough time for a run. I hoped the endorphins would do their part to wake me up. At least I was up early enough to avoid the stifling heat. This time of morning it was only just reaching the nineties.

I started out slow and eventually picked up a decent pace even with the extra weight of the gun at my side. After yesterday, I wasn't going anywhere without it. I knew the break-in wasn't meant to be personal, but the violation stung. No one was going to touch my stuff again without consequences. Bullet-ridden consequences.

I ran past one of Jed Quitman's payday loan shops. All of them were strategically located in the less affluent neighborhoods where folks had a hard time making ends meet. Again I wondered about Ronnie's very personal interest in Quitman's fate. I figured he deserved whatever he got. Last night I had put my own thoughts aside and promised Ronnie I'd help her find him. Talk about personal interest. I knew I wasn't working on this case for the money anymore. Two personal cases in one week. I must be getting soft. Maggie's favor I could understand. For years, she'd been like a mother to me. She fed me, challenged me, and would care if I was dead.

Ronnie, I couldn't figure out. She made me crazy with her evasive answers, her blind faith, her commanding sensuality. She was danger and I craved risk. Maybe the attraction was that simple. I'd already given in—no point in dwelling on the decision.

And then there was the seeming connection between these two cases. Should make for more efficient work, but I prayed any overlap was nothing more than a coincidence. Sex DVDs and murder. For Maggie's sake, I didn't want Billy to be any part of Quitman's mess, but it wasn't looking good especially since I'd learned Billy was sweet on the now dead Emily, aka Missy, the young starlet featured in Jed's productions. Had Billy gotten jealous when he leaned about Emily's side job? The DVDs were key. I needed to find them or at least find the rest of the cast to get some answers.

I finished the run and took a quick shower. I dressed in my usual jeans, boots, and T-shirt, but I dug an old blazer out of the back of the closet, partly in deference to office attire, mostly to cover my shoulder holster. On the way to Ronnie's office I almost stopped at a McDonald's to grab a cup of coffee, but changed my mind and swung into a Starbucks instead. I don't frequent the place because I think it should be against the law to pay what they charge for a cup of coffee. I wanted to bring Ronnie a drink, and I figured she wouldn't drink the swill I do. As I stood at the counter, I regretted my decision. Too much money was no longer the issue. I was plagued by too many choices. I considered the options—size, flavor, type of milk. I'd never appreciated how coffee was such a personal beverage. What would Ronnie like? I had no idea, but I felt compelled to try to figure it out.

With assistance from the tattooed, pierced girl behind the counter and my memories of the dessert Ronnie had enjoyed so much the night before, I settled on a caramel something or another. I ordered the biggest black coffee they had for myself and left before they could rob me of the rest of my money.

Maria met me at the front door. "Hi, Luca. You have your hands full." She held open the door while I walked through.

"Thanks."

"Anything I can do for you today?"

The look in her eye was suggestive. I had to cut that short, now. "I'm here to see Ronnie."

Her smile dimmed slightly and she looked at the second cup in my hand as if it contained poison. "Oh, okay. Have a seat over there and I'll get her for you."

My coffee was decent and it kept me occupied while I waited. The waiting area wasn't designed for waiting. The seats were hard plastic and the five-year-old *Time* magazines were like history textbooks. I'd started counting the specks on the tiled floor when Ronnie entered the room.

"Good morning, Luca. Why don't you come on back?"

I stood and handed her the caramel concoction. "I stopped for coffee. Picked you up a drink."

She lifted the lid and sniffed. "Smells wonderful. Caramel?"

I nodded and she groaned with pleasure. I liked the way her pleasure felt. I followed her into the office area, ignoring the eye-rolling from Maria and focusing instead on Ronnie's ass.

The deal we'd made the night before was that she would give me access to everything she had in her case files on Quitman's case. I was certain we'd find a clue about where he was in the reams of material she had. People just aren't that inventive. His habits would show through and we'd find him in some likely place, safe and sound.

Ronnie led me through her office doorway into her tiny space. She pointed to the boxes. "Everything's in there. You can use my desk if you want." I grabbed a box and folded myself into one of the chairs. She remained standing.

"Aren't you going to help?" I asked.

She glanced at her watch. "I guess I can for a little while. I have a hearing at ten." She pulled one of the boxes toward her and sat next to me. I caught a whiff of her woody, citrus scent.

"Are these arranged in any particular order?"

She handed me a chart. "I made an index when I went through them initially. It's not very detailed, just enough information to let me know if it relates to the case."

I looked at the paper and remembered why I don't do regular detective work. The chart was full of strings of numbers and vaguely worded complex phrases. I didn't know the difference between a profit loss statement and a general ledger, let alone a debit and a credit. Besides, I didn't think any of those entries were likely to lead us to Quitman's whereabouts. I traced my finger down the page until I found a reference to more basic documents: bank and credit card statements. Money talks. While Ronnie looked through her box, I replaced mine with the one containing the documents I was looking for.

Quitman had six bank accounts as far as I could tell. One for the payday loan stores, a couple were personal accounts, and the rest were listed under obscure names like Carousel Adventures, LLC and JCM Enterprises, LLC. My earlier research had already told me Carousel Adventures was the company that owned the strip clubs. The others I'd never heard of.

I started looking through the check register for Carousel. The expenses were typical. Mostly rent, booze, and tiny paychecks for the dancers. Places like that only pay the dancers aka strippers a nominal hourly wage. The women are supposed to make the bulk of their money from cash-waving customers not the hard-working owners. I set the Carousel records aside and picked up a large folder labeled in big block letters, JCM. The bank statements were a series of cash deposits and cash withdrawals. Maybe JCM was some kind of shell company, a slush fund for Quitman's other ventures. I didn't see an associated credit card account. I started to put the JCM statements back in the box but decided to set them aside instead. Something about them bothered me, but I couldn't quite catch the fleeting thought. I'd come back to them later.

I reached for another box when Ronnie suddenly stood up. Miguel was in the doorway, wearing a dark frown. All of its energy was focused in my direction, primarily at the JCM file on the corner of the desk.

"Aren't you covering the Chavez hearing?" His question was more of a command.

Ronnie's reaction was calm. "I'm ready. If I leave in fifteen, I'll be there in plenty of time."

Miguel pulled up his sleeve and made a show of consulting his Rolex. He cast another "I wish you weren't here" glance in my direction before addressing Ronnie. "Judge Slater is already mad at me about the incident last week. I'd prefer it if you were early. Besides, this is a paid in full client."

Ronnie sighed. "Fine. I'll head on over. Luca can stay here and work until I get back."

"May I speak to you in my office for a moment?"

Miguel was the master of subtle behavior. Like I wouldn't figure out he wanted to talk to her about me. Ronnie followed him out and I waited a respectable few seconds before finding Miguel's closed office door. No one could see me so I didn't mind how I looked with my ear pressed against the door.

"What's she doing here?"

"She's helping me look through Quitman's case files."

"I thought she was a bounty hunter."

"She is. The trail's run cold and I thought his files might give us some hints about where to find him."

"You hire a bounty hunter, and then you take time away from our cases to do her work for her. I thought you were more professional than that."

Ronnie's voice rose. "Lay off, Miguel. You said I could have free rein here and you gave this case to me. If you want to tell me how to run it maybe I made the wrong choice about coming back here." I was glad her anger was directed at someone other than me.

"Settle down, mija. Your mother will beat me if you go back East. You do have free rein, but Jed Quitman has always been my client. I know the man. If he has decided to skip out on his responsibilities, he has the resources to stay hidden. This woman you hired, she may not have the skills necessary to find him, and she should be doing the work, not you."

"Sounds like you're telling me how to do things. All my work is up to date, and I'm covering for you in court this morning. Quitman is my case, you need to let me handle it my way." Her voice dropped to a sweet whisper. "Please let me see this through."

"Let's make a deal. If he isn't found by Monday, we'll hire someone else. Deal?"

"Deal."

She caved pretty quickly. Busy as I was contemplating my relief to still be on the job, I didn't notice Maria had walked up right behind me. "Hi, Luca." I started to make up some excuse for standing outside Miguel's office door, but Maria saved me from myself with a whispered "She'll be coming out in a minute if she wants to be on time for court."

I nodded. "Thanks for the save." I made it back to Ronnie's office about two seconds before Ronnie burst out of Miguel's office. I spied the JCM file folder and instinct spurred me to shove it in my waistband.

❖

After Ronnie hurried off to court, I opted to continue working in the office if only to thumb my nose at Miguel. After about forty-five more snooze-worthy minutes of reviewing files, I stood to stretch my legs. I heard voices in the hall and stuck my head out the door to see if Ronnie was on her way back. She wasn't. Instead, Senator Dick Lively and Miguel walked out of Miguel's office, heads together, engaged in tense, whispered conversation. I watched them for a minute, and then stepped into the hallway. Ever since Ronnie's revelations the night before, my mental checklist included a visit to Senator Lively's office. Running into him here, away from layers of staff, was ideal.

Miguel glared daggers at me, but I ignored him. Not like his opinion of me could get any worse. I stuck my hand out and the senator reached for it, his worried expression morphing into a blazing smile. He was handsome in a generic Ken doll kind of way. Short salt and pepper hair, athletic build, and dark brown eyes. His smile didn't reach his eyes, which were hard and cold. I had no doubt the handshake and smile were pure politician muscle memory.

Miguel didn't step up to make introductions, so I did the honor myself. "Great to meet you, Senator Lively. My name is Luca Bennett. I'm a huge fan of your work." He smiled and I gushed. Both of us knew how to put on a show.

"Great to meet you, Miss Bennett. I appreciate your kind words. I hope you'll consider supporting my campaign for reelection."

"Actually, I was wondering if I might talk to you about your campaign. I know you have some very influential supporters and I hear you're really skilled at making things happen for them."

My stab in the dark hit its mark. Lively's brow furrowed and his smile faded just a touch. Miguel, though, didn't try to hide his frustration. "Luca, I think you have some work to do, and the senator was just headed back to his office."

"Oh, too bad. I have some money to invest and I'd love to talk to you more about what you have planned for your next term."

"Sure, come by anytime." He didn't mean it, but I didn't care. The invitation was too good to pass up. Miguel hustled him out of the office before I could continue the exchange. I waited until I was sure the senator was gone and Miguel was tucked back in his office, and then I ducked out with a quick wave to Maria who was busy multitasking, filing her nails and talking on the phone.

Since I knew Lively was headed back to his office, what better time to catch him? I didn't suffer under any delusions he would agree to see me, but I could try to catch a minute with him as he scurried between appointments, without Miguel at his side running interference. Plus I wanted to do something besides read through a bunch of papers.

On the drive over, I tried to figure out why a U.S. senator was slumming it at Miguel's office. Maybe he'd gotten wind of the federal investigation that was in the works and was looking for representation. Not likely he'd start with an attorney like Miguel. Lively could afford the biggest and best law firms in town. Besides, if the Feds wanted Jed to flip on him and Miguel represented Jed, the conflict of interest would prevent him from representing both of them. Of course, I wouldn't put it past Miguel to drop Jed and take the senator on as a client if he had the chance, but that brought me back to why would the senator pick a bottom-feeder like Miguel to represent him when he could have the best? I pondered the possibilities while I looked for parking close to the senator's office.

His office took up most of the third floor of a fancy Uptown building. Once I reached the well-appointed lobby, I worked my way through the first layer with ease. The receptionist seemed to think I was cute rather than crazy for wanting to see the senator without an appointment. The blazer must've put me in the "she's not a kook" category.

"He's in, but he already has several meetings scheduled with other constituents. If you'd like, you can fill out one of these cards with your information and I'll see if another staff member has a moment to speak with you about your issue."

I wasn't in the mood to pretend to have an issue, especially not with whatever just graduated from college and can't get a real job staff member they would assign to meet with the woman who couldn't be bothered to make an appointment. But since I was here, I may as well make the most of the welcome. If questions about Quitman were going to start a fire, better a slow burn than the bonfire that would come from throwing a match at the powerful man himself.

A mere twenty minutes later, a suited nerd came to collect me. He invited me into a tiny office and sat behind a desk to bolster his image. The small space didn't contain a speck of personality, no photos on the desk, no certificates on the walls, no cute matching pen cup and business card holder. I guessed it was the designated meeting with not-so-important constituents room. Was I a constituent if I never voted? I pushed the thought away and focused my attention on Nerd Boy. He glanced at a piece of paper in his hand, then folded his hands in front of him. "Ms. Bennett, my name is Donald Scurvy. What can we do to help you today?"

Scurvy? Really? Bet this guy didn't get much front time in the senator's office. I'd used my time in the lobby to come up with a story. I summoned a stern expression and let it fly. "I want to talk to you about greed."

"Greed?" I could tell by the slight tic on his face, he was thinking the receptionist had pegged me wrong, that I might be one of the crazy ones.

"Yes, greed." I leaned forward to make my point. "How much money do you think is too much for one man to make off the backs of the working class?"

He glanced over his shoulder, but the wall behind him didn't offer any advice. While he tried to decide if my question was rhetorical, I fired off another, designed to get to the heart of the matter. "When is the senator going to pass legislation to prevent the Jed Quitmans of the world from stealing the hard-earned cash of Dallas's citizens? Did you know that most of his so-called loans net him about three hundred percent profit? Again, I ask, how much is too much?"

Nerd started scribbling on the pad in front of him. "You pose excellent questions, Ms. Bennett. I have taken several notes and I plan to discuss your concerns with the senator myself." He stood. "Now, if you will excuse me, I have another appointment in a few minutes."

I remained seated. Not sure why. I suppose it just felt good to unsettle him. He was definitely flustered, which I hoped meant I had touched a nerve.

"Well, okay then. I'm going to go now." He moved toward the door and swept his arms in a gesture I knew was meant to indicate I should follow. I ignored him. By the time he reached the door, he'd run out of facial expressions to signal how much he wanted me to leave.

I threw him a bone. "Should I wait here until you finish with your other appointment?"

"Uh, well, I don't think...I suppose here is fine." He scurried from the room.

I didn't waste any time. The door didn't lock, so I shoved a chair against it to warn me of his return. Except for a few stray pens and Vote for Lively bumper stickers, the desk drawers were empty. I wasn't surprised, but I was disappointed. The trip had been a waste, for the most part. I did have fun yanking his chain, but fun wasn't going to earn me any money. As I returned to the chair to resume my act as the concerned voter, I heard a rustle outside the door. I swiftly moved the chair, fell into the seat, and prepared to assail Nerd Boy with more about my concerns. He'd apparently handed me off. A hulking figure filled the doorway. My time with the senator's staff was clearly over.

"Ms. Bennett, Mr. Scurvy won't be able to finish your meeting today. He'll call you to reschedule. Come with me."

The Hulk needed a bigger suit, or maybe he liked the way his muscles practically burst through the fabric. His professional dress didn't fool me. His job was to keep the riffraff at bay and he was here to escort me out with a minimum of fuss. I briefly entertained the idea of taking him on, but long odds were for cards, not fist fights. The thick, jagged knife scar from his ear to his collar said he didn't shy away from a challenge. Besides, I had a feeling his presence meant my deliberate shit stirring had worked. I'd leave now and find a way to watch for fallout.

He walked me all the way to the lobby, watched me while I waited for the elevator, and was still standing guard until the doors shut. I considered getting off on another floor and working my way back through the stairwell, but I didn't have a plan beyond that. Besides, I'd been up for hours and I was starving. Memories of Mother Moreno's Tex-Mex spread and the smell of lunch preparations from nearby restaurants caused me to drool. I'd grab something to eat in the car while I figured out my next move.

Ten minutes later, I feasted on a to-go order of street tacos from Primo's. I'd spread out the contents of the pilfered JCM file on the seat beside me, and made a half-assed attempt to keep salsa off the papers within. The entries on the bank statements were the same string of cash transactions I'd noticed when I first looked. Wasn't sure why I kept staring, but I did. I pulled out my phone and Googled JCM. No website, no business listing. Quitman's other enterprises had ads all over the net. This was obviously something different. The company was an LLC, so they should have a listing with the secretary of state. I'm no business wank, but I've had to learn a minimal amount as one of the tools of my trade. My oversized, now salsa-wet fingers weren't made for typing complicated searches on a tiny phone. I'd wait until I got to a real computer to see what else I could find.

While I was shoving the bank statements back in the file, I noticed a black limo pull up across the street. Senator Lively, Mr.

Scurvy, and the Hulk who'd escorted me out of the office earlier climbed into the backseat. I sucked down the last of my tacos and rolled into traffic behind them.

Today's high was a hundred and eight. A record high for July and a record thirty-one days in a row over the century mark. Frankly, once the temp gets over a hundred, it all seems the same to me, but the Bronco was feeling the extra degrees. I rolled down the windows and turned off the A/C to give her a bit of a break. Took about two minutes before I was drenched in sweat. I hoped the limo wasn't making a long trip.

It wasn't. First stop was the Federal building downtown. The senator climbed out, followed by Scurvy and the Hulk. I idled across the street. Hulk accompanied the other two to the doors, but didn't follow them in. He pulled a phone out of his pocket, made a call that lasted all of ten seconds, then strode over to a parking lot across the street.

I had a quick decision to make. Park, enter the building, and follow the senator, or trail this guy. Federal building was locked down tight. Depending on where the senator was headed, I might have to get through at least two layers of security. Even then I didn't have a clue which of the dozens of offices he was visiting. I made my choice and drove around the block to get a better view of the parking lot the Hulk was headed to.

Within five minutes, I was within a few car lengths of his dark blue sedan, headed south. A mile into the trip, the scenery disintegrated from tall skyscrapers to abandoned warehouses. As the traffic thinned, I hung back to keep from being noticed. Fifteen minutes in, he exited the highway and turned left at the light. I exited, but pulled into the shady looking convenience store on the corner and faked looking at the price of gas until he was well ahead of me before resuming my pursuit. Luckily, a few more cars joined us on the road. Just as I started to relax, he made a sharp turn onto a rocky drive in front of a rundown warehouse. I drove on by looking for a place to turn around and double back. Now I was cursing the other cars on the road since they kept me from quickly turning back. Took forever to find a place to reverse direction without killing myself or someone else. By the time I returned to the warehouse, the Hulk's car was parked in front of the warehouse and he was nowhere in sight.

The dilapidated building was lonely on a lot badly in need of mowing. The nearest neighboring building was at least a hundred yards away. From the outside it looked abandoned—no cars besides mine and the Hulk's in sight. I didn't assign any particular meaning to the apparent desolation; warehouses have a way of looking empty from the outside. I left the windows down in the Bronco. I cared more about keeping the car from becoming an oven than the remote possibility someone would steal my stuff. Besides, my most valuable possessions, my guns—except the ones I was wearing—were hidden in the secret and tightly locked compartment under the rear seat. I flicked a glance at the file on the passenger seat. My ethics may not have prevented me from lifting it from Ronnie's office, but they did nudge me to put it somewhere out of sight. I stashed it in my special hiding place, and then quietly shut the car door.

I crunched across the gravel to the first door. I turned the knob. It wasn't locked. At least I didn't have to break in. I drew my Sig and pushed the door slightly open.

I eased into the room and pulled the door shut behind me. Thin shards of sunlight from the aging roof barely lit the room. I could make out stacks of crates, a desk and chair, but not much else. I started to reopen the door to get a better look, but a muffled sound from across the room changed my mind. I stood in place and listened. Voices. Two of them. Arguing, but I couldn't quite make out the words. Hulk must've been meeting someone here. Where was the other car? I'd been in too much of a hurry to make up for lost time that I hadn't properly cased the place.

I stepped on the balls of my feet, made my best guess about where the voices were coming from, and walked toward them. Suddenly, the voices stopped and I heard feet scuffling and a thump followed by a loud groan. Then silence. I kept moving, my light steps and quick breaths were the only sound I heard. I stood still for a full ten seconds. Nothing. May as well get a good look around. I pivoted back toward the door, but froze at the sound of a guttural cry closely followed by metal crashing against the concrete floor.

No longer concerned about stealth, I ran toward the noise, making a ton of racket all on my own. In the pinpoints of light, I saw a man-shaped shadow run toward the back of the building and another headed in the opposite direction. I chose the second one and chased him, determined to get some answers about what in the hell was going on. I could barely see, but I could hear his breathing and I could tell I was gaining on him. If I hadn't tripped, he would have been mine.

Whatever I stumbled into was low to the ground and had evaded the tiny bit of light in the room. I went down hard, and my gun skittered across the floor. Running guy paused in a ray of sunlight and turned back toward me. His cap and the shadow from the backlight shielded his face, but he was about the same size as me. The Hulk was bigger. This had to be someone else. I would fight him hand to hand if I had to, but I'd rather have a weapon. He walked back toward me and I swept the floor with my hand. No gun, but I did connect with a wooden handle. Long. Probably a broom. I circled my fingers around it and tested the weight. Definitely not a broom. I hefted whatever it was and held it over my head. Hoping his visibility was as poor as mine, I announced, "Take another step and I'll beat you within an inch of your life."

Worked like a charm. Guy paused only long enough to kick my gun full across the floor before he took off toward the back of the building again. Seconds later, he opened a door and dashed outside. He left the door open and sunlight poured in. I dropped my impromptu weapon and bent over to catch my breath. The whole experience had left me more shook up than I wanted to admit. For all I knew I'd probably just scared the shit out of a homeless guy looking for shelter in what appeared to be a little used warehouse. I gulped big, deep breaths and stood up straight. When the adrenaline wore off, my other senses kicked in and their signals sent a race of dread up my spine. My hands were wet and my nosed tinged at a powerful and all too familiar smell. I turned around to the place I'd fallen and stepped to the side to see what was in my shadow. A body. Face down, which was probably good since the back of the head was a gory mess of blood and brain. Thoughts and questions tumbled over each other. Dead body. Gunshot? Fresh blood. Still alive? I shook myself and knelt to check for a pulse. I knew there wouldn't be one, but I couldn't seem to write off another senseless death. I would do what I could and then walk away. I rolled the body over, the dead weight a sure sign I was too late to do any good. Still, I searched for signs of life, using the sunlight from the open door as my guide. Took my brain a while to catch up to what was in plain view.

I'd been confident I'd find him, but not here and not like this. Jed Quitman would never again enjoy the trappings of his fancy house or the cool comfort of bought affection from his stable of strippers. As the realization of his death dawned on me, an urgent sense of awareness of my own body surged through me. I held out my hands. My palms were covered with blood. A few feet away lay a sledgehammer covered in my bloody handprints. Jed Quitman's life was over and I had a feeling mine was too. Seconds later, I was surrounded and shouts confirmed my dread.

"Police! On your knees! Now!"

CHAPTER FIFTEEN

I'd never ridden in the back of a squad car. Even last year when I got caught breaking into a jumper's house, I was given the courtesy of a trip to the hospital to X-ray my bruised tailbone before the cops questioned me and released me on my own recognizance. I figured the two stern-faced uniforms in the front seat weren't about to cut me any such slack, so I was surprised when we pulled up at police headquarters rather than the jail.

No waiting in the lobby like the other day. Cuffed, I was led through the back door and thrust into an interview room exactly the same as the one Ronnie rejected when she and I had visited to discuss yet another murder. God, I wished she were here now. I could use a good lawyer. Oh hell, who was I kidding? I wanted Ronnie for more than her legal skills. Didn't matter what I wanted. I knew the drill. I'd get my phone call when these jokers were good and ready. I could only hope she'd come when I called.

Uniform number one unlocked the cuffs and shoved me into one of the hard plastic chairs. He left with his partner. I didn't try the door. I knew it was locked. I didn't talk to myself. I didn't move. I knew my every move was being captured on video. I fixed my features into a neutral expression and squared myself for the fight ahead.

Perez waited an hour to show her face. She came alone. Sat across from me. And gloated.

"Well, Bennett, you—"

"Beat it, Perez. I've got a lawyer. Call her if you want to talk to me."

"You've got a lawyer for one case. Situation's changed a bit."

"I've got nothing to say."

"Then don't talk. Listen." She leaned in close, her breath hot and hard, and ticked off points on her fingers. "Here's what I have so far. You, standing over a dead body. Victim's blood on your hands. Murder weapon covered with your bloody fingerprints. Victim, Jed Quitman, who you've been asking questions about all over town. You, first degree murder. You're done, Bennett. Couldn't have happened to a nicer person."

Took every ounce of energy I had not to respond. She wanted me angry, off-balance. She wanted me to take a swing at her. Wanted an excuse to take me down. She wouldn't get it. Not tonight. Not ever. I said the only thing I could. "I want my lawyer."

Perez sneered. "I bet you do." She waved a hand over her head and let a few beats pass before she continued. I could tell by her words she'd signaled the camera off. "You'll get your lawyer, but she can't help you. No one can help you. I'll see to it you're locked up for the rest of your life if it's the last thing I do. This is one murder you will not get away with." Her eyes bulged and her cheeks were red with anger. She waited as if to let the full impact of her words settle in, but I refused to show fear. Finally, she assumed a calm expression, waved her hand again. She waited a few beats before assuming an even tone. "Certainly, Ms. Bennett. Once you've been processed, you'll have an opportunity to make a call to whoever you wish." She left without another word.

Another uncomfortable hour later Perez and her sheepdog partner, Dalton, retrieved me and drove me the short mile to the jail. The only words they spoke were to tell me I had a right to remain silent and the usual other stuff. I took full advantage of the silent thing. I'd been to jail dozens of times, but never on the inside—not even to visit a straying friend or relative. The experience was sobering. Didn't take long to figure out any jailhouse fantasies I've ever had were called fantasies for a reason.

Too soon, guards culled me from the herd of new arrestees in Central Intake. Big female sheriff and her smaller sidekick took their time searching me for contraband before sending me to be photographed and fingerprinted. Next, I received more of a medical exam than my noninsurance self had endured in years. I figured it would be hours before I was hauled before a judge and bond was set. Only then would I be able to contact Hardin, convince him to get me out by promising to work for free for the rest of my life. As the sidekick continued the exam, I reflected that at least I was getting my money's worth out of this escapade.

❖

I shut my eyes against the intrusion of the bright light of dawn. When they finally adjusted to freedom, Hardin's weathered face greeted me. He upended a paper cup labeled Koffee, threw it into a nearby trash can, and strode over to where I was standing. He tossed me a set of keys which I caught in midair.

"I'm parked across the street. Let's go."

Hardin's bonding agency was only a few blocks away, but no one walks in the hot Texas sun unless they didn't own a car. We climbed in his pickup and drove the short distance in silence. Wasn't until we pulled into the parking lot, he said, "Called Miguel's office. Figured you're doin' work for them, they might cut you some slack on the fee. Girl lawyer's waiting inside. She wanted to come with. Seems kinda frantic."

Ronnie. I slunk down in the seat. I had two dollars in my pocket, no guns, and no car. My Bronco was probably at an impound lot. I reeked of the sour stench of jail and I was certain I looked like I'd slept in my clothes. I hadn't slept at all and I'd worn a coarse, dingy jail jumpsuit for the last eight hours of my incarceration. Despite my current condition, I wanted to see her as much as I didn't want her to see me. I climbed out of the pickup. May as well give her a chance to reject me in person.

She met me at the door. She nodded to Hardin. "Thanks. I'll take it from here. You don't need anything else from her right now, do you?" He shook his head although we both knew it wasn't a question. Neither was her next statement, directed to me. "You look like hell. Let's get you out of here."

Her little red Mercedes zipped us home in record time. Her home. We walked through the garage again. This time my curiosity about her home was dampened by my curiosity about other things. What did she know? Why was I here?

Oblivious to my internal questions, she led me to a large room and tossed me a towel and some sweats. "Take a hot shower or bath. Take your time. I'll be in the kitchen when you're done." She kissed me gently on the forehead and left the room before I could reply.

I looked around. I was in the master suite. I crossed to the large bathroom, shut the door behind me, and locked it. After hours of exposure, I craved privacy before shedding my clothes so close in time to being forced to strip for prison guards whose eyes mocked my helplessness.

No way were these her sweats. They fit me perfectly and would've hung on her like a circus tent, but they smelled like her— the gentle wood and sharp citrus I'd come to associate with comfort. With her. I relished their soft touch against the skin I'd rubbed raw. Barefoot, I padded my way to the kitchen. I paused when I saw her. She was standing to the side. I could see her profile, but she couldn't see me as I approached. She wore skimpy shorts and a tank top. Stood barefoot at the island stove, prodding the contents of a frying pan around with a spatula in her hand. The savory smell of grilled onions hung in the air, and I finally registered she was cooking. For me?

I was starving, but food was the last thing on my mind. My hunger was deeper. I struggled to squelch it. She turned toward me and I lost the struggle. She dropped the spatula, turned off the stove, and walked over, her eyes pinned to mine. She didn't touch me, but she held me in place. I wanted to be closer.

"Are you hungry?"

I answered by stepping toward her. I was starving. Surely she knew. Not for whatever she was cooking, but for the sizzling heat that had burned between us since we'd locked looks in the crowded halls of the courthouse days before. I craved her touch, to ground me, to soothe me, to make me feel alive. For the last eighteen hours, I'd met each invasion of my personal space with threats and anger. Standing before Ronnie, stripped of pride, I wanted to feel her against every inch of me until neither one of us could mark the line between us. I prayed she could sense my need, prayed she would feed me.

She took my hand and led me back to the bedroom. When we crossed the threshold, I took it as a sign. She would give me what I wanted. I wanted her.

I twisted around and yanked her toward me. I gripped her in my arms and the blistering kiss we shared was rough, bruising. Every action designed to imprint our passion over the pain I carried. She was real, alive, beautiful. I wanted all those things. I wanted them now. I pushed her back toward the bed and bent between her legs, pressing my full weight against her slender body. Her flat palm against my chest sliced through my focus. I gasped for words. "Don't tell me this isn't what you want."

She hooked my legs with hers and rolled me over. No small feat. The simple show of strength aroused me. "I want you. I think you know that."

"Then don't stop me." I couldn't help the growl. Didn't try. I pushed back against her. Despite her actions, her words were clear. She wanted me. I chose not to look beyond the simple declaration.

"Luca, stop. Look at me."

When a lady says stop, even a rogue like me obeys. I faced her square, waiting.

"You're not used to soft and slow, are you?"

I wasn't, but I'd never given my propensity to tear through sex like a starving teenager a second thought. Even now her words hazed against my rising lust. I struggled to see through to her point. Why were we talking about it instead of actually doing it? It, it, it. I didn't give our actions a name because if I did, I'd have to examine them, describe them. The blur I felt wasn't the torrid sex I ripped through with others, surging into orgasm with no regard to emotion. Even with Jess, sex was a balm, not a cure. Ronnie's touch aroused more than a physical response, but I wasn't in the mood to dissect my feelings. I wanted release. Hers and mine. She wanted soft and slow. I'd give her what she wanted. "Show me what you want."

She didn't hesitate. Within seconds the tiny shorts and tank were on the floor and she stood, nude, at the edge of the bed. Sleek, dark, dangerously gorgeous. I craved the heat smoldering between us. I reached for her arms, to pull her toward me, but she stepped back. "*I'm* showing you. Remember?"

She showed me. Over and over.

❖

I'd fallen asleep. In another woman's bed. Had never happened before. Ronnie had never happened before. I'd spent the night more vulnerable than I cared to admit, but I still wasn't sure I'd broken her barriers. I could only hope. I stifled the slip into sentimentality and climbed out of the bed, leaving her tangled in the sheets. I yanked on the sweats she'd loaned me and prowled through the rest of the house. One hunger sated, I couldn't wait any longer to eat. Maybe all the fancy trappings in her kitchen would make up for my limited culinary skills and I could concoct a passable meal.

The clock in the kitchen told me I'd missed lunch by a couple of hours. The place still smelled of onions. A plate of tortillas sat on the counter, and I found eggs, cheese, and salsa in the fridge. Breakfast tacos. I could do this. I'd scrambled eggs for my dad and little brother dozens of Saturday mornings when my mother was off getting her hair and nails done. Appearances were more important than hunger pangs. My cooking may not look so good, but I'd never gone hungry as long as I was feeding myself. Muscle memory, don't fail me now.

I fished a bowl from the cabinet and began cracking eggs. Three for me, two for Ronnie. I doubted she ate much on a regular day. Her trim, muscular body spoke of a lean diet and grueling exercise. I whipped eggs and watched the yolk turn the mixture into a pale yellow. I'd bet all the money I wished I had that somewhere in this house a room was filled with fancy exercise equipment designed to tone and shape. I upped the portions. Our morning session had worked off more calories than I could possibly pack into this meal and I needed her strong for what I had planned for the afternoon.

I found a serrano pepper in the fridge and I went in search of a knife to release its fire. Too many drawers. All of them in perfect order. One was lined with matching towels, another with fancy utensils from a fancy cooking store. I yanked open one of my last choices and found Ronnie's one kitchen vice. The junk drawer. Wine corks, bottle caps, push pins, pens with no tops all lay in a jumble with once used twist ties and a few lonely Advil tablets. I doubted I'd find any fancy knives here. I started to shut the drawer, but several words on a half-folded piece of paper caught my attention. "We're pleased to offer you a position with our firm." A souvenir from her first job? I scanned the heading. The letter was dated a week ago. Sent from D.C. Allowing time for snail mail, she'd probably received it yesterday or the day before. I couldn't help myself. Well, I didn't try, anyway. I lifted the single sheet from the drawer and unfolded it. The bottom half referenced a fully detailed job offer which was attached. It wasn't. I leaned against the counter, letter in hand, and considered. I'd seen her office, her house. Ronnie was organized, methodical. If there was a job offer, she'd either thrown it away or placed it somewhere more prestigious than her kitchen junk drawer. I didn't need to search the trash. Everything about her current situation signaled she was out of place—with the low-budget law firm, with her traditional family, with me. She'd saved the job offer, no doubt cush, and was strongly considering it. The realization stung. I dropped the cover letter back into the drawer and quietly shoved it shut.

She'd leave. I knew she would. The bout we'd shared? Sex was all it was. Our connection had been off from the beginning. I suspected she was hiding more than the job offer, and she knew more about Quitman than she wanted me to believe. I don't know why I was surprised. She'd done her best to elude all my attempts to penetrate her badass lawyer persona, but after spending the last twenty-four hours naked and vulnerable, I'd been stupid to let myself warm to the idea of waking up with her, sharing breakfast, starting another round. Sex had always been enough before. It wasn't now and there wasn't a damn thing I could do about it.

I scrambled the eggs, layered in the peppers, onions, and cheese. Wrapped the concoction in a warm tortilla and arranged it on a plate. I'd never been as careful preparing a meal. I found a pen and paper, not in the evil drawer, and jotted a short "thank you for the good time, so long, I'll find help elsewhere" note. I wanted to sneak back and watch her until she woke, but I'm not big on wanting things I can't have. I found my own clothes without distraction and let myself out.

Chapter Sixteen

Took me three hours to walk home in the heat. At least I didn't get rousted by any cops along the way for looking like a vagrant. My Bronco was parked outside my building—an unexpected surprise. A simple note from Hardin was stuck under the windshield. *Thought you might need this. Left the keys with your landlord.* I thanked and cursed him. I did need the car, but I didn't want to run into Withers looking the way I did. Couldn't be helped. My apartment keys were on the same ring. Amazingly, Withers didn't ask a bunch of nosy questions. I bet Hardin warned him I'd be in a foul mood.

I showered for a long, hot time. The extended luxury was the only one I'd afford myself today. I didn't want to stay at home any longer than I had to. I didn't want to be anywhere Ronnie could find me if she decided to follow up on my note. I also didn't want to be waiting around here, hoping for a visit that might never come. Clean body and clean clothes, I packed up the essentials. Guns, laptop, cash. The coffee can yielded three hundred dollars. Wouldn't get me very far. I considered my options. I was currently avoiding Maggie, at least until I had something intelligent to tell her about Billy besides the suspicions Perez had planted in my head. I wasn't ready to face Chance again, and no way would she make room for a suspected murderer at her place. I knew of only one other cheap option. Well, cheap monetarily.

As I walked out the door, I remembered the bag of receipts I'd gotten from Quitman's apartment building. I hadn't had time to look them over in between being hit on the head in my apartment and arrested at the warehouse. I snatched them from the kitchen drawer and tossed them in my bag.

I didn't call first, but I did stop at Red Coleman's and bought a "hey, I'm staying with you, but this should take the edge off" gift. When I arrived at my destination, I didn't ring the doorbell. Instead I fished the key from under the flowerpot, went straight to the fridge, and put the twelve pack next to a nicely-wrapped casserole. I hoped Mrs. Teeter wasn't lurking somewhere in the house, waiting to share dinner with dear old dad.

She wasn't. I found him sprawled in his favorite easy chair, a newspaper spread across his lap. He snored the loud, uninhibited sounds of way past buzzed. I breathed a sigh of relief. I wouldn't have to explain my sudden reappearance. Two times in less than a week was out of the ordinary. And since it would be several hours before he woke up, the beer I'd just bought would last longer than I'd expected.

I stowed my stuff in my old room and considered my next step. I spread the bag of receipts out on the bed and spent an hour going through them. Too many John and Jane Does to count. Apparently, no one has an imagination anymore. The names I thought might be real didn't ring any bells. After a few passes through, I shoved them back in the bag.

I checked my cell phone, which I hadn't done since before I'd arrived at the warehouse over twenty-four hours ago. The voice mailbox was full. I'm usually not that popular. I scrolled through the numbers. Maggie, Ronnie yesterday and today, several numbers I didn't know, and Chance. Jess had called an hour ago, before I'd switched the phone back on. Doubtless she'd found out about my arrest. Was she calling to chew me out? To say she never should've stayed my friend after I fucked up the first time? I didn't want to hear any of it, but maybe I could absolve some of my guilt by letting her vent. I shut the door to my room and punched the numbers. She answered on the first ring and didn't waste any time getting to the point.

"Damn you, Bennett! How're you going to get out of this scrape?"

I bit back a retort. We both knew my current situation was way more than a scrape. One I couldn't see my way out of. I wanted help, but I didn't want to admit it. Especially not to her. She'd stuck her neck out for me on too many occasions before and I suspected her efforts were taking a toll. Professionally, if not personally. "I'm fine. Don't worry about it." I started to say see ya later when I remembered why I called. "Hey, you called me. Did you need something?"

"Don't be an ass. You're not fine. Perez is on the warpath and it sounds like she has more than enough to get an indictment. You need a good lawyer, but more than that you need a good story or you'll end up back behind bars. Tell me why you just happened to wind up at another murder scene? Two in one week seems a bit much, even for you."

I ignored her last question and the sarcasm she served up with it. "I can handle Perez. Seriously, Jess, let it go. You've done enough. Look where it's gotten you."

"Shut up, Luca. Look, I need to know what you were up to. Spill."

I hesitated. If I started talking, I had to tell her everything. She was the only person I trusted completely, but that didn't mean I should take advantage to put my mind at rest. She interrupted my thoughts.

"Where are you?"

"My dad's place."

"Give me the address. I'm coming over." I'd never been able to resist when she bossed me around. I only ever let one other woman do the same, but I'd left her lying in a bed across town. On the right side of the tracks, where she belonged and I never would. I shrugged Ronnie from my head and gave Jess the address. She could help me put a serious dent in Mrs. Teeter's casserole.

I spent the next thirty minutes picking up the place. Beer bottles, dirty dishes, stacks of junk mail, and several weeks worth of papers I was certain Mrs. Teeter supplied since Dad was too cheap to subscribe on his own. I gently woke him and nudged him to the shower, with the promise of dinner if he complied. He grumbled, but I heard the water running within a few minutes.

When the doorbell rang, I gave up. Not sure why I even cared. It wasn't my house and for damn sure Jess had seen my place in worse shape. Maybe it was because he was going to like her instantly and I didn't want her to see him for only what he'd become. He deserved a clean slate with someone. Jess was a cop. What he'd wanted me to be. Because law enforcement was respectable, good benefits, full retirement. Jess was the daughter he'd wanted. I was the daughter he'd wound up with. Despite everything he'd lost—his wife, his health, his job—Dad hung tight to his dreams. He'd want to impress Jess, and I wanted him to have that opportunity. In spite of himself.

Jess looked like shit. Black circles under her eyes, mussed clothes. Maybe I'd made a mistake cleaning up the place on her account. I motioned her in.

"Dad'll be out in a minute."

Weird. I hadn't realized until that moment how much I'd compartmentalized my life. How had I known Jess all these years and she knew nothing about my family other than my parents lived apart—a simple matter of geography. I knew nothing about hers either. Our strong bond didn't extend to anything outside creature comfort. I knew her favorite food, drink, her favorite position in bed, but I didn't know other things. Things I'd never considered important to know about a person. Like what kind of family she had, when did she come out, why did she become a cop? The kind of things I wanted to know about Ronnie. The kind of things I would never know about Ronnie.

Focus. "You look terrible."

She raised her eyes to mine. "Lot going on. I may look terrible, but you're the one who's got trouble." She jerked her head to the living room. "Does he know what's going on?" She lowered her voice to a whisper. "From what I hear, you're lucky to be walking the streets and you won't be for long." She cocked her head. "How'd you afford the bond?"

Questions. Details. Ones I wasn't prepared to share and ones I didn't know. I hadn't asked Hardin any questions. We talk business, not personal stuff. Here the two intersected, which definitely made any conversation off-limits. When I was arraigned, my bond was a quarter of a million. High for a first time offender, and I'd figured Perez had been to blame. She'd probably whispered something in the judge's ear about another murder they hadn't been able to pin on me yet as a reason to up the ante. Hardin's normal fee on the bond would have been at least twenty-five grand. I'd never be good for that kind of cash. I shook my head. Money wasn't the issue, at least not as it related to me staying out of jail. But I was sure money had something to do with Jed's death, at least business anyway. I needed to get rid of Jess so I could think. Letting her come over had been a bad idea.

"Look, I'm not feeling so well. Go home and I'll call you tomorrow."

She wasn't going anywhere. Well, except the kitchen. She hefted a brown paper bag. "Don't think so. I have a lot of time in the bank. I'm taking a couple of weeks. Where's the fridge?"

I sensed there was more to her decision to take time off than having too many comp days racked up. I imagined Perez was making her life hell on account of our friendship, but she obviously didn't want to talk about it, and I wasn't going to press. I was glad she was here. I put the beer in the fridge and became the picture of domesticity, heating up plates of casserole for Dad and my guest. A better hostess would have been able to find more than two plates that matched. At least the food smelled good. Good enough to draw Dad into the kitchen, his hair still wet from the shower.

He slumped into a chair. "Luca, hand your old man a beer, would you?"

I shot a look at Jess, who acted as if nothing was out of the ordinary. "Hey, Dad, we have company."

He followed my gaze and attempted a quick transformation. The hasty hair combing and shirt straightening didn't change anything, but he puffed up as if it did. He stood and thrust his hand in Jess's direction. "Joseph Bennett. Nice to meet you."

She shook his hand hard. "Jessica Chance. Nice to meet you too."

He was still standing, as if unsure of the next line in polite society. I intervened before he fell over. "Sit down, Dad. Jess is a friend. She's staying for dinner." I pointed at the oven. "That casserole's pretty new, right?"

He nodded, but he didn't look at me. He was still focused on the shiny object in the room. "What do you do for a living, Ms. Chance?"

Ms. Chance? Jess opened her mouth to answer, but I saved her the trouble. "She's a cop. Homicide detective. Call her Jessica."

"Sure. Ms. Chance, you staying for dinner? You know I tried to get Luca here to become a cop. She didn't stay on too long. Decided it wasn't for her."

"I know. She and I went to the academy together. I was there when—" I cleared my throat. Loud. Beyond the bare details, I've never talked about that night with my dad. No way did I want to open the door to a discussion now. Jess looked over at me and changed direction. "I was there when she started, and we've been friends ever since."

"Police work's solid. Respectable. Good benefits, good retirement." Dad spoke with authority, praising benefits that had eluded him. After years in the automotive industry, he'd been laid off. At half what he'd expected for a pension, he barely had enough to make ends meet. He worked various odd jobs, mostly for the widows in the neighborhood, to stay in six-packs and poker money. Most responsible children might encourage their parents to give up vices for security. Not me. I firmly believed his indulgences were the only thing that got him through each day. Our similarities were the reason we got along just fine. I couldn't help it if he didn't want me to be like him. That ship had sailed.

"Dad, Jess and I need to talk for a minute. We'll eat in a few minutes."

He didn't budge. I didn't want to discuss my current chaos with a living image of the future chaos that awaited me sitting across the table. Jess had different ideas. "Maybe your dad will have some ideas. Couldn't hurt to have an extra brain on the project."

Hell. Wasn't like I had anything to hide. Sex DVDs, murder, fraud. I had no compunction about sharing any sordid details with Dad. My hesitation was more about the prospect of sorting through his hare-brained ideas. He's a talk radio junkie and no stranger to conspiracy theories. I may not know what was behind the killings I'd stumbled on, but I strongly doubted an intricate web of deception. More likely someone was sending a simple message. Figure out what the message was and I'd find the killer, clear my name.

Jess wrote notes on the back of a junk mail envelope while I told them everything, from my first meeting with Ronnie at Foxy Lady to the moment I was handcuffed in the warehouse, Jed's still warm body only a few feet away. I included my search for Billy and his connection to Quitman, the dead stripper and her connection to Billy, the DVDs, the warning, Miguel's desire to replace me on the case, Ronnie's persistent desire to find Quitman, my visit to Lively's office, Lively's visit to Miguel's office, and Ronnie's certain belief that Lively had something to do with Quitman's disappearance. The only details about my recent activity I left out were the several hours I'd spent wrapped in Ronnie's arms this morning.

When I quit talking, they both stared at me for a moment then Dad blurted out, "Where's Billy?"

He was the anti-help. I shook my head and glared a "see what I mean?" look at Jess. She played along with him. "Yeah, Luca, where's Billy?"

I sighed. "Wish I knew. My gut says his connection to Quitman runs deeper than an odd job here and there. He had a thing for one of Quitman's girls, she winds up dead, and now Quitman's dead while Billy's still in the wind."

"I guess you didn't see who else was at the warehouse before you got nailed?" Jess asked.

"Billy didn't have anything to do with this."

"You know that for sure?"

I didn't. I shook my head. "I don't know anything for sure."

"Let's go talk to Maggie again. She's his sister. She may know more than she thinks."

"Damn it, Jess. I haven't seen Maggie in days. I'm not going to show up at her place trying to pin her brother for a murder."

"Don't worry. We'll eat here before we go so she won't think you're taking advantage." She stood and walked to the oven. "Didn't you say something about a casserole?"

I sighed. Murder was making me lose my appetite. Almost.

CHAPTER SEVENTEEN

Maggie's place surged with activity. When we saw the overflowing parking lot, I told Jess to park at my place. No one would recognize her car and it was a short walk. I'd brought along the bag of receipts I'd conned from the apartment manager and I shoved them under my seat. I kind of figured Jess might take me home with her after Maggie's, and we could take a look at them together if, make that when, we weren't busy with other pursuits.

Friday nights at Maggie's were an odd mix. Local regulars, mostly sweaty softball players, celebrating victory or drowning defeat, combined with college students who'd heard rumors she was lax about carding. She was. Her theory was if you were old enough to get to a bar, you were old enough to drink. I warned Jess not to send out big bad cop vibes when we entered the bar.

She'd never been to Maggie's, which was kind of odd considering how long we'd known each other. I'd never brought anyone here with me. Purposeful decision, but I'd never considered the why behind it. As we walked through the doors tonight it hit me. Maggie's was a safe place, a solid signpost on my wayward journey through life. I didn't want to clutter it with stuff or people that might not stick around. As I prepared to grill Maggie for more info about her brother, I didn't feel so safe anymore.

Maggie's face lit up when she saw me. Probably assumed I had news. I had news all right, but none she'd want to hear. She rushed over and gave Jess a once-over, finishing with a questioning look in my direction. I opened my mouth to blurt out the reason for our visit, but Jess stilled my arm and fired off the first words. "Maggie? Luca's told me about this place, and I had to see it for myself. Can we get a couple of beers? I'm buying."

Maggie beamed at the compliment. I relaxed and let Jess take the lead. Maggie showed us to a booth—normally I didn't merit the extra space—and brought over a couple of icy cold Blue Moons. I drank half mine before the bad news kicked in. Jess glanced around the bar. "Busy night. Do you think you can spare a moment to talk to us? I'm helping Luca with some of her current…projects."

Maggie gave her a sage nod. "No problem. I've got a new guy working the front tonight, but chaos will be good for him. I'll be right back." She shot me a conspiratorial wink before she leered at Jess, just out of her eyeshot.

A few beers delayed my reaction time, but I caught on fast. She thought Jess and I were an item. Holy shit. Any filter I had was dulled by the slight buzz. "She thinks you're my date."

Jess shrugged. I'd expected a reflection of the abject horror I was sure my expression conveyed. Just to be clear, I said, "Well, we're not."

"I know that." Her tone signaled indifference.

"I just wanted to be clear."

She leaned across the table. "If we dated, we'd kill each other." She served the words with a grin. She was trying to get me to lighten up. I took another deep swallow of beer, but the liquid didn't drown the persistent feeling that I was coming out of my skin. No small wonder. In the last twenty-four hours, I'd found a jumper that I couldn't collect on, been arrested for his murder, bonded out of jail by a woman I was hot for, made love to said woman more times than I cared to recall, found out she was on her way out of town, moved in with my father, and decided one of my best friend's brothers might be responsible for at least some of my predicament. Relaxation was out of reach. I tried to ignore the real reason Maggie's assumption bothered me, but recent memories of Ronnie writhing beneath me were a painful distraction. I fought for control. Jess and I were solid. Neither of us wanted more between us than what we had. I spoke the only commitment I knew how to make. "I don't want to kill you."

"Good thing."

Maggie interrupted our sentimental exchange. She slid into the booth on Jess's side. "So what do you do for a living?" I answered before Jess could open her mouth. "She's helping me. I seem to be busier than usual. Chance is good at finding people. We want to ask you some more questions about Billy."

Jess took over. "Do you know if he ever did any personal work for Quitman?"

"Well, not Quitman, himself, but he did some odd jobs at some of the clubs. Billy used to tell me stories about the crazy stuff that went on in those places."

I interrupted. "Crazy stuff? Why didn't you mention that before?"

"Not crazy like you're thinking. Just interesting. You know what I mean."

I didn't. Wasn't sure I wanted to, but a nagging feeling pressed me to ask more. "Tell us. You never know what might be important."

"One of the places had a locked room, decked out with all that dungeon crap, like you see in movies." She looked around and lowered her voice. "He only saw the inside of the room once, but some of the people he saw visiting the place? You wouldn't believe."

"Try me." None of this was surprising, but I wanted to hear her take on it.

"You know Senator Lively?"

I nodded, resisting the urge to tell her to speed up the story.

"His biggest contributor is that Randolf woman. You know, Caroline Randolf. She showed up at the club. At least Billy thought it was her. She was wearing a scarf that nearly covered her face, but he said he'd know her anywhere. He recognized her from the homeless shelter. She makes a big show of volunteering at The Right Path. She's on the board, you know."

The things I knew were increasing by the second. I'd barely heard Maggie's last comment. I was fixated on the name and the scarf. I'd seen Randolf recently, even recognized her despite her face being covered. But when I saw her, she wasn't wearing a scarf. No, she'd sported a leather mask over part of her face, and wielded a cat-o'-nine-tails, much to the pleasure and pain of one Jed Quitman. Now I knew for sure who owned those piercing blue eyes. What was a wealthy heiress doing with the likes of Quitman? Maybe Ronnie had read too much into Senator Lively's motivations. Quitman's death might have been a message from Randolf about keeping certain acts of pleasure to themselves.

I shook my head. As cynical as I was, no way did I believe socialite Caroline Randolf had anything to do with the bloody mess I'd stumbled into at the warehouse. The brutal beating was too much like the vicious stabbing I'd happened on earlier in the week. Another strange coincidence. No wonder Perez had a bead on me. Two murders, victims who knew each other and the same person found at both crime scenes—me. I'd arrest me too. Perez was probably standing over some forensic schmuck, urging him on while he pulled my prints off the sledgehammer that had killed Quitman.

Jess's voice cut into my thought drift. "Anything else you can think of about Billy and his work history?"

I almost laughed. Good thing she'd aimed the question at Maggie. The words "Billy" and "work history" weren't ones I was likely to put in the same sentence. Still, the guy had to earn some bucks and sometimes petty thefts are hard to come by. Okay, so he'd worked for Jed. I still didn't believe he had anything to do with Jed's death or the stripper's for that matter. Still, there was the apartment building, which Perez insisted was owned by Quitman, but the manager professed to not have a clue who he was. Billy had been seen there, listed it as his address on bond papers.

Maggie reeled off a list of jobs Billy had worked for an hour or two at a time over the last year. The minute she finished, a mini brawl broke out across the room over the remote control to the flat screen TV. Jess and I pushed out of the booth, ready to take on the troublemakers, but Maggie waved us off. "Keep your seats. I got this." She didn't move, but her bellow echoed across the room. "Cool it or you're cut off!" She shook her head as the fight died down. "I should go over there. Make them order some food. You got any more questions?"

"No." I spoke for both of us. I was tired and ready to head out. Jess flipped her notebook shut and took Maggie's hand. "Thanks for your help."

Maggie cradled Jess's hand in both of hers. "Pleasure to meet you. You're welcome here anytime." She pierced me with a look. "Luca, you bring her back here. Okay?" Wasn't really a question, which was good because the answer was too complicated.

As we strode out the door of the bar, Jess asked, "Where to now, Bennett?"

"I'm bunking back at Dad's, but I want to check my place. Make sure there were no more break-ins." I took quick strides down the street.

She quickened her pace to keep up with me. "Sure you don't just want to make sure a certain sexy lawyer hasn't stopped by. Maybe left you a sweet note?"

"Back off, Chance."

She didn't. "Rumor has it you got cozy with her at her parents' house earlier this week."

"You been following me?"

"Not me. Perez has a big mouth."

No sense trying to hide what was obviously public knowledge. "Cozy no. Dinner yes. We were talking about my case. You know, the first one, where Perez thinks I killed a stripper who'd been dead long before I found her."

"Sure. Whatever."

The light outside my apartment wasn't bright enough for me to assess her facial expression. Her tone was casual. She'd warned me off Ronnie from the start, but I hadn't read anything into it. I knew she didn't like Miguel. Figured she didn't like Ronnie by association. Ronnie hadn't been in town long enough for Jess to know her very well. She had no way of knowing Ronnie was nothing like her uncle. She was sharp and professional where he was all flash and no substance. She was tender, he was rough. She was beautiful and he was a dog. He made me feel like I needed a bath. She made me want to bathe with her. Suddenly, it was very important to me that Jess not judge her too harshly. My defense came pouring out in three simple words.

"I like her."

She pulled up short and turned to face me. "I know," she said. Then she squeezed my shoulder and tacked on, "Be careful."

Too late. My attraction to Ronnie wriggled deep under my skin. Her alluring combination of aloof and penetrating had me tied in knots. Not like it mattered since she wasn't sticking around. She'd take the sweet job back East and go back to a life I'd never be a part of. Never want to be a part of. Why I cared was a mystery.

When we got to the door, I fumbled in my pocket for my keys, a lot sore and a little drunk. When I finally fished them out, Jess grabbed them and pushed me out of the way. "Here, let me." As she turned the key in the lock, I heard a throat clear behind us. Memory of getting bashed in the head crashed through my buzz. I whirled around, ready to face the brazen attacker face-to-face.

CHAPTER EIGHTEEN

Brazen yes, attacker no. Ronnie stood a few feet from my doorway. When we turned her way, she stepped out of the shadows and took a step toward me, a hopeful expression on her face. A nanosecond later, she flicked a glance at Jess who stood really close and held my keys. Ronnie stepped back as if she'd hit a force field. I searched her face. Ronnie hadn't struck me as the type who'd go chasing after a woman who'd left her bed. Close inspection told me she wasn't brazen at all. She was unsure, hesitant. For a second, I wanted to pull her close. Drink in her scent, the memory of a morning filled with nothing but us. No murders, no missing persons, no jail time. I squelched the desire to pull her close and erase the insecurities with reassurance. She could exit without my fond farewell. I settled on a casual question. "Any news about my case?"

The expression in her eyes changed from insecure to sharp as she shifted gears. She looked again at Jess, who looked at me. I lifted my shoulders, signaling I had no idea what was going on. Wasn't true. I knew exactly what was going on. I'd bailed and Ronnie wanted to know why. She apparently didn't possess mind-reading skills. Guess she wasn't so perfect after all. No way was I getting into whatever was going on between us with Jess standing right there watching. Good detective that she is, Jess read my mind and gave me what she thought I needed. She shoved my keys into my hand and said, "I need to check my phone. Left it in the car." She disappeared before I could protest.

Ronnie stayed in place until the sound of Jessica's footfalls faded away. "We need to talk."

Faced with the proposition, I balked. "Not me. I'm good." I jingled the keys, faking coordination I didn't possess. "It's late." I couldn't bring myself to tell her outright to leave, probably because I didn't want her to. I wanted her to come inside. I wanted to wrap her in my arms and wipe away the traces of doubt I saw etched in her face. I wouldn't. I had my own doubt, scary doubt. I'd wanted things before, things I couldn't have. Wasn't going to start down this path with her. Her path led elsewhere. Away from me and what I wanted. No point in pretending otherwise.

She pushed the point. "I woke up and you were gone."

"Yep."

Both of us stating the obvious, but dancing around the real issue. Why we'd come together in the first place. Why I'd left. I didn't want to dig any deeper. Digging usually unearthed more than anyone went looking for, but I couldn't help it. I laid my cards on the table. "You're one to talk about leaving."

Her eyes told me she didn't know what the hell I was talking about. I grasped a piece of hope from her puzzled expression before I realized she probably just needed a little more context to bring it home. "The job in D.C.? When do you start?"

She opened her mouth, but not to protest. "Like I said before. We need to talk. Invite me in?"

I stared at the keys in my hand. Say no. The door isn't open. You've opened more doors than you should've lately. I clenched the key ring in my fist, determined to keep her out. She reached over and put her hand on mine. My traitorous fingers loosened. I looked into her eyes and my resolve betrayed me as well. I opened the door and she followed me inside.

I motioned for her to sit, but I stood near the door, ready to escape my own house. She scooted around on the couch, clearly uncomfortable that I wasn't joining her. I didn't care. She wasn't staying long enough to be comfortable. "You have something to say?"

"I haven't decided about the job."

"I don't care."

"Why did you leave?"

Couldn't answer without making myself out to be a liar. I opted to fire off a question of my own. "Why do you care?"

"I do. Does that matter to you?"

"No," I lied. "Guess I thought we were done."

"Luca Bennett, you may be good at most things, but you are a horrible liar."

I'm not, but apparently she could see through me. Besides, I wasn't in the mood to protest. I wasn't in the mood for this conversation at all. Matters between us had gotten too complicated too fast. In the span of a week Ronnie had become my employer, my lawyer, and my...

I wasn't sure how to fill in the last blank. And that was a huge part of the problem. Until I could define our roles, I wasn't interested in more than hot sex. Way hot. Hot enough to sear through my bravado and into the cracks of insecurity I hid from the rest of the world. She'd been a fantastic lay, but she was nothing else to me. Again with the lies, but simple non truths kept me grounded, kept me sane. Not going to dig any deeper. I teetered on the edge of my own destruction. At the brink, I tested the edge. "Is it a good job?"

Inane, but too late. She lit up at my apparent interest. "It's like what I used to do, but for the other side." She scrutinized my face, but I gave her nothing. Taking my lack of response for permission, she kept talking, the words spilled out fast and furious. "I worked for a big firm in New York representing the richest of the rich. We made sure they stayed rich. I was a rising star, youngest associate to make the partner track. Billed twenty six hundred hours my last year." She offered a humorless grin. "That's a lot."

I nodded. She'd started filling in the holes, and I wanted to know the rest more than I wanted to protect myself from any hurt she could send my way.

"I knew everything about my clients. All the scars and skeletons. Their secrets were my secrets. I was their protector. I was very impressed with myself and my power."

She stopped. Perfect opportunity for me to ask a question, urge her along. I didn't. I wanted her to tell it to me because she chose to, not because I asked. She fixed me with a stare and started again.

"The last case I worked was my biggest win of all. Big pharmaceutical company sued by a huge crowd of plaintiffs. They suffered horrible illnesses and claimed their maladies were the result of the super drug to treat depression, a drug my client manufactured."

I knew the commercials, cheery men and women discussing their newfound lease on life for a full five minutes followed by a syrupy-voiced announcer reciting the potential harm in a singsong litany designed to lull the listener into apathy.

"They brought a huge class action suit. But they couldn't prove the connection. The side-effects were all over the map. Their case was on the verge of being tossed in a pretrial hearing, when I found a report proving the plaintiffs' claim had merit."

"Did you turn it over?"

"Wasn't that easy. The report had been compiled at the request of a partner at our firm, under the guise of attorney-client privilege. They wanted to know if the claims were true, but used the law to cover up what they found."

"Shady."

"We were paid big bucks to be shady. I'd just never realized what lengths the other lawyers at my firm would go to keep their biggest client happy."

"So what did you do?"

"I implored the partners I worked for to talk to the client, get them to settle for something reasonable. With a confidentiality clause, they never would have had to share the details in the report."

"I assume they didn't go for it."

"Not a chance. So I leaked the information to the other side."

Invested now, I asked, "So they won and you got fired for telling your client's secrets?"

She laughed. "Your ideas about justice are pretty simplistic."

I scowled at her and stepped back. "I'm no lawyer, but I know what's right and wrong."

"Oh, really? Well, check out what really happened. I leaked the information, and the court ordered the other side not to use it because of how they obtained it. I was fired and then quietly disciplined by the state bar. The only people who won were the fat cats who developed the drug and hid its evil secrets, the same ones who would have won if I'd kept my mouth shut in the first place." Her voice rose and her accent became more pronounced. "If I'd done nothing, I would've still had my job, my stellar reputation, and an exemplary record. Where's your right and wrong in all that?"

I joined her on the couch and answered by pulling her into my arms. She resisted for a minute, then gave in to the gesture. Once she was there, I didn't know what to do. She'd gotten screwed for sure. She acted so tough all the time, I hadn't gotten a glimpse of this woman, broken and kicked to the curb. I had a ton of questions, but I let her sob it out first. When I thought she was done, I stood and said, "Promise me you'll stay here for a minute."

"Where are you going?"

I hesitated. I wanted to find Jess, let her know everything was okay, that I needed a little time. For some reason, I didn't want to mention Jess to Ronnie. She felt no similar compunction. "She's a cop, isn't she?"

An easy question. Seemed harmless to answer. "Yes."

"Be careful."

Funny to hear Jess's words from Ronnie's mouth. "She's helping me with something. Not on the job." I stopped rambling when she placed a finger against my lips.

"Still. It never hurts to be careful."

I stared into her eyes, but the elusive undercurrent of her warning didn't surface. Oh well. Careful isn't one of my better traits. I kissed her on the cheek and hurried out the door.

Jess stood, leaning against her car. Someone who didn't know her would think she was relaxed. I could tell she was wound up tight. She spoke first. "Took you long enough."

"She has a lot to say."

"You were talking." She fake coughed. "Right."

"I'm going to stick around here for a while."

"Of course you are."

I did my best to ignore her dig. Time for her to go and me to figure out what was going on with the other woman in my life. "I'll call you tomorrow." She turned and started to walk away, but she stopped when I called out. "I left that bag of receipts under the seat in your car. You might want to go through them. I didn't find anything, but maybe you'll have better luck."

"I assume you trust me enough to take them to my place?"

"Don't be a jerk. Of course I trust you."

"You should be more careful who you trust."

As if her words weren't signal enough she was annoyed, I also caught a tone. More than the earlier warning, but less than a shout of danger. "I'll call you later."

"Yeah, no problem."

As she drove away, I realized I no longer had a ride since we'd left the Bronco back at my dad's. I'm sure Jess noticed. Her not reminding me was probably her way of saying told you so. Whatever. I wanted to make it back upstairs before Ronnie bolted.

She'd made herself comfortable. I couldn't decide if that was a good sign or a bad one. Fancy sandals were strewn on the floor and her linen jacket hung on the back of my rickety kitchen chair. I sat a safe distance away from her and said, "Sorry, it's so hot in here. I turned the A/C way up before I left."

"You aren't staying here?"

"No." She waited for more, but her disclosures didn't make me feel compelled to do any sharing of my own.

"I wondered when I didn't see your car."

I ignored the invitation to disclose. As far as I was concerned, we were still on the topic of her. I had a ton more questions on that front. "Did you know Senator Lively was at your office Thursday after you left for court?"

"My office?"

"You know, the office where you work, where Miguel works."

"Oh. Was he?"

She knew what I meant. I recognized her question for the stall tactic that it was. "Yes, he was. Any idea what he was doing there?"

"Let me think. Um, yes, I remember now. Miguel mentioned that Senator Lively came by to offer his assistance with Jed's case. Guess he didn't take me seriously when I told him we didn't need any character references after all."

She was lying. She wouldn't meet my gaze and the pitch of her voice rose with every word. But I sensed something more than deceit. I felt her fear. Like I'd suspected from the beginning, she knew way more than she let on, but whatever it was scared her. Jess's advice "you should be more careful who you trust" buzzed in my head. I decided against backing Ronnie into a corner, and changed the subject instead.

"Did you think working for Miguel was your only choice after what happened in New York?"

"I work *with* Miguel, not for him."

"That's not how it sounded the other day."

"What are you talking about?"

"I listened outside the door when you were talking to him."

"You're a sneaky one, aren't you?"

"I thought you wanted me to investigate. I was investigating."

"Who? Me?"

"Whoever. Look, I listened. I know he's your uncle, but he gives me the creeps. I don't see anything in the way of a family resemblance and I don't get why you're working beneath what you're obviously used to."

"You've met my family. You know my roots. I'd say I'm doing exactly what I'm used to." She spewed the words and I almost ducked to avoid the force of her anger. I'd touched a nerve, but I still wasn't sure about the source of her pain. Should I look deeper? Did I care?

Curiosity, never a strong impulse before, propelled me to move to the couch, pull her close, and whisper, "I don't get it. But I want to."

She melted against me. No turning back now.

"I had an expensive apartment in the city. Fancy clothes, flashy friends, a top-notch career. When I lost my job, I lost my friends, my career. Everyone knew my license was suspended and why. I was blackballed. I had enough money saved to maintain the trappings of my lifestyle, but the substance was gone. My mama, she said, 'Come home, we'll take care of you here.' Home. An old East Dallas bungalow with jacked up cars and broken appliances in the backyard. I'd worked hard to break free from that past. I came back, but I spent every dime I had on my house. Problem was I needed to work to maintain it. Miguel. He fixed things. I don't know how, but the state bar approved my request to transfer my license, gave me credit for the suspension, and I was free to work. The deal was I had to work for him. The terms of our arrangement were never spoken out loud, but I owe him and he's family. I'll never break free as long as I stay here. This D.C. firm contacted me out of the blue and suddenly, I have a way out. Can you blame me for considering it?"

I couldn't. I had no concept of what she'd gained and lost, but I could imagine. I'd already gotten the sense, while at her parents' house, she resented her humble past. I'd seen my mother's resentment simmer for years until she boiled over. She'd left my brother and me to seek out the shiny side of life my father had never been able to provide. At least Ronnie stayed in touch with her family. I couldn't remember the last time my mother and I had shared a meal. Ronnie had left her family to make something of herself, unlike my mother who sought her fortune by jumping from marriage to marriage. Still, the similarities stung. I'd heard her out, now I was ready for her to leave.

"Ronnie, it's late. I think you should go." I added a yawn to emphasize the point.

She reclined on the couch. "You don't want me to."

"I do." I walked toward the door, motioned her to follow.

She didn't move. "Don't you need a ride somewhere? The cop who gave you the ride home left, didn't she?"

"Her name's Jessica." The minute I shared her first name, I wanted to take back the detail.

"Okay, Jessica. She left, right?"

The tiniest hint of jealousy filled the space between us. I should clear the air. I started to, but stopped and didn't consider why. Instead, I ducked her question. "I'm good. Maybe I'll sleep here tonight."

"Alone?" She was up off the couch and striding toward me. I knew before she crossed the room, I wasn't going to sleep at all.

I let her unbutton my shirt, slide her arms inside, wrap herself around me like a python seeking warmth. And then I took over. I had a lot to take and I took it all. She hung on tight and I led her to the bedroom, loosened her grip, and leaned her back on the bed. Control was the goal and I wrested it from her. Before the night was over, she would scream my name and I would be her hero. I was done being rescued. It was time for me to do a little rescuing of my own. Judging by the strength of her cries, she needed all the rescuing I could deliver. I didn't think about Jed Quitman, Billy, my arrest for murder, or U.S. senators and their benefactors. The only thing on my mind was how much pain we could fuck away. We writhed until dawn.

I woke up alone. She hadn't made me breakfast, not that she could have since the random packets of ketchup and mustard in the fridge weren't good omelet material. She did, however, leave a note. "Thanks. You were exactly what I needed. Funny, I'm not always good at figuring out exactly what I need. I don't know what my future holds, but I think I'd like you to be a part of it. Ronnie." Then she'd written and scratched out "your lover" and wrote "your lawyer."

I would've gotten more satisfaction from an omelet.

CHAPTER NINETEEN

I ran for way longer than I intended, sweating the scent of Ronnie from my skin. Had to shake her somehow since I apparently didn't have enough self-control to pack her into her pretty red car before she found her way into my bed. After a night of strenuous exercise, I was amazed I had the strength to make it back to my apartment. After a quick call to my dad to let him know I hadn't died—didn't want him to think he could keep the Bronco—I jumped in the shower. Blistering hot water burned away all thoughts of Ronnie, murder, and money out of my head. A heavy pounding on the door, brought them all screaming back. I considered ignoring whoever was there until I realized it might very well be Perez. If she was here to harass me I wanted to be dressed for the occasion. I reached for a towel and kind of dried off. I shouted at my morning visitor. "Hold your horses, I'm coming." I half wished Ronnie was around to run interference.

I tugged on a pair of jeans and a T-shirt and shook my wet hair for good measure. The pounding increased, so I didn't bother with shoes. Hopefully, Perez would find it in her heart not to haul me in barefoot. I swung open the door and almost got a fist in my face.

Jess, hand in mid-knock, looked as surprised as I did. "I've been knocking forever. What the hell are you doing in here?"

"I live here."

"Smartass."

I looked at her non-knocking hand. She was holding a cardboard tray with two steaming cups. "You brought me coffee?"

"There's only two cups and one of them is for me. Are you alone?"

I briefly considered the implication that she assumed Ronnie would stay the night or that I'd still be here this morning. She read my thoughts. "I figured you might need a ride this morning. Wasn't sure if the girl would stick around."

"She didn't."

Her only reaction was to shove a cup my way. I let the fine black brew scald me into fully awake mode.

"Drink up. We have stuff to do."

"Really? What's on the list?"

"Caroline Randolf's hosting an event at the Dallas Museum of Art. Benefit for Dick Lively. We're working security."

The coffee didn't taste as good coming back up. "What?"

"You heard me. You need work don't you? Gail scored the gig and she's holding spots for us." She looked me over. "Got any khakis?"

She knew better and I should've known better than to indulge this crazy act. Apparently, my life was full of should haves. "I can get some."

An hour later we were headed downtown. On the way over, Jess informed me she'd stayed up late looking over the receipts from the now infamous room three nineteen. She confirmed my initial opinion that they were a dead end.

"Most of the names on them were probably fake, but even so, I didn't see anything worth a second glance."

As she talked about what she had found, a thought occurred to me about what we hadn't found. "Do you think it's strange that there's no receipt for either Emily Foster or Billy? I mean we know both of them were there recently."

"I guess that's strange, but maybe neither one of them paid to be there. They could've been bunking in on someone else's dime."

The only person I could think of who both Billy and Emily were connected to, that would've been able to provide them access was Quitman. Then I remembered that the apartment manager didn't even know Quitman owned the place, making it pretty unlikely that Jed made a habit of throwing his weight around to comp rooms for his strippers and errand boys.

My aha moment didn't seem to lead anywhere so I focused on where we were headed. The new downtown arts district was going to be a showplace. At least that's what Jess told me. All I could see was a ton of construction and some funky shaped buildings, all part of Lively's pet project to revamp downtown Dallas. The museum we were headed to was one of the only buildings in the area that wasn't new. I didn't spend a lot of time indulging the arts, but the DMA was a regular stop for elementary school field trips, and I had vague memories of my own youth and spitball fights in the atrium. My mother had been appalled at the note the teacher sent home. I could still hear her: "Luca Bennett, I didn't raise you to be a hoodlum." I suppose I wasn't as much of a hoodlum as she thought or I would've replied that she didn't raise me at all. My dad had faked a stern expression, but I had been able to tell by the twinkle in his eye he was proud of me for wreaking a little havoc.

The museum was about the same as I remembered, though that didn't mean much. We met Gail at the front entrance. She clapped me on the shoulder, then straightened the collar of the newly purchased light blue oxford shirt Jess had made me buy. "Hey, Bennett. You clean up nice. Maybe you'll consider a regular spot on the team."

Team. Not my favorite four letter word. I'd be burning these clothes as soon as we were done here. "Sure, Gail. Whatever." I knew she was teasing. On the ride over, Jess explained she'd confided in Gail about the real reason we wanted on today's detail. She'd also explained that Gail had the gig through her contacts at the museum, not the senator's office. We were backup to Lively's regular security team and wouldn't have to be cleared through his office. Good thing, since I didn't think a murder suspect would make it through a background check.

Gail gave us lanyards with plastic badges and positioned us near the bar. Even at lunchtime, contributors needed to get their drink on before they emptied their wallets. I briefly wondered why

Lively required such a large contingent of security. Maybe it was the venue. I couldn't for the life of me imagine why anyone would want half the pictures hanging on the walls, but the museum obviously considered them valuable. Maybe our presence was necessary to make sure the folks in line at the bar didn't try to use fake drink tickets to get more than their fair share. I didn't really care, but I was wishing I had a few drink tickets of my own when Jess poked me in the side.

"There's Randolf." She jerked her chin toward the podium a few feet away. "Striking woman."

"You should see her with a whip in her hand," I whispered. "Smokin' hot." Up close and in person, I was certain she was the woman in the videos. Still I couldn't figure out the why. Why with Quitman? Why on DVD? She had limitless funds. Surely she could indulge her prurient interests more privately than the back room of one of Quitman's clubs. Limitless funds. Enough to buy off a blackmailer? Quitman had the DVDs at his home. Had he tried to leverage them into a way to fund his defense? But what was Lively's connection? Jess's voice interrupted my jumbled thought process.

"Speaking of hot, look who's headed our way."

I followed Jess's gaze. Even with a lot more clothes on than when I last saw her, Ronnie did indeed look hot. The only thing that detracted from her beauty was the man who held her arm. Miguel Moreno. Everything about him screamed sleaze, from his too shiny, slicked-back hair to the date-like way he clung to his beautiful, and much younger, niece. I stared daggers at him, but Ronnie noticed me before he did. She locked eyes with me, then zeroed in on Jess. I read surprise, jealousy, anger. The surprise was the one emotion we shared. No way had I expected to see her here. Not with Miguel, not by herself. Was this event the reason she'd slipped out so early this morning? I'd figured she thought it was easier to leave a note than to lie in bed naked, trying to figure out what else to say. What would she have to say now?

I didn't have to wait long for my answer. Ronnie whispered something to Miguel, then she strode over to where Jess and I were standing. She stared Jess down. Jess, in turn, looked at me for a signal. I nodded, and Jess walked a few feet away. I was pretty sure she was still close enough to hear whatever Ronnie had to say to me, and I was kind of glad. Couldn't put my finger on why, but I felt like I needed a witness.

I opened the conversation with Ronnie by waving a hand at the assembling crowd. "Guess this explains why you had to hurry off this morning."

"Miguel is one of Senator Lively's staunch supporters."

I looked around and observed, "He's in good company." My words sparked a reaction. Ronnie's eyes reflected discomfort. Odd. Why should her uncle's support of a popular politician make her uncomfortable? Was it because she thought said politician was responsible for the disappearance of her client? If that was the case, what was she doing at an event designed to raise money for the perpetrator?

Suddenly, pieces of the puzzle started falling into place. The "good company" I'd referred to included the following players: Miguel Moreno, Caroline Randolf, Senator Lively, and Jed Quitman, and the connections extended far beyond senatorial campaigning. Miguel represented Quitman in court, Randolf punished Quitman in bed, and Lively took Quitman's money, and, according to Ronnie, was more than a little involved in silencing him to keep himself out of trouble with the Feds. All signs pointed to a dead man. A dead man I'd been hired to find and happened to be accused of killing.

I cared about clearing my name, but the more pressing question was what did Ronnie know about all of this? She'd seemed surprised when I told her about the sex DVDs, but was she really? Was her work at Miguel's office really happenstance, or was she more involved with this sketchy crowd than she'd led me to believe? Doubt clouded everything she'd told me. After all, she was the one who asked me to find Quitman, bring him directly to her. I didn't believe for a second she was at this event just to accompany her uncle. Her connection to this group was stronger than that. The cloud of doubt grew larger. Now I doubted not only her, but myself and my judgment. I made a habit of letting pretty women blur my vision, but never with so much at stake. Of course, she wanted to be my lawyer. What better way to make sure I took the fall for Quitman's death?

Now it was more than the outfit making me feel claustrophobic. Ronnie must've noticed too. She acted relieved to turn the focus away from her, from this event and back to me. "Luca, you don't look well. Are you sure you should be working?"

She reached to place her palm on my forehead. I stopped her midway. "I'm fine."

"I have to admit I didn't expect to see you here. Do you work security often?"

"Have to do something to make ends meet. Especially when the people I'm looking for wind up dead." Would my deliberate vagueness draw her out?

"People?"

"Well, I don't know that they're both dead, but since one is and the other one worked for him, it seemed like a pretty good guess. Anyway, can't collect bounties on dead folks."

Her expression was flat. Either she didn't know anything about Billy, or she was a fantastic liar. I didn't trust my judgment well enough to distinguish the difference. I wondered if I was wasting my time. Talking to her, being here, when I could be beating the streets looking to clear my name. Her next words made me wonder if she could read my mind.

"The grand jury is scheduled to meet on your case next week."

Jess stepped back toward us and made no secret of the fact she'd been listening to our conversation. "That's quick. Too quick."

Ronnie frowned at Jess, then turned her attention back to me. "Detective Perez convinced the ADA handling the case that it's a slam dunk." She focused on Jess again. "Apparently, cops in Dallas are no strangers to rushing to judgment."

I felt Jess bristle and I put a hand on her shoulder. The act didn't escape Ronnie's notice. She glared at my hand and delivered a dazzling and completely insincere smile to Jess. "Perhaps, you can help your *friend* avoid prosecution, *Detective*. I'm not sure my skills are what she needs. Or even wants for that matter." She leaned in, kissed me on the cheek, and strode back to Miguel who stood across the room watching our little tableau with more than a casual interest.

❖

The event ended a grueling two hours later. I'd have ducked out way before the final thank-yous, but Jess assured me Gail was actually paying us to stand around and look formidable. Except for the crowd, the speeches, and the uniform, it wasn't a bad day's work. Bonus would be a few minutes with Lively. Not likely, considering how many others were vying for his attention, but maybe my plastic badge would work some magic.

The senator had left the room, but he was still in the building, judging by the big black limo waiting at the VIP rope. I told Jess I was going in search of a restroom and went on a hunt for the politician. I wandered out of the reception hall and looked for a private spot. Somewhere the senator might powwow with his most select contributors, like the lovely sex kitten, Caroline Randolf. The corridors were packed with couples strolling arm in arm and families pushing strollers. Weekends were apparently busy times at the museum.

In my search for a posh private room, I stumbled across a space I was certain wasn't being used for official business. The coat check closet. We were thirty-nine days into over a hundred degree temps, and none of us could imagine wearing coats ever again. I stepped behind the long, unmanned counter and walked toward the closet door. I started to open it, but the sound of voices inside stopped me. Apparently, someone else realized this was a perfect place for a private meeting. I ducked behind the counter and strained to hear.

"I don't want to know anything about it. I only want the problem solved." A man's voice. Might've been the senator, but I could barely make out the words and wasn't quite sure it was him.

"I thought it was," a woman responded. "Why is it your staff has to bungle everything? I should have taken care of this myself. Lord knows the two of you are no help at all."

"Back off, Randolf." A different male voice than the first one. Thanks to him, I knew for sure the female voice was Caroline

Randolf. "You're the one who created the problem in the first place. Besides, you're off the hook for Quitman. A certain bounty hunter happened to be in the wrong place at the wrong time."

I'd know that voice anywhere. Shades of his accent shadowed his niece's speech patterns. Either Miguel Moreno was a bigger contributor to Lively's campaign than his sleazy little law firm would indicate or he was in business with the senator, not unlike the equally sleazy Quitman. Miguel sounded proud, like he was taking credit for pawning Quitman's death off on me.

For a man with a clean-cut image, Senator Lively sure did run with a rough crowd. Except for Randolf. She was all sharp and refined. Except in the bedroom. Or sex den at the Foxy Lady. Or wherever else she'd administered punishment for play. Assuming her actions were play. I didn't trust my own judgment anymore. I stopped trying to evaluate the words and concentrated on memorizing them.

"Look, I don't care who did what. I want it fixed." It was the other man speaking again, and based on the comments of the other two I was certain it was the senator. "Obviously, someone still has those DVDs and I want them found. What would constitute simple embarrassment for Caroline would be devastating to me. None of you want that. Am I right?"

At the word "DVDs" I almost let my resolve to process this information later go by the wayside, but I resisted the urge and waited to see if this little band of thugs dropped any more juicy hints. The wait paid off.

"That idiot Jed hired to get them probably doesn't even know what he has. If he did, you can be sure one of us would have been paid a visit by now. Don't worry. Your man will find him. It's just a matter of time."

I didn't care what else they said; my mind was racing to process what I'd just heard. Not a complete surprise, since I'd always figured the thug who broke into my place was hired by Quitman, but that Quitman had never gotten the DVDs back was a revelation. Who had them? And why? The thug probably wouldn't have gotten paid for the job if he didn't finish it. Was he holding out for more? Apparently, these three didn't have a clue, but they were desperate for answers. I was willing to bet not only were they behind Quitman's death, but they'd be willing to kill whoever had the DVDs if they had to in order to get them back.

The haze started to clear. The more I'd learned about Quitman, the more I'd questioned my assumption that he would want the DVDs back out of personal embarrassment. Hell, he was the only big name to appear in the kinky movies who hadn't been wearing a mask. He'd been proud of his starring role. On the other hand, Randolf's motive to retrieve the tapes was clear, but still not quite strong enough to merit murder.

I flashed on an image of the only person in the videos I hadn't yet identified. The masked masochist with the mini dick. I dug deep to remember other details about his appearance, his voice, and shuddered when I struck gold. Salt and pepper hair, muscular build, deep, but gentle voice, even as he asked to be punished. I'd heard the voice at Miguel's office two days ago and its owner was in the coat closet now. Holy shit, I'd just discovered who had the most to lose if Quitman's DVDs surfaced.

Suddenly, I realized they weren't talking anymore. I glanced at the door and saw the knob turn. Time to get the hell out of here. I fast crawled my way out from behind the counter, trying not to sneeze from all the dust I was kicking around. I didn't stand until I reached the farthest end. By the time the door opened, I was striding down the corridor, in the opposite direction. Totally focused on looking like I was doing security guard type things and hoping no one would notice the dirt on my knees. My laser focus didn't prevent me from running smack into the Hulk from Senator Lively's office.

He pushed off me and patted his side. Of course, he'd be carrying. Well, I was too. We could have a shoot-out right here by the—I looked around and my eyes landed on a sign—Impressionists. Probably not wise. Besides, I didn't want to hang around long enough for him to recognize me. As much as I hated the blue shirt and khakis, I didn't think they were much of a disguise. I took advantage of a lady in a stroller who looked lost and volunteered my services. Surely, big guy wasn't going to accost a museum employee helping one of the patrons.

"Ma'am, may I help you find something?"

She turned toward me and her face brightened. "Thank you. We're looking for the Native American art display."

I returned her smile and led her away. Big guy was losing interest in a fight since I wasn't in his direct path anymore. I made a mental note of the handwriting on his "Hello my name is…" tag, and then faked disinterest. I could tell Lloyd Pitts had made me, just didn't know what to do about it. I walked the woman and her toddler around in circles until I finally found someone who looked like they knew their way around the place, and then I handed them off.

Time to find Jess and get started on finding whoever had those DVDs. Once we had those, I had a feeling we'd be able to piece together the rest of this puzzle.

CHAPTER TWENTY

I spent the car ride filling Jess in on what I'd learned about the videos and my suspicions about Lively.

"That's pretty huge." She shook her head. "Lively, huh? Never would've figured him for the type. You still have one of those DVDs, right?"

"Yep, but not the right one. The one with Lively is gone, but maybe we can figure out a way to use what I've got. How about I buy you dinner and we can talk about it?" I was feeling flush after our job. Who knew working security for rich folks paid so well?

She blew me off. "Keep your money. You're going to need it."

"What's that supposed to mean?"

"You heard Moreno. Grand jury's meeting next week on your case. Doesn't sound like your girlfriend's going to be offering her services for free much longer."

I ignored the girlfriend comment. "I don't need a lawyer. I just need to clear my name."

"Dumber words were never spoken. You need a lawyer and you need a good one."

Neither of us stated the obvious. Ronnie was a good lawyer, at least judging by the number of zeroes she was capable of pulling in. But I couldn't be sure she'd put my interests ahead of her uncle's. After the suspicions she'd shared with me about Lively, her appearance at his fundraiser today was too strange for me to write off as a mere coincidence. I couldn't help but wonder what she knew about the senator's extracurricular activities. Maybe she'd played me from the get-go.

We rolled up to a red light and Jess turned in her seat to face me. "I've got some money I've put back. It'll be a loan. You'll pay me back when you can." I opened my mouth to tell her no, but she shut me down. "Think about it. But think fast. Okay?"

I nodded. No way was I taking her money, but I'd pretend to think about it rather than hurt her feelings. I could also feed her dinner, gratis. "Take me to my dad's. I'm pretty sure there's some of the casserole left over. He likes you. He'll want you to stay. He likes cops."

"Yeah, okay. Sounds good." She delivered the words with the appropriate degree of enthusiasm, but I could tell she wanted to say more. We rode in silence for a few more minutes before Jess punched right into the topic that hung in the air. "You ever tell your parents why you quit?"

"No." A simple answer designed to deflect a complicated explanation. Or maybe it only seemed complicated because no one had ever asked me about it before. My parents knew I'd been shot. Kinda hard to hide since the story made it into the metro section of the daily news. The rest I'd kept from them the same way the department had shut out the press. The higher-ups at DPD had a vested interest in keeping secret the fact a cop to whom they wanted to give a medal had refused the honor and turned in her badge. I didn't want the hassle of having to explain to my dad that police work with all its rules, misplaced loyalties, and politics wasn't for me. Guess I was also pissed because I figured he should've known me well enough to know that about me in the first place. My mother? She'd sent flowers to the hospital. Expensive ones. And a card, one of those tiny ones, held in place by a plastic pitchfork. *Get better soon, darling. Jackie*. She called about a year later. Guess she figured that was soon enough. Anyway, when she finally did call, all she wanted was to talk about her life, not to ask about mine.

I looked across the seat. I owed Jess more than my flat answer. I rustled up as much detail as I could stand to share. "Dad wouldn't understand. He spent his life craving all the benefits of steady work.

When he finally found it, he got laid off in a matter of a few years. My mom? She always thought police work was a dirty business. Not becoming. She probably thought my getting shot was the best thing that ever happened to her."

"Rough."

"Yeah."

A few minutes later, we pulled up in front of my dad's place. Jess parked behind my Bronco. I'd missed my own ride, driving myself around. Even though the police had seized all the firepower I kept inside, riding in the driver's seat of my own car felt safe, secure, powerful. I vowed to take her for a spin after dinner. Get some of my mojo back.

As if she could read my mind, Jess spoke up. "They'll have to give you your guns back eventually. It's not like they can tie them to the crime."

I laughed. "Perez will figure out something. Of course, maybe she wasn't smart enough to find them all." I'd have to check out the hidden floorboard compartment and see how clever she really was. The second I had the thought, a memory surfaced. I'd stuck something else in that compartment, minutes before I'd stumbled over Quitman's body. The file I'd lifted from Ronnie's office.

We entered the house and found Dad napping in the living room recliner, a drained beer bottle and a half eaten plate of casserole balanced in his lap. We tiptoed past, headed for the kitchen to see if he'd left us any beer and food. Barely.

A few minutes later, Jess and I pored over the JCM file at the kitchen table. Just like I remembered, there wasn't much to look at. Jess asked if I'd brought my laptop.

"Yes. Cross your fingers one of the old biddies on this street has a wireless connection."

Jess shook her head, but didn't try to stop me from stealing service from the neighbors. Once we were connected, she drove, searching the Texas Secretary of State's website for any info she could find on JCM, LLC. She got frustrated fast. "The corporation is owned by several corporations and those corporations are owned by several other corporations. None of the names seem familiar, and

I don't recognize any of the names of the officers." She slid the computer my way. I looked at the jumble of names, but I didn't know any of them. She pulled the computer back toward her and clicked on the keys some more. "Wait a minute. Here's something. Look who's listed as the registered agent."

I stood over her shoulder so we could see the screen at the same time. She pointed out the name: Miguel Moreno. My adrenaline spiked, then plummeted back down to earth. "I'm not sure that means anything, Jess. Ronnie told me that Moreno handles most of Quitman's business. Isn't the registered agent just the guy who accepts service for lawsuits and stuff?"

"Yeah. Damn, I thought I was on to something." She scrolled down the page, and I started to sit back down, but a line on the screen caught my eye.

I jabbed at the words. "Check this out!"

She stared where I was pointing, and shrugged. I recited the address on the screen below Miguel's name. It wasn't his office, but I knew it well. "That's the warehouse. Quitman's last stand."

I continued to stare at the screen as if I could find some meaning to the connection if I tried hard enough. I was on the verge of a breakthrough when a sharp ring pierced my concentration. My phone vibrated on the table, and Maggie's name and number lit up the display. Anyone else and I would've ignored the call. But Maggie never called me. Had to be important. I punched the phone to answer. "Bennett here."

"Luca, it's Maggie. I need you to come by the bar. Right now."

"I'm not at home. Can we set something up for later?"

"No. Has to be now." She lowered her voice to a rough whisper. "Billy's here, he's scared shitless, and we need your help."

CHAPTER TWENTY-ONE

I'd insisted on driving. Jess wouldn't have broken quite as many traffic laws. When we entered the packed bar, Maggie was pacing by the front door. She offered Jess an approving nod, and then grabbed my arm and pulled me toward the back. Jess had to double-time it to keep up.

I managed a question on the run. "Where is he?"

"Harry's with him in the office. He's telling some wild tale." She stopped short in the middle of the crowd and turned to face me with a fierce set to her jaw. "He may be in real trouble this time. Promise me you'll help him."

I looked a question at Jess over the top of Maggie's head. Billy had an active warrant. I needed to know she wasn't going to go all law-and-order on me once we got him cornered. She nodded, a silent signal telling me to promise whatever I had to, and we'd sort out the rest.

"I promise."

She motored us back to her office and motioned for us to wait outside the door. She cracked the door and exchanged a few words with Harry. He gave up his post, and Maggie thrust us over the threshold.

As the first one into the room, I'd expected a reaction from the scruffy guy in the corner of the room. Relief that help had arrived, agitation about not being on the lam. The wide-eyed horror on Billy's face wasn't at all what I'd expected. I walked toward him and he shook like I was coming to take him away. I tried to calm him down. "Billy, settle down. We're here to help you out, man."

He backed away from me and shouted at his sister. "What the fuck, Mags? Are you trying to get me killed? I thought you said you called for help."

I glanced back at Jess and she jerked her head toward the door. Both of us moved to block the exit. Nobody was leaving until we figured out what had Billy so jacked up. I sized him up. Not as hungry and tattered as I expected a homeless guy on the run to be. About my size. I could fight him hand to hand if I had to...

The thought trailed off, replaced with a vague sense of realization. I pulled my gun, ignored Maggie's protests, and backed Billy into a chair.

"Where the hell have you been?" I had to repeat the question a few times before I got a response.

"Like you don't know. Just take me in. I don't want to talk to you." He spat the words and delivered a venomous look at his sister.

I used the gun as a pointer and directed his attention back to me. "I'm not a cop and your sister didn't turn you in. We're here to help you, and strangely enough, I think you can help me too."

Jess spoke from directly over my shoulder. "What's going on, Bennett?"

I ignored her question in place of one of my own. "Billy, where were you Thursday afternoon?"

"I look like I have a day planner?"

I cocked the revolver in my hand. "Do I look like I'm fuckin' around? You better tell me everything you know about Quitman's death or you won't have any plans for the rest of your life." I heard Maggie gasp, but I didn't budge. I had a hunch and only Billy could tell me if I was right. I wasn't putting the gun away until I had answers.

His eyes darted around the room, but it didn't take him long to realize he wasn't getting past me. Maggie stepped closer, put a hand on my arm, but when she spoke it was directly to her brother. "Billy, you can trust her. Talk."

He looked into her eyes, flashing a glint of admiration for her, probably because she showed no fear in the face of my badass self. "Okay, okay. But for crying out loud, put the gun away. At least until you hear what I have to say." I lowered the revolver, but kept it in sight. He put his head in his hands and his whole body shook a prelude to his story. I waited until he was ready to talk, but despite my hunch, his first words surprised me.

"I didn't mean to hit you. I didn't know it was your place."

Took me a few to sift through what he'd said. Earlier, when I'd sized him up, I figured he was the guy who kicked my gun away in the warehouse where I'd found Quitman's bloody corpse. That would explain why he was scared to death of seeing me again. But his confession was a disconnect. Hit me? My place? Slowly, my brain kicked into gear. Stranger in my apartment. Toaster to the head. Missing DVDs.

I pointed with my gun hand and raised my voice. "You? You broke into my place and took Quitman's home movies?"

Jess walked into the middle of our cluster. "Let's back this up. Would you two care to fill us in?" She motioned for me to put the gun away, but I was beyond angry now. I spent the better part of a week looking for this fool and he'd been under my nose the whole time. Not only that, he'd been in my apartment, rifling through my shit. Oh yeah, and the blow to the head. I'd haul him to jail myself, except I wanted answers more than I wanted revenge.

I looked at Maggie who was staring back and forth between me and Billy. The looks she gave us were exactly the same. She cared about us both and didn't want us fighting. Billy may be a pain in the ass and a poor excuse for a human being, but she loved him anyway. Me? Well, I was a pain in the ass in a different way, but I knew she loved me too. Hearing Billy out would be a small price to pay for all the food, talk, and friendship she'd sent my way over the years. I pulled up a chair, lowered the gun onto my thigh, and waved my free hand in the air. "Start talking."

Billy started slowly. He'd met Quitman while working at one of his bars. Billy'd never been on the payroll, but he'd dropped by on occasion when he needed some cash.

"Quitman hired you himself?"

"No, but he showed up at one of his places a lot, the Foxy Lady. Nice guy. Always smiling and he tipped really well. I cleaned the back rooms and he went out of his way to tell me I did a great job."

I tried to imagine the sleazy payday loan god as a friendly big tipper in the back room of a strip joint. Jibed about as well as the image of him spread-eagle on a bed taking whatever socialite Caroline Randolf felt like dishing out. Anxious to get this story moving, I prodded, "Let's get to the part where you broke into my place."

"I didn't know it was your place," he said, as if that was the most important part.

"Tell me how you got the job. Who paid you, everything."

"Quitman. He said someone had come to his house and stolen something valuable. Said he would pay me good to find his stuff and keep it safe for a while. He gave me your address. Lock was easy to pick and the box he described was in your closet. You don't got much else in there. I was only in your place a minute or two." He shook his head. "Can't believe you showed up."

I rubbed the bump on my head. "Yeah, thanks for the souvenir." I wondered how Quitman had known I'd taken the DVDs and how he'd gotten my address. Had Ronnie decided to give her client some inside scoop? But she hadn't known for sure I'd had the DVDs before I told her, and that was after the break-in. Damn, every time I thought I was getting closer to the whole story, the truth slipped through my fingers. "What did you do with the DVDs?"

"Stowed 'em. I got places."

"I bet you do. Speaking of places. You know anything about a dead stripper—" I searched my brain for her name, "Emily Foster aka Missy Bloom?"

"I know she's dead. Nothing else. Whoever killed her cost me a place to crash. Cops were crawling all over the place when they found her body."

Well, they hadn't been crawling too long since I'd been able to roust the manager a couple of days after. Billy should've hung around. Maybe then I would've found him before he got mixed up in Quitman's cluster. I was confused. Billy's break-in at my place had happened well after the murder at his old place. Was Missy's death related to Quitman or not? "Tell me what you know about Missy. I heard you were sweet on her."

"I told you already. Nothing. I saw her at the club sometimes, and Jed made her let me crash at her place. He wanted me to keep an eye on her, but didn't tell me why. He mostly wanted to know who else she hung with. Missy didn't talk to folks like me. She had a lot of airs for a girl who takes her clothes off for money."

I didn't like the tone of his comment, but his expression didn't convey any particular feeling at all for the dead girl. For now, I'd believe his story. "Okay, let's get back to the DVDs. What were you supposed to do with them?"

"Jed got word to me to meet him to hand them over."

"And?"

"And I did."

This was painful. I decided to go ahead and ask the big question, but I prefaced it with my guess to let him know I was onto him. "I saw you at the warehouse. Saw you take off right before the police showed up to find Quitman's dead body. Did you kill him?"

His face twisted into a painful grimace, but he didn't say a word. Maggie's loud voice broke the silence. "Luca Bennett, my brother's not a killer. Tell her, Billy. Tell her you didn't do it."

We all waited. I didn't really think he had killed Quitman. Why would he? But there'd been two other people besides me and Jed in that warehouse and he was one of them. Billy was involved somehow, and I had a bunch of reasons for wanting to know why. Clearing my own name topped the list. My fingers twitched around the gun in my hand. I didn't want to have to threaten him again, but neither of us were leaving here until I knew the truth.

Jess pulled up a chair and gently eased me out of the way. I watched while she did what she did best. "Billy, look at me." When he raised his head, she eased a hand into her pocket. "I'm going to show you something." She pulled out her detective shield and placed it in his hand. He started out of his chair, but Jess pushed him back, waving me off with her other hand. "It's all about trust, Billy. I need you to trust me just like I'm going to trust you to tell us what we need to know. Luca's in trouble. She needs your help. You help us, I'll help you. Trust me?"

After Jess overplayed her hand, I glanced at Maggie who shot daggers my way. I'd brought a cop into her place. Her place. Where she didn't always follow the rules and where her fugitive brother was hiding out. Her message was clear: I'd lied by omission. It would be a long time before she'd trust me again. Jess'd better know what the hell she was doing.

In contrast to Maggie's anger, Billy merely seemed resigned to his fate. "I don't got anywhere else to go. They're looking for me."

I perked up and almost interrupted, but Jess kept it one-on-one. "Who are they?"

"I don't know. Quitman got word to me he was ready for the DVDs. Took me with him to that warehouse. Said we were taking a short trip for a long payoff."

"Any idea why he didn't just get the DVDs from you and show up on his own?"

"Said he wanted a witness."

"Witness for what?"

"He gave me five hundred bucks for getting them." Billy offered an apologetic look in my direction. "I didn't ask a lot of questions."

"Okay, so what happened when you got there?"

"He parked around back, then we went in together. There's this guy waiting. Big guy, all dressed up in a suit like a businessman, but too rough for the part." Billy sounded proud to know the difference between a professional and a poser.

"Rough how?"

"He's got a scar the length of my hand down the side of his neck. Knife fight, I'd say."

Pitts. Had to be him. Jess and I exchanged looks. I widened my eyes to convey my impatience, but she shook her head at me and kept slowly mining for details.

"Any idea who he is?"

"Never seen him before. I hear he's been asking around about me the last few days. Guy like that, asking questions? Word gets around real fast."

Jess nudged him back to the story. "You and Jed meet this guy. What happens next?"

"He pulls Quitman aside and they talk. I didn't listen, figured it wasn't my business. They were arguing though. About money. Quitman told him his offer wasn't good enough." So much for him not listening. "Next thing, Quitman asks me to wait by the car. I was only out there a minute, when I hear this horrible scream, like someone's being skinned alive."

"What did you do?"

"I'm not gonna lie. I wanted to run, but I didn't have the car keys. And Quitman had promised me another five hundred when we finished with his business. I snuck back up to the door and tried to see what was going on inside. I couldn't see a thing, so I ducked in and hid behind some old furniture until I could get my bearings. I didn't see Quitman, but the other guy barreled out the back door. When he hit the light, I could see blood on his hands and he was jabbing at his phone. Freaked me out. I bolted in the opposite direction and that's when I ran into you." He pointed at me.

"Thanks for sticking around to help me out," I said.

"Give me a break. You had a sledgehammer in your hands and you threatened me."

"All true. I couldn't see well enough to tell it was you." I didn't stop to wonder whether it would have made a difference. "Where did you take off to?"

"I stood outside for a few, trying to work out a plan. When I heard sirens, I took off into the woods behind the place and kept going. Found my way to a convenience store and bought myself a ride back."

"Who called the cops?"

"Dunno. Could've been the other guy, I guess."

We hadn't made much progress. Up until now, I managed to block out the possibility I'd be indicted for murder, but this dead end clinched my fate. No way was Perez going to buy Billy's

• 217 •

story about the argument between Quitman and Pitts, especially the version where Billy was present, but wasn't directly involved. And she sure wasn't going to believe Lively's motive for sending Pitts to take care of Quitman—not without proof. Bottom line, Billy hadn't seen the senator's enforcer kill Quitman, and his sketchy history with law enforcement meant his credibility was in the tank. What he had seen—me, standing over Quitman's body, wielding a sledgehammer—was pretty damning. The grand jury would meet in a few days to decide my fate. Short of a miracle, there was no way I could clear my name in time. Unless...

Unless I could find a way to flush out the real killer.

"What about the DVDs?"

"Huh?" Billy looked confused by the question.

"Quitman's DVDs?" I needed the one with Lively to have any real leverage, otherwise I'd just get myself killed. Randolf and the senator didn't have them. They'd said as much in the coat closet at the museum. Had the senator's enforcer hidden them in an attempt to drive up the price? Or could there be another possibility? I didn't dare even think the complete thought, but I did ask again, "Do you know where Quitman's DVDs are?"

Billy stood and reached for his waistband. Jess and I both twitched at the movement, and I raised the gun I'd never bothered to reholster. He lifted his shirt and did nothing more dangerous than point at the envelope tucked in his pants. "I got 'em right here. Safe and sound."

CHAPTER TWENTY-TWO

I'd never suffered the dread of Monday mornings that folks with regular jobs did. Until today. I lay, half-awake, on the same twin bed where I'd first necked with a girl, and reviewed the plan Jess and I had hatched the day before. A plan so crazy it just might work.

I reached for the alarm clock. Seven thirty a.m. Jess wasn't due to arrive for another half hour. No time for a run, but a shower should wake me up. Judging by the quiet, Dad wasn't stirring yet. Fine by me. I didn't want to have to explain what we were up to.

At eight sharp, while I stood in the kitchen trying to figure out where Dad hid the coffee filters, I saw Jess's car pull up in front of the house. She climbed out, shouldered a medium-sized duffle bag, then reached back in and pulled out a cardboard tray full of coffee cups. I sighed in relief and met her at the door before she could ring the bell. I reached for the tray of salvation. "Here, let me take those."

She shoved it in my direction. "Don't drink mine. Your plain black tar is clearly marked. The extra one's for your dad."

Sweet. Not a trait I'd ever assigned her. I hoped it wouldn't stick. Sweet wasn't going to get us through today. I led her to the kitchen where we both sank into chairs and drank the expensive brew in silence.

She waited until I'd emptied my cup before bringing up the plan. "You still want to do this? We could take the DVDs to Perez. Maybe once she sees the cast of characters she'll get off your back and hold out for a bigger prize."

"She'll try to say I was part of the whole deal. I don't trust her to back off. Do you?"

We'd spent the day before working out the details. At our direction, Billy had placed a call to Pitts and arranged a meet. Jess and I cased the location and worked out a strategy. Billy wasn't going anywhere near the place, but I was. My initial idea was to show up early with enough firepower to blow the guy to bits, but Jess had a different take on the situation. Her plan was, of course, more sensible—use the meet to clear my name. The more I considered it, the more I liked it. Besides, if the senator's reach was as long as I believed, Perez might be convinced to cover up his involvement. This adventure wasn't just about clearing my name. I wanted to bring Lively down.

By way of answering my question about whether she was still in, Jess opened the duffle bag and pulled out the equipment she'd brought. "Let's get you wired up."

Normally, when a woman pulls up my shirt and traces her hands along my chest, an orgasm, for at least one of us, isn't far off. Guess I was too keyed up thinking about our plans to focus on the usual. Jess taped the tiny voice-activated digital recorder to my skin without any interruption from me.

She stepped back to observe her work. "Looks good, but if he frisks you, he'll be able to tell."

"If he frisks me, he'll be dead." I ignored her disapproving look, and pushed on to other subjects. "Where should I meet you later?"

"There won't be any later. I'm coming with you."

"No way." She'd put enough at risk by helping me as much as she had. Whatever was about to go down was going to be one-on-one, me and Pitts. "It'll be bad enough when he shows up expecting Billy and gets me instead. If two of us appear, we're not likely to get anything out of him."

"Give me a little credit. I'll be hiding out, but you can bet this guy will show up ready to kill Billy as soon as he gets what he wants. I'm sure he'll have no qualms about killing you instead." She glanced away, but not before I glimpsed worry in her eyes. "I'm leaving now so I can find a place to hide out." She put a hand on my arm. "I got your back. Don't do anything stupid."

I hoped those two sentiments weren't mutually exclusive.

I had just finished my coffee when Dad shuffled into the kitchen. I pointed out the cup Jess had brought for him, black like mine. "Hey, Dad, I'm headed to take care of some stuff." I fumbled with what to say next. If I don't come back, you can have my car, seemed a bit abrupt. Don't know why I came down with a sudden case of the sentimentals. Maybe staying in his house, this house where a lifetime of memories added up to nothing more than old and lonely, touched me, made me sad. Whatever it was, I wasn't inclined to share what Jess and I had plotted, but I did want him to know he was more than a place for me to crash when the going got tough. I boiled my feelings into a few words. "Take care of yourself, okay?"

He barely looked up from his coffee. "Sure, Luca. No problem."

I started the Bronco and pulled out my iPhone to type in the address Pitts had given Billy. Jess had driven us by the building yesterday, and although I was pretty sure I could make my way back, I may as well let technology be my friend. The phone rang in my hand. Ronnie. Her sixth call since yesterday. I'd let the others go to voice mail and I hadn't listened to any of them. I didn't trust myself to judge which Ronnie I'd be dealing with. Strong, capable lawyer or tender, vulnerable lover. And then there was the smooth-talking vixen, the one who I suspected knew more about her uncle's involvement with Senator Lively and Caroline Randolf than she cared to let on. After reflecting on the past week, I was forced to admit I felt used. What frustrated me the most was not knowing why. If shutting Quitman up was the ultimate goal, why had Ronnie seemed so concerned about his safety? Face the facts, Bennett, she set you up. You found Quitman and now he's dead. Of course, I'd only found him after he'd died, which meant the senator and Randolf were even more motivated to find him than Ronnie had been. Maybe her motives had been pure.

I shook my head. I'd probably never know the answers. Wasn't sure I cared. The phone continued to ring. What the hell. I clicked it on and raised it to my ear. "Bennett."

"Luca, thank God. I was worried. I've been trying to reach you since yesterday."

"Have you? I've been busy. Hadn't noticed you called." The lie came easy because I wished it was true. Frankly, I was a little pissed about the way she'd acted at the senator's reception. She owed me a dose of sucking up.

"Are you okay?"

The question seemed odd. Not the words so much as the worry and anxiety behind them. She had no reason to think I wouldn't be okay. Unless she thought our little tiff at the senator's reception had left me pining for her. I'd set her straight. "I'm great. I'm really busy though. Did you need something?"

"Well, no. I mean, yes."

I waited for her to decide on a final answer.

"I suppose I only wanted to tell you I'm sorry."

Not what I'd expected, and my surprise spurred me to ask, "Sorry for what?"

"That day at lunch? When you mentioned Jed and, uh, sex?"

I didn't have a clue where this was going, but I wanted her to move it along. "Yes," I said impatiently.

"When I got back to the office, I mentioned what you said to Miguel."

She had my attention now. "And?"

"And he asked me a bunch of questions. I didn't understand at the time, but he kept asking me about DVDs." She paused. "Like did you have them, did I know what was on them? I didn't think it was important at the time."

"And later, when I told you about them, you still didn't think it was important to tell me about Miguel's questions?"

"I'm sorry, Luca. I should've told you. Have you figured out who took them from you?"

In my anger, I let the non sequitur slide. "Don't you worry about me or the DVDs. We're both safe and sound. Now, why don't you

go back to doing your uncle's bidding. I can take care of myself."
I clicked off the line and threw the phone on the seat next to me. I
was riled and I needed to settle down before I met with Pitts. Being
emotional would only get me in trouble.

❖

I parked a few blocks away and walked to the location Pitts had
chosen. The abandoned building gave me déjà vu. I offered a silent
thanks to Jess for insisting on joining me for this stunt, even though
I had no idea where she was hiding out. My brain chanted, please
don't let there be any dead bodies, please don't let there be any dead
bodies. No amount of good lawyering would get me out of this mess
if I turned up near a third corpse in less than a week.

Pitts had instructed Billy to take the elevator and meet him in
the third floor lobby. I wasn't thrilled about the prospect of being
trapped in an elevator, but he could be anywhere, watching me, and
I didn't want the plan to go off track before I got him talking.

I wore the same sweaty cap Billy had on at the warehouse and
I kept my head ducked low as I made my way into the building.
Hopefully, Pitts was far enough away that even if he was watching,
he wouldn't notice I was here in Billy's place. Not yet, anyway.

The elevator was fairly modern. The building had probably been
a victim of the failing economy rather than old age. I stepped inside
and punched the number three. As the car rumbled to its destination,
I scouted out an escape plan. I was tall enough to reach the ceiling
panel that led to freedom, if crawling along the top of an elevator
car can be called freedom. Hopefully, dangerous exits weren't in my
future. I didn't have much time to consider my prospects before the
elevator doors slid open to reveal an empty third floor lobby.

I eased out of the car and waited. I expected Pitts to greet me
when I arrived, not be the last to show. I took the time alone to
poke around. The lobby led to what used to be office space, judging
by the random assortment of desks and chairs in evidence. I idly
wondered who owned the building. Probably one of the many shell
companies Senator Lively and his cohorts had arranged to hide their

incestuous business practices. I glanced around, wondering if Jess was hiding somewhere in this space, when I heard a deep voice from across the room.

"I told you to wait for me in the lobby."

I'd made the mistake of turning my back on the entryway to the office space. Probably for the best, since I would look more like Billy from behind than I would when I turned around. I moved slowly, so he wouldn't think I was up to anything and also so I could catch the look of surprise on his face when he saw me in Billy's place. When I finally faced him, I was the one who was surprised. Pitts held Ronnie Moreno in his arms, a gun pointed at her temple.

I took a step forward, but stopped when Ronnie warned me off. "Luca, don't. He'll kill us both."

He grinned. "Listen to your girlfriend. She's smart."

I forced a casual tone. "Not smart enough to choose better friends."

He laughed and looked at Ronnie as if expecting her to join in the fun. I took the opportunity to send with my eyes all the messages I couldn't say out loud. *You'll be okay. I'll get you out of this. Trust me.* The fear she reflected back hid any other response. I still didn't know her role in all this, but the gun at her head bought back some of the trust she'd lost.

He turned his attention back at me. "Did you bring what you were supposed to?"

I held up the envelope in my hand. "Right here." I needed to stall. My initial plan had been to engage him in conversation, get him to confess to something. Anything. Now that he held Ronnie at gunpoint, the plan was an imperative. No way would I let her be a casualty of my careless plan. "You don't seem surprised to see me."

"I'm good at my job. I had one of my guys follow you after the benefit. He's been watching your every move. He saw you and your former cop friend squirrel away that junkie Quitman hired to do his dirty work. I put that bit of intel together with what your girlfriend here was willing to spill about your interest in those DVDs, and no, I'm not surprised to see you here. I am surprised you're still talking though." He pointed his gun at a desk, several feet to his right. A shiny portable DVD player sitting on its surface contrasted with the rest of the dusty, abandoned furnishings in the room. "Start up the movies. When we're done watching, I'll let her go."

If only it were that easy. I wasn't stupid enough to believe he'd let us walk out of here. Now might be a good time for Jess to drop from the ceiling and pull a Rambo. Of course I still hadn't gotten anything decent on tape yet. If Jess was waiting in the wings, she'd give me time to get what we came for. Time to step it up. I started with a deflection.

"She's not my girlfriend."

"Right."

"Seriously, I don't even like her that much. Not crazy about her uncle either."

"Guess you're not a fan of the senator either."

"I like him okay, but again with that company you keep thing. Lively should pay closer attention to all the dirty business his big donors are into. Or is he too busy trying to keep his own dick out of the news. I mean, fraud's bad enough, but flashing his Johnson while taking a beating from a stripper, that's headline stuff."

Pitts jerked Ronnie's hair. "Fraud? She tell you that? Lawyers should be better at keeping secrets, don't you think? After the senator pulled strings to help her get her license in order, you'd think she'd be more grateful."

That explained how Ronnie was able to start up shop here in Dallas with a clean record, but she shouldn't have to pay for professional success with her life. Whatever her involvement, I was getting her out of here. She might not like me when we were done, but she'd be alive.

"Maybe she thinks she's above getting her hands dirty." I did my best to ignore the hurt expression on Ronnie's face. The pain of my words was nothing compared to what would happen if I didn't figure out a way to get us both out of here. "You and me, we're not afraid of a little dirty work, right? Like at the warehouse. Quitman was getting too greedy wasn't he? The senator's help with his case wasn't enough. He wanted money too, right? As if he didn't have enough."

If I'd thought it would be easy to goad Pitts into talking about his personal involvement in Quitman's murder, I'd been wrong. The guy stayed locked up tight, but everyone has their weak point. I had to keep poking until I found his.

"Sloppy kill, though. I thought the same thing about the stripper. Knives and sledgehammers? I would've thought you'd be a crack shot. Why the blood bath?"

"Guns leave too much evidence." My prodding had worked and the flow of information continued. "Didn't want it to look too professional."

I had what I needed, but I couldn't resist a final question while I ciphered a way for Ronnie and me to get out of this mess, alive. "Why the stripper? I never did get why she was worth anyone's time."

"She wasn't worth anything, but she thought what she knew was. I taught her different. You think Quitman would've gotten the point, but he had to overreach too." He pointed the gun at me. "Enough talking. Put the envelope down and walk to that wall." He jerked his chin to indicate my final resting place. I followed the first instruction, but ignored the second. After I tossed the envelope on the desk, I started walking toward him, hands in the air.

"Back off, Bennett."

"Hey, Pitts, I thought we had a deal. DVDs for the lady."

"I think I'll keep this particular lady. Why don't you take off?"

Jess, now would be a good time for you to make an appearance. I didn't have a lot of options. In the time it would take me to pull my gun, he could blow Ronnie's head off. I had to get his focus off her long enough to take action. I used the oldest trick in the book.

"I think I'll stick around. Especially since help has arrived." I waved at a big bunch of nothing over his shoulder. Not many can resist that maneuver. He jerked his head and the tip of his pistol followed. Not much leeway, but I'd take it. I lunged, aiming for the fraction of a space between him and Ronnie. She fell and I landed on top of her. Hard. Pitts managed to stay on his feet, but he weaved while he caught his balance. I pushed myself off Ronnie, hugged his shins, and pushed him back, hoping he'd drop the gun on his way down. He didn't.

I gasped at the searing pain in my shoulder, but I didn't have time to dwell on the pain. While I scrambled to get off him, Pitts was only too happy to help. He shoved me hard and I groaned as my shoulder hit the floor. I watched him rise to his feet, still gripping the damn gun. I snaked a hand down to my boot, but I knew I wouldn't have time to get off a shot. He pointed the gun at my chest. I didn't give him the satisfaction of seeing my fear. Instead I turned toward Ronnie. She was only inches away, but paralyzed by what had just happened. I tried to catch her eyes. Let her know that even though I'd broken my silent promises, I'd given it everything I had.

She wasn't looking at me. Her stare was laser focused over Pitts's shoulder. I almost laughed at her attempt to use my trick. No way would Pitts fall for the same ruse twice in a row. I had to admire her spunk. What the hell, I looked too. Just in time to see Jess step out of the shadows and aim her gun at Pitts. I heard a shot. A second flashed before I felt the sharp, stinging, gut-wrenching pain. Everything swayed in slow motion as I grasped for clarity. Jess was too late to save me, but she could still take Pitts down, rescue Ronnie, clear my name. Me? I couldn't help anyone. I closed my eyes and surrendered.

CHAPTER TWENTY-THREE

Another day, another scar.

Make that two scars. The news of my death was exaggerated and premature. I'd exposed the truth this morning when I woke up, hours out of surgery, in the ICU. At the time, I hadn't been convinced I was alive. I'd awoken to the sounds of Maggie arguing with the nurse about why she couldn't get in to see her niece. Had a nice ring to it, but definitely not reality. I'd given back in to the pull of sleep. Or the afterlife. Until the pain meds kicked in, I didn't really care which.

When I woke again later, traces of my dream remained. Except Maggie was actually sitting next to my bed. Reading the *National Enquirer*. I struggled to sit up, but she barked, "Don't you move, Luca Bennett, or I'll kick your ass." Her fierce expression told me she might be worthy of such a feat. I wasn't really in any position to fight even her scrawny self. I rested back against the pillows and assessed my situation.

I was broken, but alive. Tubes ran from various places on my body to machines that pumped and buzzed signals of my status. A long curtain roped me off from other patients. The room was tiny with barely enough room for the chair where Maggie had taken up sentry duty. She'd dressed up for the part. Spiked red patent heels, a short black skirt, and a flowing blouse with a loud paint splatter pattern. Bright gold earrings and a colorful beaded necklace rounded out the image. Maggie's version of high fashion. I was willing to bet a handsome doctor was on duty. I probably should bet since I seemed to be blessed with an extra dose of luck. Last thing I remembered was looking at Jess while Pitts fired off another round in the direction of my chest.

Ronnie and Jess. Were they all right? As my eyes darted around the room, Maggie read my mind. "Your lady friend's just fine. She's been pacing the halls for hours while you were in surgery. I told her to go home so her raggedy self wouldn't be the first thing you saw when you finally woke up."

I didn't bother protesting even though I knew she meant Jess. The trace of affection in her voice signaled she'd forgiven me for involving a cop in her brother's trouble. Still, I wanted, needed to know if Ronnie was okay. Maggie may not know, but Jess would. "Do you know when she's coming back?"

Maggie checked her watch. "Won't be long. She left about an hour ago and she made me promise to wait here. As if I need to be told what to do by some young thing with a badge."

She didn't fool me with her stern tone. She liked Jess despite her aversion to authority figures. I guess they'd bonded while I was sleeping off my bullet wounds.

Seconds later, Jess plowed through the curtain. Her first words were to Maggie. "That nurse is a piece of work. Had to flash my badge to get back here. Seems like you have first priority since you're her aunt and all."

Maggie started to retort, but I pulled the attention back to me. "Hey, Jess, in case you're wondering, I'm alive."

She glanced my way, the hint of a smile at the corner of her lips. "Oh hi, Luca. Good to see you again."

Whatever. She could pretend all she wanted; Maggie had blown her nonchalant façade. I was so glad to be alive, I didn't care if she acted happy to see me. Besides, I wanted answers more than I wanted sentiment. "Spill, Jess. Tell me everything."

She stared at me for a long time, as if assessing my stamina, before she answered. "She's okay. Not hurt. I imagine she'd be here, but she's being debriefed and that's going to take a while. Billy's with Perez and a couple of Feds." She shot a look at Maggie. "No worries. With what he's spilling, he'll get another chance on the outside. I've already vouched for him, and I told them he has a sister who'll make sure he stays on the straight and narrow."

"What about Pitts?" I asked.

"Flesh wound. I didn't want the bastard to miss out on a prison sentence. Plus, now he has strong motivation to give up the big players. Lively, Randolf, and Moreno are in for a big surprise this afternoon when the Feds show up with search warrants. Turns out they were all in business together—secret, quid pro quo business, not including Randolf and Quitman's sex games. When the DA's office came after Quitman, the rest of them dropped him like a hot potato. He decided to use his video to buy some assistance for his troubles. Unfortunately, the others decided Quitman was expendable. If the video of the family values candidate hit the news, their behind the scenes business connections would be worthless."

I nodded, too tired to take it all in right now. I'd like to debrief Ronnie myself, but who knows if I'd ever get a chance to find out how involved she was in her uncle's not so legal business dealings. I supposed I should feel used, but I only felt a little sad. No sense dwelling on what could've been. Ronnie had been a splash of color, a spark of heat, but right now I craved normal, boring, not getting shot at days. I responded to Jess with one word, a blanket to cover saving me, bringing me news about Ronnie, and her rush to get here before I woke up.

"Thanks."

❖

I couldn't believe they were letting me check out without paying the bill. Jess told me not to worry about it. I figured she'd used her badge to help me bypass the patient administration desk, but I was still too weak to protest. A week of lying in bed with no action wasn't my idea of restful. I'd watched the news of the investigation, supplemented by Jess's inside scoop. A grand jury had convened to review a long list of charges involving Miguel,

Caroline Randolf, and Senator Lively—fraud, corruption, bribery. Ronnie wasn't in the grand jury's sights. She was a witness and had relayed her suspicions and the information she'd discovered about her uncle's business practices in exchange for assurances she wouldn't be swept up in the rush to justice. Perez was off my ass, at least for now, after Jess presented her with Pitt's taped confession to both murders.

I was ready to be home, ready to work, ready to return to normal even if normal was an old SUV, an empty fridge, and a coffee can with a few dollar bills.

Jess spoke casually as she wheeled me to the hospital lobby. "Your dad's expecting you. I told him you'd be staying with him until your first follow-up visit."

She ignored my murderous glare and kept moving. I let it go. Dad had been a constant presence over the last week. Half sober and somewhat well groomed. Judging by the way he looked at Maggie while he'd been here, I sensed his evolution had little to do with impressing his daughter. Still, whatever his motivation for staying by my bedside, I could repay the favor by hanging with him for a few days. Hell, maybe we'd sneak off to Bingo's and catch a game together like old times. Playing cards was as much risk as I could handle right now.

The elevator doors opened to the lobby and risk of a different kind. Ronnie leaned against the information desk, her eyes locked on mine. None of the scenarios I had conjured up for us to meet again involved me in a wheelchair. Not sure why I was surprised. Nothing about me and her fit within my brand of normal. She constantly threw me off-balance. I liked it and I didn't. Guess it was time to decide which feeling was stronger.

She walked toward us. I could feel Jess stiffen, but she let Ronnie speak first.

"Hello, Detective. I was hoping I could take Luca home."

"Hello, Miss Moreno." Jess spoke in polite, clipped tones. She shot me a look that left no doubt as to her feelings, but she didn't interfere. "I think that's up to Luca."

I looked between them. The safe thing to do would be to get in the car with Jess, ride to my dad's, and heal. Ronnie wanted bigger and better things than she'd ever find here in the shadow of her humble roots. Ronnie was probably headed out of town, away from her uncle's disgrace and on to a six-figure job at a fancy D.C. firm. Ronnie was trouble.

I didn't have to think it through. I'd already decided. One last ride with the lady.

THE END

About the Author

Carsen Taite works by day (and sometimes night) as a criminal defense attorney in Dallas, Texas. Her goal as an author is to spin plot lines as interesting as the cases she encounters in her practice. She is the author of five previously released novels, *truelesbianlove.com*, *It Should be a Crime* (a Lambda Literary Award finalist), *Do Not Disturb*, *Nothing but the Truth*, and *The Best Defense*. She is currently working on her seventh novel, *Beyond Innocence*. Learn more at www.carsentaite.com.

Books Available from Bold Strokes Books

Slingshot by Carsen Taite. Bounty hunter Luca Bennett takes on a seemingly simple job for defense attorney Ronnie Moreno, but the job quickly turns complicated and dangerous, as does her attraction to the elusive Ronnie Moreno. (978-1-60282-666-3)

Touch Me Gently by D. Jackson Leigh. Secrets have always meant heartbreak and banishment to Salem Lacey until she meets the beautiful and mysterious Knox Bolander and learns some secrets are necessary. (978-1-60282-667-0)

Missing by P.J. Trebelhorn. FBI agent Olivia Andrews knows exactly what she wants out of life, but then she's forced to rethink everything when she meets fellow agent Sophie Kane while investigating a child abduction. (978-1-60282-668-7)

Sweat: Gay Jock Erotica edited by Todd Gregory. Sizzling tales of smoking-hot sex with the athletic studs everyone fantasizes about. (978-1-60282-669-4)

The Marrying Kind by Ken O'Neill. Just when successful wedding planner Adam More decides to protest inequality by quitting the business and boycotting marriage entirely, his only sibling announces her engagement. (978-1-60282-670-0)

Dark Wings Descending by Lesley Davis. What if the demons you face in life are real? Chicago detective Rafe Douglas is about to find out. (978-1-60282-660-1)

sunfall by Nell Stark and Trinity Tam. The final installment of the everafter series. Valentine Darrow and Alexa Newland work to rebuild their relationship even as they find themselves at the heart of the struggle that will determine a new world order for vampires and wereshifters. (978-1-60282-661-8)

Mission of Desire by Terri Richards. Nicole Kennedy finds herself in Africa at the center of an international conspiracy and being rescued by beautiful but arrogant government agent Kira Anthony, but is Kira someone Nicole can trust or is she blinded by desire? (978-1-60282-662-5)

Boys of Summer edited by Steve Berman. Stories of young love and adventure, when the sky's ceiling is a bright blue marvel, when another boy's laughter at the beach can distract from dull summer jobs. (978-1-60282-663-2)

The Locket and the Flintlock by Rebecca S. Buck. When Regency gentlewoman Lucia Foxe is robbed on the highway, will the masked outlaw who stole Lucia's precious locket also claim her heart? (978-1-60282-664-9)

Calendar Boys by Zachary Logan. A man a month will keep you excited year round. (978-1-60282-665-6)

Burgundy Betrayal by Sheri Lewis Wohl. Park Ranger Kara Lynch has no idea she's a witch until dead bodies begin to pile up in her park, forcing her to turn to beautiful and sexy shape-shifter Camille Black Wolf for help in stopping a rogue werewolf. (978-1-60282-654-0)

LoveLife by Rachel Spangler. When Joey Lang unintentionally becomes a client of life coach Elaine Raitt, the relationship becomes complicated as they develop feelings that make them question their purpose in love and life. (978-1-60282-655-7)

The Fling by Rebekah Weatherspoon. When the ultimate fantasy of a one-night stand with her trainer, Oksana Gorinkov, suddenly turns into more, reality show producer Annie Collins opens her life to a new type of love she's never imagined. (978-1-60282-656-4)

Ill Will by J.M. Redmann. New Orleans PI Micky Knight must untangle a twisted web of healthcare fraud that leads to murder—and puts those closest to her most at risk. (978-1-60282-657-1)

Buccaneer Island by J.P. Beausejour. In the rough world of Caribbean piracy, a man is what he makes of himself—or what a stronger man makes of him. (978-1-60282-658-8)

Twelve O'Clock Tales by Felice Picano. The fourth collection of short fiction by legendary novelist and memoirist Felice Picano. Thirteen dark tales that will thrill and disturb, discomfort and titillate, enthrall and leave you wondering. (978-1-60282-659-5)

Words to Die By by William Holden. Sixteen answers to the question: What causes a mind to curdle? (978-1-60282-653-3)

Tyger, Tyger, Burning Bright by Justine Saracen. Love does not conquer all, but when all of Europe is on fire, it's better than going to hell alone. (978-1-60282-652-6)

Night Hunt by L.L. Raand. When dormant powers ignite, the wolf Were pack is thrown into violent upheaval, and Sylvan's pregnant mate is at the center of the turmoil. A Midnight Hunters novel. (978-1-60282-647-2)